THE

RANCHER'S WIFE

By
Sharon R. Hunter

ALL RIGHTS RESERVED
Sharon R. Hunter copyright © 2012
Amazon ISBN#
ISBN -13:978-1477579220
ISBN -10:1477579222
All rights reserved. No part of this book may be reproduced, used or stored in a retrieval system or transmitted, in any form or by any means without the prior permission in writing of the publisher.
PUBLISHER NOTES:
This is a work of fiction. All characters, places, businesses, and incidents/happenings are from the author's imagination. Any resemblance to actual places, people, or events is purely coincidental and is not to be considered real. Any trademarks mentioned herein are not authorized by the trademark owners and do not in any way mean the work is sponsored by or associated with the trademark owners/company. Any trademarks used are specifically for descriptive capacity.

To my husband, Jeff Hunter, thank you for letting me fly and being there to catch me. For Lauren and Beau, my children, for letting mom have computer time.

> For all their hours of help and reassurance
> Annette Dowling
> Amy Rohaley
> Carol Pritts
> Stephanie Yanovicz
> Ann Ulrich Miller

And all those who believe in me.

A special thank you to Lynn & Jack O'Day for a crash course in "Horse Care 101"

And to Mrs. May, my tenth grade Creative Writing teacher.

Chapter 1

New Orleans

After attending this overrated culinary convention, the highlight of my day awaited me, a night out on Bourbon Street. Pampered, mood swinging cater-to-me chefs, mostly men, surrounded me for a full eight hour day. A week in New Orleans, who better to be stuck with than my sister Allison, and Gina, my sidekick of a friend and sister chef. On the flip side, just my luck, a cattlemen's convention or whatever rancher farmer people call it was also hanging out in the Big Easy. The town was filled with ten gallon hats and cowboy boots who shared the sidewalks with the white apron society. Tonight's club choice, 'The Funky Pirate' picked by none other than me. I wanted nothing more than a smooth glass of red wine and the soulful sound of jazz music. Anyone who could tickle the ivory or wail on the sax would perk up the end of another dreadful day.

"Well would ya look at that," Gina breathed out in her sultry vocals. "Stud cakes, beef cakes, whomever they are…I want a bite. Just a little nibble."

My sister, Allison, nudged her hard in the ribs, snapping her back to civilization. The group of blue jeaned, leather belted men heard her loud and clear. The four of them seated themselves at the bar, ordering beers and shots of whisky.

"Aubrey, you're staring. Who's captured all that attention of yours?" Gina smirked with eyebrows wiggling up and down, sliding a napkin over the table top. "You're drooling girly."

"Him," I pointed with my pinky finger sipping my wine. "The one with the long braid down his back. Black hat." I sighed, "That's nice. Very nice."

"Thought you swore off men?" Her eyebrow wiggling peaked to a short stop.

"Never said I swore off men. Just the games they play." My eyes drifted from Gina back to the stranger sitting at the bar.

Safely tucked in our corner table, we eyed the group of men as if they were our main dish on a freshly created menu.

Gina, married and divorced three times over, still enjoyed prowling for men. My sister Allison widowed at the young age of thirty-nine, and me, the old maid. Forty-four and never married, I have a permanent engagement with my career. I dated. Did the relationship thing for a while. Married? No one wanted a chef whose main hours consisted of the nightshift.

"When was the last time you got laid, Aubrey?" Gina spouted smugly. Her fuchsia lipstick enhanced her nasty lipped comment. At least the music muffled Gina's voice.

"We all know you did last night. And the night before. How about the first night here?" I cracked back at my overly free spirited friend.

"Hey, I use protection." Gina announced as if it was her badge of honor.

"Gina, how many guys did you…you know?" Allison tapped danced around using the word 'sex' while sipping her wine.

"Great. My heart's getting broken. Look. Blonde bimbo rubbing on my cowboy." My heart really did sink. This guy just had my…well he was entertainment to my senses. The tingle of those senses stirred from their deep valley of sleep just watching this cowboy in my quiet way.

"Oh my god, he refused her," Allison gasped, "She's one of those pretty things guys dump ya for in a heartbeat."

"She's got a frickin' chicken neck and I bet her boobs are fake too." Gina, never one to mince words, tossed her cutthroat comments on the table. "Your chance is still open. Go talk to him."

"Are you insane? He just dumped Ms. Hottie Tottie, with big ole boobs popping out of her teeny tiny sweater. You really think he'd give me the time of day?" Horrified at the thought of attempting to chat up a man I didn't know, I sulked in my glass of wine. Bravery just isn't my strong side and I was so out of practice on the dating scene. "He won't even give me a second look if I walked by."

"How do you know Aubrey?" Allison glanced back at him. "Maybe Ms. 'Hi. Do-ya-want-to-meet-my-nice-big-boobies' isn't his type."

"Oh please, what guy won't snap her up? Just let me admire him from afar. We need more wine." I shrugged off the whole cowboy thing, waving to our waiter.

Forget ordering by the glass, we just ordered the bottle. At ease and relaxed, I propped my feet up on the chair next to me. My eyes weren't the only one keeping tabs on the four gents at the end of the bar. I liked men. I loved men. But seriously, I didn't think I stood a chance with the particular cowboy sitting in my sights. His outer ruggedness appealed to me, but what did I have to offer him? I'm tall, not super model tall, body tailor fitted with curves, wild red hair and over forty. With another sip of wine, I leisurely drank in his body of thick, hidden, hard muscles. His exposed forearms rippled with outlined muscles, it was my only glimpse as to what could possibly be hidden under that flannel and jeans he wore. He wasn't body builder muscular, just well maintained and sculpted. He used his muscles for the skill of his profession.

The club wasn't overly packed, so my viewing entertainment went uninterrupted. An occasional glance our way, I felt was most likely for Gina. She had what I called 'The Signal.' The 'I want to get in your pants' neon sign flashed on her entire body. She bathed in the scent of 'which man shall I bounce on tonight.' The dreamy look oozed from her salutary blue eyes to her pouting lush lips.

"That wine's playin' with your head again, isn't it?" Allison asked grinning.

My restless sign sank me. Yes, I know the wine was playing with me. I cooked with it daily, and enjoyed my evening goblet of sweet red to wash the day down.

"So glad this place offers up a dazzling sweet chocolate red." I grinned at my sister, sneaking another peek at the cowboy and his friends.

The man at the piano let his fingers dance out an old Harry Connick Jr. song. Just hearing it perked me up, letting me sway to the soft tones.

"It's Harry. I love Harry." Allison swayed along with me. "Would I love to dance with the cowboy to this."

"Get off that skinny-boned ass of yours, and ask the man to dance." Gina downright demanded. "Go on girl. You'll never know unless you ask him."

"But, no. What, what if he says no? Total humiliation." I groaned while my sister shoved me off my chair. "He turned down the blonde bouncy boob chick."

"Go." Allison handed me the last of my wine.

"Great. I can't believe I'm not drunk enough, but stupid enough to do this. You better order another bottle; I'm going to need it for when he shoots me down." I made my fingers into little imaginary guns shooting them both at my own head.

One fast look over the shoulder. I need a boost of encouragement. Yeah there it was, big thumbs up, beaming smiles, and a mouthing from Gina, "Just do it." I had my own cheering section.

"Well, here goes nothing." I muttered running my hands over my jeans.

Just as I expected, the nervous moisture clung to my skin as I inched myself closer to him. Directly behind him, my panic gripped me. "Escape now," my conscious mind warned. I nearly ran for the ladies room, but stopped short. Am I crazy? I can't compete with those young pretty petite things. Suddenly, my hand tugged lightly on the end of the braid dangling halfway down his back. The man in the black hat swung around to face me. Fury fired from his enticing brown eyes. Motive enough, he just wanted to bust whoever yanked his hair. His eyes met the brewing terror in mine, both of us shocked. I stepped back ready to run, but his hostile glare instantly softened. The lump of nervousness built in my throat. Wine, oh how I wished badly for a glass to wash it down. A good swift push on the vocals and I uttered something reasonable.

"Hi. Would…would you care to dance with me?" My offer made, I waited to get shot down. Waited for rejection, like the kind super boob girl got.

"Dance? I…um…well, I…." He stammered with words worse than I did.

"Ya, dump ass. Say yes. Did ya forget how to hold a pretty woman?" The man directly to his right laid into him with a verbal assault. "What are ya waitin' for ya fool? Songs goin' to be over before ya can have a little spin with her."

This sassy man tossed me a grin of hopefulness. My nerves finally broke free, and I laughed out loud at this strange man's outburst toward his friend.

"I really like Harry Connick Jr.'s music. But if you don't want to…I understand." I slipped another step back. Tail between my legs. I was heading, no, I was ready to run back to the girls table.

"Now wait a minute. I didn't say no." He grabbed my hand, pulling me back to him. "I'll take ya up on that dance."

From the quiet corner I'd emerged from, a scream of cheers and a wolf whistle echoed over the soft piano music. I don't think Gina and Allison could see my expression of "shut the hell up" in my eyes when I tossed a glare back at them. A warmth of rough callous engulfed my hand as he led us to the dance floor. He didn't hesitate to pull me close, a little closer than I expected. An affection I missed, being held in the arms of a man. I cuddled into his warm body, resting my chin on his shoulder. His intoxicating scent of spice, woods, and the wide open plains had me inhaling deeply. The heat from his massive hand, placed on the small of my back, a warm tingle raced its way up my spine.

"So who do I have the pleasure of dancing with?" He asked, his voice smooth, deep.

I grinned, drinking in the depths of his eyes. Brown; a sugary honey, brown coated my senses. "Oh sorry," I muttered, drawing myself back to his attention. "I'm Aubrey, Aubrey Hunter."

"Nic Ravenwood." He pronounced clearly, moving me even closer. "Sorry about Bones, he can be a little…overbearing."

"Bones? Your friend's name is Bones?" I asked, trying not to crack a laugh. The man who sat beside him resembled nothing of what a pile of bones should look like. Large, round, and jolly. I'd say 'Santa Claus' fit his description better than 'Bones.'

"Yeah. He's my ranch foreman."

"Ah, I take it you're here for the cow or farm or what do you call it convention?" Great I think I just stepped in cow crap with him all ready.

"Agriculture convention, city girl." Nic fired back fast with a grin.

"Born and raised a city girl and I'm a chef from the city, too." A simple smile eased the nervous tension between us.

"So you're down here in New Orleans for a cooking convention?"

"Yes. But we call it a Culinary Convention."

"Friends of yours?" Nic nodded toward Allison and Gina.

"The cheering section over in the corner, my sister, Allison and fellow partner in crime, Gina. We design and create gourmet food daily."

"You're a cook?" His eyebrows arched in question.

"Well technically, I'm a chef at the Blue Point in Cleveland. Rated with a five star, elite."

"You're from Cleveland? Cleveland, Ohio?"

"Yes, Cleveland, Ohio. You know, home of the Cleveland Browns." I grinned hoping football would forge us together. "So you're a rancher. From where? Do you ranch cows or..." I did it again, just insulted the man with a question.

Laughter escaped him like the wind circling in tree branches. "Aubrey Hunter, have you ever been on a farm?"

"No." I answered. "The closest thing to a farm, um, well does the farmer's market in downtown count?"

"No. It doesn't count at all." He smiled brushing a strand of hair from my eyes. "I'm from Wyoming. Got about 50,000 acres. That's land, honey."

"Oh very funny, smarty…I know what acres are. That's a lot of land."

"Raise and sell beef cattle. Have about thirty purebred horses. Show some. Breed and sell some of them. And there's some little farm animals."

"Horses? All those cows and you have horses too?" I paused, a little pale, I'm sure, "When I was a kid, I was thrown from a horse. Just a little intimidated by them."

"Some get spooked easily. Most are pretty tame. We have several different breeds. Gorgeous animals. You'd like the ones I have." Nic showed his confidence. "Got ta say, horses are so easy to train."

"I have a cat. He was easy to train, or I should say he trained me." I grinned still swaying to the music with him.

"I've got a barn full of those damn things. All colors, all kinds. You could have your pick."

My head rested easily on his broad shoulder. His flannel shirt, soft to the touch on my cheek, I don't know why it surprised me. This time, he didn't even mind when I weaved my fingers around his braid. Three songs later, I was still in Nic Ravenwood's arms. Of course a good moment always seems to end. The piano player decided he needed his break time. Nic pulled back from me, staring down over me. Do I run? Do I stay put? So I waited for him to say something as the people on the dance floor cleared away.

"You don't look like one of those high maintenance chicks who only tosses down those fancy little drinks, Aubrey."

"Really? What makes you think I'm not some high maintenance chick from the city?" I wasn't sure if I should laugh or be offended.

"Starters you talked to me." He winked.

"Wait a minute. I saw you brush off that little blonde..."

"I'm old enough to be her father. Blondie, couldn't have been more than legal age. How old are you?" He eyed me over trying to guess my age.

"Why? Nic, you don't ask a..." he interrupted me, again.

"Please don't be some twenty-something. Are you at least close to thirty-five?"

My breath caught, my smile spread wide over my face. I know the lights were dim, but this was great. "I think I love you." With crazed laughter I grabbed onto him hugging him. "I'm forty-four. Your turn"

"You tell me."

Nic wanted me to guess his age? Please let me be kind. "You like playing games, don't you?" We hadn't even made it off the dance floor. "Ok fine. You've got to be in your forties. But you feel like you're in your twenties." My hands swept over his hard muscled arms. Now I did it, I really hope he doesn't want an explanation.

"Forty-seven." He paused, grinning as my hands rested on his biceps. "You're sweet Aubrey. You don't have ta leave yet?" he glanced over to where the girls were sitting, "Stay. Have a drink with me?"

"We cracked a bottle of wine back at the table, come join us?" I pulled at his hand still attached to mine as he looked back at his buddies. "They can join us too. If they want."

Gina's arm suddenly wrapped around my shoulder, "Hey, girly." She handed me the bottle of wine and two glasses. "We're heading back. You be ok?"

"I'll make sure she gets back to your hotel safely ma'am." Nic stepped in so politely.

"I should really…" My protest went weak to the ears.

"Call if you need any help Aubrey." Gina winked at Nic. She kissed me on the cheek and let her cat walk of a swagger lead her out the door.

"Nic, we're headed back. Mind your manners with this one, she's a lady." His friend, Bones, slapped him on the back and the three men clomped their way out of the jazz club behind my sister and Gina. My eyes followed them; they all left, leaving me alone with Nic. The clinking of the two wine glasses in my hand and meeting Nic's eyes again, my mind went blank. Great, the awkward moment crept in and the cat got my tongue.

"What kinds of wine do you like Aubrey?"

I loved the way he said my name. "It's a sweet red, hope you like it." I sat the glasses on the table pouring out the wine.

I'm sitting here with a total stranger from Wyoming, but he felt so comfortable to me. I really hope it wasn't all the wine shrinking my brain into a mush pile. I learned an amazing amount about ranching and how a ranch operates in our short time together. He had me in stitches when I thought he said "slapping" the hogs and it was really "slopping" the hogs. I amused him with the stories on my one lone animal, Mr. Perfect, my Siamese cat.

"Nic, it's past midnight. I've got to get back. I've got a class to teach at eight."

His feet were resting up on the adjacent chair, his black suede hat propped on the edge of the table and my little clutch purse lounged beside it.

"We're ya stayin'."

"Just two streets over….The Hotel Montelone."

"Isn't that the one with a haunted floor?" He asked, winking at me.

"Yes were staying on it, but don't tell Gina, she'd flip."

He stood up, grabbing my hand, pulling me with him. "I'll walk ya back. No way I'm letting you roam these streets by yourself."

"Thank you. Are you staying far from here?"

He picked up his hat, handed me my purse, and offered his arm. "Another street over from where you're staying."

We stepped out onto Bourbon Street. Music belted from just about every doorway we passed. Happy people danced in the streets while beaded necklaces dropped from the balconies above. With a conscious effort Nic pulled me closer to him as we weaved our way amidst the crowd to my hotel. The Hotel Montelone settled itself on a side street. No traffic, no wild party goers, a pretty quiet street for one in the morning. A doorman still kept watch at his post as we approached. Nic and I stepped inside the grand entrance of the hotel. Under the fully lighted crystal chandelier, I'm sure I showed my true age to him.

"Thank you for asking me to dance. I haven't…it's been so nice being in your company Aubrey."

"Thank you." My nervous laugh displayed itself. Come on I thought, you've got to do better than that. "I'm really glad you didn't turn me down." Another nervous giggle surfaced. "Are you free tomorrow?" I just blurted it out, I wasn't thinking. He's going to think I'm too forward. Too pushy. I never noticed the streak of gray in his hair. His skin tan, weathered nicely, and I found myself falling into those deep brown eyes. Nic's hands rested around my waist; his fingers silently played into my curvy hips like the piano player at the club. Still waiting for his reply, I couldn't help myself. I leaned up on my tiptoes putting my hands on his weathered face and kissed him. He didn't resist. Nic took over my initiative. No power struggle from me, I just followed his lead. Oh how I forgot what it was like to be kissed by a man. The icy coolness of my fingers flamed with heat from the touch of his skin. His hand left my waist reaching for the back of my hair while his lips crushed harder onto mine.

"Aubrey," Nic's lips left mine. "I'm free tomorrow night. Dinner, I'll be here about six." He stood there grinning, not even bothering to wipe off the lipstick I branded him with.

Starry eyed, like some high school girl, who just got her first kiss, I clenched my fingers deep into his biceps. A little dazed from wine, more from the kiss, I felt myself swaying. Immediately Nic's hands clinched around my waist, steadying me.

"You alright there Aubrey?" He asked not having to wonder why.

"Yeah. Yeah, I'm. Do that again." Politely, I asked for a repeat kiss.

"Do what again?" Amused by my question, Nic didn't need to figure out what I wanted.

"This." I grabbed him, landing my lips right on his. The wine must have given me an extra edge. I twisted his braided hair around my hand, letting my other hand slid over his flannel shirt. Flannel, who'd ever thought it be so soft to the touch. Out of left field my sensible self appeared. "Oh. I'm, I…"

"I believe I should be saying thank you." Nic laughed at my embarrassment. "Where's your phone?"

"Phone? In my bag." Puzzled, I was still relishing in his kiss and I wanted more. "What do you want my phone for?" For carrying a small clutch purse, my fingers fumble pulling it out. Nic slid it from my hand and programmed his number into it. "I've found a high tech rancher." I stared at him a little amazed.

"Your turn." He handed back my phone and waited for me to rattle off my number.

As quick as I recited my number, he zipped it into his phone. Then Nic handed me a little brown business card. Titled at the top in thick black ink it read, "Ravenwood Ranch."

"Wait. I've got one too." Giggle, that's all I could do as I handed him one of my business cards.

"You're an Executive Chef?" He flipped the card over, "You really do live in Cleveland?"

Before I could answer, his lips captured mine again. The heat filled my cheeks and I didn't bother to ease myself back into his kiss. I eagerly took more. "Ow." A sudden sharp pain stabbed my stomach and poked my flesh deeper. I cringed in pain backing away from our kiss.

"I think your 'belt buckle' just attacked me." Still breathless from his kiss, I tried to regain my sweater back.

"Yep. You're a little stuck on me," Nic tried as gently as possible to unweave the delicate yarn. "Like to hear you explain this one to those girlfriends of yours."

"Gina, she'd be proud of me." Freed at last. My purse shielded me from Nic's offending belt buckle as I kissed him goodnight.

"You look good in "coffee" lipstick," I joked.

"Miss Aubrey, I'll see you at six for dinner. If you get a break from all those cooking classes tomorrow, give me a call."

My body curved back into his, savoring the deep embrace between us. One last kiss and he headed for the door. "Goodnight Aubrey."

I watched Nic slip through the double doors and out into the darkened streets of New Orleans. My feet barely touched the marble floor as I floated over to the elevator. My imagination enjoyed torturing me as the elevator doors shut with a quiet thud. Did I really meet, dance with, and kiss a rancher from Wyoming? Would Nic Ravenwood really show up for dinner tomorrow night?

Chapter 2

Oyster Shucking

My alarm screamed beside my buzzing head. Five-thirty in the morning. No, it's not time to rise and shine. I've only been asleep for a few hours. I wanted my dream back. Nic's lips dancing on mine. His hands wrapped securely around my waist again. Dream? I lived the taste of his lips on mine, then even dreamed about him. Snooze alarm just jolted another body jumping reminder; get out of the bed, chick, you're teaching a culinary cooking class in a few hours. I slapped at the alarm, finally ending the annoying buzz. Like a ten year old protesting going to school, I sat myself on the edge of the bed not budging. Piled under the pillows, I could see the outline of Gina's 'dead to the world' body. She had dropped right into bed with her clothes still matted to her lifeless figure. She wasn't even back when I came in. Had to wonder who her 'catch of the night' had been. I'm sure she'd be frying up a story and serving it to me on a platter when she'd surface to the light of day.

"I'll make ya coffee if you dish on Mr. Rancher." Allison sat up next to me.

"Deal." I headed toward the bathroom needing a steaming shower.

My head pounded. I knew I didn't suck down that much wine. But then again, I drained one bottle with the girls and a second with Nic. "Nic." My head didn't seem to hurt as bad when I said his name out loud. Misty hot moisture filled the bathroom and the heat of the water beaded over my body. Coffee, a brewing aroma of my tranquil drug was only steps away. Didn't know how Gina did it night after night. Drank. Met men. Drank more, and did the dirty little deed with the men she played with. She collected men for that one sole purpose…sex.

"Aubrey, you've got a phone call." Allison invaded the bathroom.

"Who's calling me this early?" I protested peeking from behind the shower curtain. In one hand Allison pushed my phone towards me. The other hand, she held my cup of life.

"It's him." She whispered, holding back her excitement.

"It's him?" I shut the water off reaching for my phone. The little neon green screen announced Nic Ravenwood's name in large bold black letters. "It's him."

"Hurry. Wrap up in a towel, silly. Say good morning." Allison whispered tossing me another towel for my dripping hair.

"It's not like he can see me over the phone, Al." I whispered back, holding the phone next to my towel-wrapped body.

"I want details." Allison hissed a whisper.

In return, I gladly waved her out of my private space.

"Morning." I tried not to sound too perkily pleased that he called.

"Just wanted to say mornin' to ya. Felt a little bad, kept you out so late." His voice was smoother than the coffee in my hand.

"How sweet," The man had me melting at six in the morning for him. "You're up early."

"Sharin' a room with old Bones. Man snores like a freight train." A ripping of what could have been some kind of bizarre thunderstorm echoed over the phone line.

"So I hear." Another round of snoring poured between our words. "Ever just want to put a pillow over his head?" Jokingly, I asked.

"Yep, done that a few times. Doesn't help. Ya should try sleepin' in the same room with him." His laugh mingled with a swallow of his coffee.

"So what do you have on tap for the day?" My voice cracked between sips of my own coffee.

"Besides meeting you tonight?" Warm tingles shot over my damp body just hearing those words leave his lips.

"Oh, I didn't forget." Another sip of my coffee stifled my excitement.

"Usual stuff, vet clinic, organic feed for the cattle."

"A vet clinic?" I asked.

"We take care of our own animals. Only call in the regular vet when it gets too bad for us to handle."

"Amazing. You give them shots and do all that stuff?" I formed a new respect for my rancher.

"Aubrey, you'd be a treat to have out on the ranch."

"A treat? What kind of a treat?" I asked hesitantly.

"Think you'd really love being out on the ranch with me." Nic's smoothness kept me wanting more.

"The big wild open country, where the sky is endless. I'd like to see that some day, other than on PBS." I melted faster for him than the cream in my coffee.

"You'd love it there. I'll see ya at six. Try not to keep ya out past midnight again. Hope causal is ok with you."

"Causal is fine. I'm looking forward to seeing you." Eager, ugh, was I being to darn eager? "Promise I won't be a food snob and get all judgmental over dinner."

"Good. You'll like the place. You have a good day, Aubrey." Nic clicked off, leaving me overheated in the steamy bathroom.

"Allison. Allison, get in here." I gave up whispering and shouted for her.

"Was it him? What'd he say? What, what happened? You're still seeing him tonight?" Allison danced around the crowded bathroom. Coffee splashing from the cups as she carelessly poured.

"He just wanted to say good morning to me." Allison and I giggled like we were teenagers back in our high school days. "I've got a dinner date with a rancher."

My day couldn't fly fast enough. Geared and pumped for a simple demonstration of breakfast cuisine, my culinary skills out shined themselves. Of course my thoughts weren't on the food preparation or the people gathered around the burners.

He said a causal night dining. Causal, how casual? Jeans and tank casual? Or simple skirt and flats casual? This is why I cooked and didn't pursue a career in fashion. Me, I designed food to tantalize the palette. A gift to hold your senses captive while you dined under the glow of candlelight.

Finally the end neared. My last class, nothing more to do than observe and critique. Simple enough, done, over, and freedom belonged to me. I had an hour and half to primp and polish myself for my casual dinner date. Another fashion problem...being clothes challenged. And just my luck, neither Gina or Allison were back yet. My suitcase found itself emptied and strung out over the bed.

"Oh what the hell, I'll just call him. Let's see what Mr. Ravenwood's description of casual is." Under the pile of clothes I retrieved my phone.

A click on the address book and there his number popped up. I giggled. I haven't giggled this much in years and I giggled over looking at a man's name on my phone. Dial pressed and I waited.

"Aubrey." A wave of a velvety smoothness caressed my ear.

"Hi Nic." I suppressed the girlish giggle. "I hope I'm not interrupting."

"You're a nice break to end this dragging afternoon on. What's up?"

"Would you, um...describe your version of causal? I...I don't know what to wear tonight." My simple words tangled over my tongue.

"You own a pair of jeans, city girl?" He questioned with attitude.

"Yes, of course. Doesn't everyone?" I'd hoped he was joking.

"Good. Wear your jeans. Be comfortable. It's not a fancy place. Take my word on it."

"Jeans it is. I'll meet you in the lobby at six." I gushed. Didn't mean to. But that whole puddle melting thing happened again. Just hearing his voice and I'm jellied.

"Jeans, jeans, jeans. Ha, found you." I grabbed up my nicest pair hiding in the pile.

I didn't think Allison would mind if I borrowed one of her knock off designer labeled tops. "It fits. Thank you Al." I checked my causal look in the mirror. All curves tucked away, with a modest hint of my pale skin revealed. Tastefully revealing, leaving my rancher to use his imagination.

"Well look who's all hot to trot tonight." Gina stood in the doorway of our hotel room downing her umpteenth cup of coffee.

"Is it too much?" I couldn't hide my panic from Gina. It'd been years since I'd been on a date.

"You kidding? Ole cowboy ain't goin' to know what rode him after tonight."

"Gina. Stop that, you're so not funny." Nervous, me? No not at all.

"You got protection? Here put this in your purse." Gina handed me a handful of condoms, laughing.

"You're insane. It's just a dinner date." I squirmed with the little silver wrapped packages slipping through my fingers. "When did dinner turn into sex?"

"Ya never know Aubrey. That man looks like he could ride all...night...long." She scooped up the unmentionables. "You better get saddled up girly. Take these."

"Gina? Seriously?" Reluctantly, I snatched them from her hand hiding them in the bottom of my purse.

Sex, now that was action I didn't see much of. I swear, just hearing Gina talk about her romps, it'd make you want to kick back and have a smoke, after her wild details.

"Gina...Do...do I look all right? He said casual, really informal."

"Aubrey, honey you look great. He thought you were somethin' last night in that tank top and what did ya call it skirt?"

"Prairie. You know a Prairie skirt." I attempted to add a little color to my face as we discussed my date.

"Wait till he see's you now." Gina tried to do something with my hair, but again like my clothes my hair resisted. "Why the heck are you so nervous? You were sucking his tonsils out last night."

"I know, that was...Nic's a good kisser." Girly giggles spilled out of my mouth, again. "I...I'm just so nervous. It's like I've never been on a date in my life."

"Do you want me to count how many months since your last date?" Gina got her jab in helping me finish my causal look. "Perfect. You'll be fine. Be yourself, you're a natural."

"It's like, ten till six. I told him I'd meet him in the lobby. Should I wait or go now?"

"Calm down," Gina rolled her eyes laughing at me and my nerves. "Better get a move on there little cowgirl."

"Stop that." I did the one more check over in the mirror. "Wish me luck."

"You don't need luck. And remember use the damn protection." Gina demanded.

"What no 'how to tips'?" I slammed the door in her face before she could offer up her how to tips of sex.

"Elevator or stairs? Elevator or stairs? Stairs would let me calm down, but elevator would get me to him faster. Oh crap what if he's not there? What if he doesn't show?" Really I need to stop these one sided chats with myself.

"Don't worry sweetie, he'll show." An older grey haired gentleman stood directly to my right side.

Where did he come from? How long had he been standing there next to me while I had a conversation with myself?

"And if he don't show, he's a fool. I'll take ya to dinner myself." My gray-haired friend gave me a wink.

"Ding, Ding" the elevator announced its arrival and slid its massive jeweled doors open. My new friend motioned for me to step in.

"Thank you." I said pressing the 'L' for lobby button.

Instantly he struck up a conversation with me, "Did you ever notice how elevators move so fast? You leave your stomach on the floor you just left and it takes all night to catch up with ya." The silver fox had a sense of humor.

The doors slid open, once again, and the massive marbled floors and glittery crystal lights beamed. "Hope that fellow meets ya Miss."

"Thank you." Silently, I wished for the same.

My eyes toured over the enchanted lobby bustling with people. Slowly, I moved away from the safety of the elevator. Nervously, I slipped through the late afternoon crowd of guests. If your heart can really skip a beat, mine did. Nic patiently waited by the fountain in the center of the lobby. No ten gallon black hat tonight. No trailing braid. His hair hung freely below his shoulder blades. Longer than I'd remembered. The solid grey streak, the one I wanted to wrap my finger around, accented the cool blackness of his hair. Worn blue jeans, leather belt, with the attacking buckle that tried to eat my sweater last night, and a simple deep blue pullover, sleeves bunched to his elbows. Deep blue heightened the sight of his eyes. Mahogany eyes smiled back at me.

"Aubrey."

"Hi. Have you been here long?"

"You look…." He paused reaching for my hands.

"Is it ok? Too causal? Not causal enough?" I stuttered around my words trying to stay calm.

Instantly his lips found mine repressing all my worry. My insane intensity slowed to a mellow glow feeling the light brush of his chest over mine. I guess I'd never know if it was or wasn't causal enough. But, really, who cared? All the clatter of people passing by disappeared. I didn't even hear the cascading water in the fountain beside us. My silly school girl dream flashed back, Nic Ravenwood's arms surrounded me again.

"You look perfect Aubrey. I just got here a few minutes ago." His thump whisked away my new shade of coca cream lip gloss.

"Oh good, I mean thank you." Great, I can't even talk straight. My mouth formed words, but the brain commanded other signals. Like how about another kiss cowboy.

Another huge hug circled around my body. Ah, his scent, fresh, so outdoorsy, even a hint of burning wood.

"You're not nervous are you?" Nic asked teasingly.

"No. Yes. It's…I haven't been on a date in a really long time." My cheeks instantly flushed.

"Great, makes two of us." He didn't miss a beat. "Nice color of pink." His fingers gently passed over my blush of embarrassment.

"You ever hear of a place called the Oyster House?" Nic asked, trying to get me back to comfortable.

"Yeah. Isn't it a few streets from here?"

"Yep. We're shuckin' oysters tonight." He grinned, slipping his hand around mine.

The door opened compliments of the automatic response of the doorman. "Hail you a cab sir?"

"No thank you. Too beautiful of a night." Nic nodded to the doorman.

Another night back on Bourbon Street. Secretly, I promised myself to drink no more than two, maybe three glasses of wine. I had to set a limit and I definitely needed to keep my wits about me.

"You ever shuck oysters before?" Nic asked as we weaved our way along the bustling street.

"Well, yes," I started, "You've got to shuck them to prep them for whatever dish it is you're creating."

The chef in me took full stage. Detailed explanation of several different ways to prepare and eat the delicate oyster rolled out of my mouth as we mingled along. Nic stopped me in front of a busy little hole-in-the-wall diner. The door slammed on its hinges while people buzzed in and out as we stood on the sidewalk.

"Have you ever shucked them and washed them down with a beer?" Nic asked, chuckling and pointing to the sign above the door.

"Oyster House, Shuck Me, Suck Me, Eat Me Raw." I gasped, momentarily speechless at what I just read out loud.

T-shirts hung in the windows with the famous quote framed on them. Nic tried to gage my reaction to the risqué suggestion of the diner's sign. I stammered for words as the double meaning of the sign hit me. "I've never eaten raw oysters before."

"You've got to be kidding me? You're a chef." He opened the door ushering me in. "You're going to love it."

"Two beers, platter of oysters, hot sauce and bring the largest bucket of fries." He gave his order to the waiter like a pro. "Hope you got room in that pretty little figure of yours for all of this." Nic's hand poked around my pouching tummy, kicking a giggle from me.

"You come here often?" I asked crawling up on a bar stool beside him impressed by his one, two, three order. "You eat these raw? I've, I...I cook them. There, they're appetizers. You really eat them raw?" Nic laughed and slid me a very long tall glass of beer, foam slopped over the sides.

A plate, no, a huge-ass platter of raw oysters on the half shell plopped down in front of us. A bottle of hot sauce nearly bounced off the counter into my lap. Slapped down next to me, a metal basket that looked like it just surfaced from the deep fryer. Sliced golden fries heaped over the edge of the basket landing on the counter.

"Another round of beer for ya two?" The skinny waiter asked wiping grease from his hands.

"Bring two more; she's going to need it." Nic grinned reaching for the malt vinegar. "I'd like an executive chef's opinion on shucking, sucking and eat'n raw."

Nic just ended the sentence. My jaw dropped, you could've shoveled the whole basket of fries in my gaping mouth. Let alone how my eyes must have bugged out at his question.

"You mean the oysters, don't you?" Innocently asking, I reached for the nearest beer, I didn't care if it was his, mine, or whoever was sitting beside me.

"Why, Chef Aubrey, you've never downed an oyster raw?" This time he took his beer from my hand, and handed me back my lipstick marked glass.

"No." My voice turned mild, so meek, and I never knew beer could taste so good.

"Pick up an oyster." He dabbed hot sauce in the center. "Ya just suck it off and swallow it...whole."

Nic downed the thing whole. Not even chewing, he swallowed it. Then washed it down with beer and adding a shit eating grin for me.

"Your turn Aubrey." He dotted my oyster with hot sauce. "Just open up, suck it down."

Cold, wet, and slimy, an oyster perched itself in my fingers with hot sauce dribbling over it. I hate hot sauce. I looked at my oyster, then at Nic. "You swallow it raw?" Never in all my days of being a chef did I ever see anyone suck down a raw oyster.

"Come on Aubrey you can do it." Nic taunted me with a sly smile. "Just let it slide."

"Ok. Ok, stop rushing me." My lips snickered into a you've-got-to-be-kidding-me twist. "Ok, here goes nothing." One more look at the ugly slippery oyster, back over to Nic, and I put the oyster up to my lips. My lips refused to give in. My month wouldn't open. Nic put his arm around me, rubbing my shoulders.

"Just open up. Let it slide in." Casually Nic flipped my hair over my shoulder. "Just suck on it honey."

I didn't think those were words of encouragement. Mr. Shuck'm, Suck'm cowboy, even dared to wink at me after suggesting the two way statement. The oysters slid over my lips. A salty rubbery glob danced on my tongue and bounced itself in my mouth. The hot sauce only made it worse. Nic reinforced the 'don't chew, just swallow' rule. My one hand grabbed for his arm, pinching deep into his flesh. The other hand pounded the heck out of the side of the bar as I managed to swallow the slime.

"Holy Shit! What did I just suck down?" I grabbed the beer out of his hand and drained half the glass. "That has got to be the most god awful thing I've ever put in my mouth." I gagged again wiping the slime from my lips.

Nic erupted with a roar of laughter and reached for two more oysters. He handed me another one, "Show me what you're made of Aubrey Hunter."

Then he counted to three and I let another slippery salted oyster slide down my throat. Nearly three beers downed and our platter heaped over with empty shells.

"The basket of fries, let me guess, calms the stomach so you don't puke the oysters back up?" I asked him as he sucked the last oyster down.

"Somethin' like that sweetheart." Nic plastered a beer, oyster and greasy fries kiss on my lips. "You can go back and tell that wild legged friend of yours you've been shucked, sucked and ate'm raw. That'd keep her wondering about what I did with you."

"Nic." I busted out laughing. His take on Gina, direct and to the point. "You won't believe what she..." I stopped dead in my sentence remembering the fashion accessory Gina insisted I take was neatly hidden at the bottom of my purse. I reached for my beer not finishing my sentence. No way was I blurting out 'Gina gave me a handful of condemns and told me to ride you all night long.'

"I won't believe what?" Nic eased back on his bar stool, waiting for my answer. "You know I swear I saw her coming out of one of my buddy's room the other night."

"Good chance." Saved, I hope. "Gina enjoys men." I shrugged my shoulders grinning and I left it at that.

"How long are you down for?" Nic asked, passing me more fries.

"Allison and I are going back on Saturday. Gina is staying till Monday. You?"

"Leaving late Monday." His eyes shifted over me, "Any chance I can get you to stay the weekend?"

"Um," A little floored by his forwardness, I struggled for an answer. "I...I could...I could rearrange, I..." A new shade of blush red flushed over my entire body.

A man that I've only known for two days just asked me to stay the weekend with him and I'm blushing. Please be a hot flash.

"It's only Wednesday," I toyed with the idea and wished for my original coloring, "I'm sure I can change my flight, and…Gina is staying till Monday. You actually want me to stay till Monday?" I leaned deeply into the frame of the bar stool, relieved for the support of the back catching me, still in disbelief of what Nic just asked me.

"I'm not ready to let go of you Aubrey. It's…I just…I just want to keep you around me." Nic's fingers filtered through a tangle of my curls. "God, hope I didn't just scare you off." He frowned and shifted back from me.

"No. No you didn't." I jumped to answer him. I let my hand slid softly over his thigh, and hoped I could lure him closer to me again. I wasn't scared. I was still reeling about the fact he wanted me to stay till Monday. "Nic, I'm flattered you want me to stay." This time I engaged his lips for a kiss.

"You two need another round?" The skinny greased covered waiter interrupted.

"Two more." Nic answered, annoyed.

"Truth be told, I've never been married." My turn to level with him. "My so called relationships…few and far between. Difficult, being a chef and all, I pull late nights, even later on weekends."

"Relationships?" Nic scuffled. "Most woman want noth'n to do with ranch life. Long hours, dirty work, animals always need cared for." He eased over brushing my shoulder with his. "Not a glamorous life at all."

"At least your animals don't throw their food at you when it's not up to their palette's standards." He cracked a smile at me.

"I've had my share of women. Ends up the same." Nic drank the last of his beer. "But you, you're a breed all of your own. I just want to take you home with me."

"Well now the Ravenwood Ranch would have its own executive chef." My snappy comeback left him relaxed and me still bewildered.

"Saw that on your pretty little card. So tell me, you play with food all day?" Nic waited for me to spill my guts on chef life. "You said you work nights."

"Yep, I do. Went to culinary school, graduated with honors and worked my way up in a world of mostly men. I've been at the Blue Point for over thirteen years and climbed the ladder out cooking the 'so called' greats." I sipped slowly at beer number four. "I'm rated in the United States in the top ten of the "Who's Who in chefs," I came in at number four. Like you, I'm very much married to my profession. Those few and far relationships I've had, I found that men resented the fact I pulled a nightshift. I'm gone from about five till one or two in the morning."

I sighed in my own disbelief, facts are facts, I'm married to my career choice. I glanced up at Nic. He studied me, arms folded over his chest, his mind piecing together everything I just spit out.

"What time do you have to be up?" He questioned sharply.

"I've got a class to teach at eight." My heart sank to the depths of my oyster filled stomach. I blew it. Too candid for the cowboy who I just sucked oysters with.

"Hum, nine thirty." He watched me fidget in my chair. "You won't turn into a pumpkin till midnight, right?"

My head snapped up, "My late night lifestyle doesn't bug you?" He still wanted to be with me. I thought it was over. Half expected him to say, it's been nice but...

"Honey, I shovel cow shit for a livin'." Nic leaned in for another kiss.

Chapter 3

A Casual Yes

I sat alone in the open air café waiting for Allison. Half glad that she was running late for our lunch date. My rehearsal, I practiced over and over, "Oh by the way Allison, I won't be on Saturday's flight. The cowboy from Wyoming, you know Mr. Rancher? He asked me to stay the weekend…with him." My sister's mind fell open to just about anything. So why was I getting all knotted up over telling my kid sister I wanted to do something totally outrageous with someone I barely knew? Me, the safe one. I'd never stray from the safety net of the inside of my practical boxed life. How would Allison accept this? Please don't let her turn into our brother Phil. I cringed, sipping my iced tea. Allison wasn't only my sister, but my best friend. We shared nearly every detail of our lives with each other. The knot twisted around in my stomach again. This really wasn't about telling Allison. Nic Ravenwood had me twisting for him. In less than three days I knew more about him and ranch life than any of the guys in my so called long term relationships. Up front, and to the point, Nic hid nothing from me. Everything about himself; he spread out on the table. An only child, his mom passed away a few years back, dad still lives on the ranch with him. We got all the small important details out of the way in two nights. Sharing my family dirt kept Nic amused. I just couldn't wait for him to meet my unmentionable brother Phil and his suffocating wife Dee. We had a simple and basic family life. The three of us kids had been dumped on Gram when our parents needed to 'find themselves.' Small details of my upbringing left Nic scratching his head. I envied Nic; he seemed to have the package of a normal family life. I liked that. Even more, I wanted it for myself at times. I carved mental notes into my memory bank of every signal this man offered me.

Men like Nic were too good to be true. Red flags knocked at my skeptical brain and kept me dwelling on the negative. Could he just be pretending? Playing me along till he got me in bed with him? Then hit me with the usual lines: 'Great to have met ya. It's been real, but, you know,' or 'you'll forget about me. Have a nice rest of your life.'

But he left me clinging to certain repeated emotions that kept tugging at my heart. 'How he didn't want to let me go. He couldn't wait for me to see the ranch. How I'd love the animals.' Let's not forget, the last few days, morning wake up calls, even afternoon 'Hello's.' Yeah, yeah, yeah, I know it could all just be a fling for him, but could it? Both of us were here for a reason, something more than the conventions we attended. Could Nic Ravenwood be the piece missing to my empty heart? For once in my life, please don't let him be a desperate, lonely cowboy just wanting a bed buddy. Obvious fact, neither one of us mentioned. We came from two different worlds; city girl meets dreamy rancher man and then the whole thing of a long distance romance. I'm back East and he's smack dab in the middle of the West.

"Aubrey." Allison's voice broke my 'lost in thought' moment. "Your mind is a millions miles away. It's written all over your face. Spill it." She slid the chair out next to me and hovered waiting for details.

"Let's order first." I kept skimming the menu.

Allison and a menu meant I could spend the whole afternoon detailing every dish to her.

"Deep fried platter sound good to you?" I knew it was a safe choice for both of us.

"What, no raw oysters today?" Allison smirked over the top of her menu. "Oh, look, look, look. Split one of those black'n bleu burgers with me. Bet it's not as good as yours."

"Diet city when we get home." With a chuckle, I handed the menu to our waiter.

"So what's on your mind? You've got someone toying in that brain of yours? Any chance his name is Nic Ravenwood."

Allison, right as usual. We trusted each other so much, depended on each other, and always backed one another. I let a long sigh out and played with the straw in my iced tea.

"Aubrey…"

My great planned rehearsal just spilled out. "Allison he asked me to spend the weekend with him. He doesn't fly home till Monday. Gina's staying till Monday too, so I think I'm…" Allison waved her snapping fingers high in the air, dancing in her chair.

"You're staying the weekend with him? Aubrey, I can't believe it. Well yes, I can believe it. Do it. Just say yes to the man."

I didn't really expect a blue ribbon overwhelming reaction. Well, I didn't know what kind of reaction Allison would hit me with.

"Aubrey, I haven't seen you this happy in years."

"No mushy crap. Set it aside. Be serious with me for a moment." I had to rope Allison back into my nitpicking bring me back to reality side. "What if I'm setting myself up for disaster? What if all this sweet talk is for just one thing? Take a roll in the hay with the ranch man. Then what? He goes back to Wyoming and I go home, alone?"

"So, enjoy him. Who says you can't have a week long fling if you want?" Allison raised her eyebrows, she had a point. "But the memories you'll have. Can you see it now? We're in our eighties, rocking away at the nursing home, and you recall your romp with Nic Ravenwood." My crackled laughter at Allison's animation, turned peoples heads staring in our direction.

In the back of my mind, the red flag city jumped out all over the lunch table. Just surfacing, the ugly 'what if' questions. Seriously, I didn't know how I'd feel being a week long fling for him. The good ole 'Wham Bam Thank You Ma'am,' just kept pounding at my temples.

"Aubrey, you're over analyzing again. Stop worrying. If the man wanted you for nothing but sex, he would've offered it up the first night you met. You two were pretty shit faced after all that wine." Allison laughed at me. "You never drink that much."

"I know. I know, I only cook with the stuff and look at me now…beer and raw oysters. The man's corrupted me." The black-n-blue cheese burger melted in my mouth. "Oh, this is good.

"Look at me." High flying drama halted as Allison turned all serious on me. This would be hard to swallow, watching her scoop up a mouth full of cheese and onions, but she went on. "You're forty-four years old. Think about it Bre, you haven't been in a relationship in years. You're down right taken by this man."

"But Allison, I've been in these so called love affairs. It starts off rolling on a high and then it splatters. It hits the bottom because I won't give up my career for some guy's whiney needs."

"Aubrey, Nic is no whiner. He's nothing like what you've dated before. Just hear me out. I saw something. Don't laugh, it was like magical." Allison rolled her eyes all dreamy like. "When Nic walked into the bar, your eyes glistened, you sat there smiling. You've never responded to a man like that. And you didn't even know him yet."

"So what are you telling me?" Sister approval, always a must.

"I'm saying if I felt this guy was a jerk, I'd be facing off with you about it." Allison laid her burger down and tapped her greasy fingers on the back of my hand. "Aubrey I'm telling you, Nic is the guy for you."

"You never talk like this. You're better at bashing the ones I go out with." My sister's disposition changed from sharpness to tenderness.

"Remember when I met Ray? You told me that night he was the one for me." A tear slipped from Allison's eye.

Ray, Allison's late husband, he was a gift from heaven sent directly to her. Seventeen years of marriage until the cancer stole him from her. Stole him from all of us.

"Do you see what I mean? I took that chance with Ray. Take that chance with Nic."

"Thanks Allison, I needed to hear that. I better get busy and get my flight rearranged."

"Don't forget to call Maria. She'll be pissed you won't be back for Monday night." Allison snickered, retreating back into her mouth watering burger.

We all knew how Maria hated when I was gone. Her junior chefs drove her to drink, literally. My flight rearranged and a fast phone call to work to say "Hey, I met this hot stud muffin cowboy and I won't be reporting till Tuesday night." But best of all, I planned on waiting for dinner to spring it on Nic. One last person to surprise, Gina. She had wanted me to extend my time in New Orleans with her; this would be music to her ears. Not only would I be hanging out with her, but I'd be staying for Nic.

Casual dining with Nic seemed to be suiting me fine. Another off beat hole-in-the-wall place. This time I found myself sitting next to him in what seemed to be a grocery store-turned diner. At the checkout a cat laid curled sleeping on the counter top under the "next register" sign. Mismatched chairs, old metal tables with brightly colored tile tops and condiments packed heavily in a scrappy wooden box adorned the table tops. At a hand's reach, your choice of accessories waited to compliment the deep fried delights. Greasy fingerprints stained the paper menu we had just ordered from, but I had to scan over it again. Mental note…get myself a good southern cookbook. Instead of the usual wine or beer, I grabbed us two grape sodas from the help yourself cooler. Nic was on his third napkin trying to wipe away whatever remainders were stuck to the table top.

"I haven't had grape soda in years." I slurped it right from the bottle.

"It's Friday…you leavin' tomorrow?" Nic ignored my bubbled hiccup. Catching his drift of sternness mixed with sadness, I didn't hold my excitement back.

"Well, um, I…" Great, another hiccup, then the giggles hit. "I changed my flight. I'm leaving on Monday afternoon."

"When were you going to tell me?" If brown eyes could twinkle, Nic's just did.

"Yo. Red. Your order's up." The baby faced boy behind the food counter bellowed for my attention. I jumped up to retrieve another swimming in grease, deep fried seafood dinner, grinning at Nic. "I left you a message this morning."

"You just said you wanted to have dinner tonight."

"I know. So I changed my plans. I'm staying the weekend. Kind of hoped, I could hang out with you." My first bite of crunchy fried fish left my tongue burning.

"You really changed your plans?"

I loved his disbelief. "You asked. Watch the fish is really hot. Be careful." I took another swig of pop and padded the grease from the basket with a napkin.

"You're really staying?" Nic asked again, grinning.

"It didn't take me long to decide. I want to." My chair squeaked under my squirming body. "You're a very interesting man, Nic Ravenwood."

Malt vinegar, a smudge of ketchup, and beer batter dip crossed my lips. Greasy finger tips slipped over my jaw, Nic definitely enjoyed kissing.

"How'd your sister take it?" He was so casual.

"Allison. She's ok with it. She likes you." Between not being able to sit still and grease covering my chin, Nic yanked on my chair, pulling me closer to him.

"Aubrey, am I making you nervous?" He enjoyed the new shade of blush that casted over me.

"Just say, in a flattering way, yes you do."

"Good." He moved on to another bite of fish.

The whole meaning explained itself in Nic's eyes. Call it lust, love, I don't know what, but my heart just fell deeper for the rancher.

My fingers gently outlined a tattoo peeking out from under Nic's t-shirt. "What's this?" I asked wanting to see more of the colorful artwork on his arm.

"Got a few tattoo's. Have to show'em to ya sometime." Nic grinned and exposed one more to me.

"How many are there?" I shoved at his shirt sleeve revealing another display of inked color.

"Like I said, there's a few. You got any to show me?" Nic teased enjoying the basket of fried shrimp.

"No. No, I don't…you love this deep fried stuff don't you?" Quickly, I changed the pace of conversation.

"Love seafood. Any way, raw, deep fried, broiled. I'm sure you can cook up something spectacular with it." Nic winked at me. "We don't get much fresh seafood out my way." Nic's hand planted on my knee, he kept my fidgeting at bay.

"Seafood, delicate and temperamental to work with. Depends on what it is." I shook my head at the many disasters I'd saved over the years. "I still cry when I put a lobster in a pot of boiling water. I swear you can hear them screaming."

"Kind of like when we cut the heads off the chickens. They run around headless."

"Nic that's…that's not true? Is it?" I couldn't tell if he was lying or not.

"You're the chef." He winked, egging me on.

"My chickens, they come to me all fresh, cleaned, and ready for the pan. You really chop the chicken's heads off?" He could see the city girl shining through in me.

"Oh, I can't wait to get you out on the ranch." Nic's fingers squeezed deep into my knee, making me jump.

"Making fun of me?" I reached for the inside of his bicep and pinched deep into a fleshy spot of muscle for teasing me.

"What was that for?" He yanked his arm back.

"Teasing a city girl. So not allowed." I shoved a piece of fish in his mouth before he could protest.

Chapter 4

The Rancher, The Gentleman

"Where to tonight? Another shuck'm, suck'm, eat me raw night with the cowboy?" Gina couldn't resist snickering. "Does he have a friend? I'm lookin' for a weekend buddy."

"Gina, you're unbelievably bad. What would the good sisters at Holy Chapel Rosary think of you?"

"Years of being a 'goodie two shoes' 'tis the reason I'm the way I am. Dress fitting?" Gina called through the bathroom door.

I pulled. I tucked. I shoved. I boosted and rearranged all my curves to fit into Gina's little black cocktail dress.

"Ta-da. It fits." Happily, I whirled myself in a circle showing off my fabulous curves. "Look, it works with all of my bumpy bulges and rolls," My hand flowed over the shear black lace. "Thanks Gina. Think it's too low? Too short?"

"Nonsense. Fits you perfect," Gina tossed me a silk shawl, "Take this too, unless you're planning on stud cakes keeping ya warm all night."

"Thanks." I shot her a half grin. "Are you sure I don't look like a stuffed sausage?" I tried to smooth one more curve that wouldn't flatten.

"For the sake of Pete, would ya stop worrying." Boots in hand, Gina flopped down on the bed. "Aubrey, the man is crazy over you."

"You're in rare form tonight," I checked over my appearance in the mirror, "Almost forgot to tell you, Allison called. She got your mail and took care of Herman the Cat for you." I touched up my lips with pink gloss.

"That girl is way too sweet. You ever think she'll get married again?" Gina slipped her long legs into the black knee high boots.

"I don't see it happening soon. I miss her already and she just left this morning." I pointed to Gina and her half way up the legs boots. "Where did you get those?" Our hotel room had turned into glamour central.

"You like? Attention getters, ya think?" Gina smiled and zipped up her glove fitting mini skirt.

"You seeing the same guy tonight?" I asked as she pushed me out of the way to hog the bathroom mirror.

"Don't wait up for me. If I don't come back, don't worry. I'll see ya in the morning." A dazzling smile spread over her olive skinned face. She looked hot and perfect; she should have been a runway model.

"Seein' the same man or ya sampling a new dish tonight?" I asked again. She'd been keeping it with the same guy for three consecutive nights.

"Same one. He's not a cling-on. I like this one. The sex, raw, rough, and good." Her denim jacket tossed over her shoulder, Gina headed for the door.

"Just be safe." I wasn't trying to lecture, just caring as she shut the door.

Oddly, Nic asked if I minded dressing a little fancy for him. Said he found a quiet restaurant off of St. Charles Street. Casual wear took a backseat for tonight, but I liked doing just that with him, casual.

Ever since Tuesday night, the water fountain in the main lobby became our romantic place to meet. Gina referred to it as my 'splashing hot spot for a hook up.' Fifteen minutes early, how'd I manage that? It was Nic who ran early. Kind of disappointed he wasn't standing here when I stepped off the elevator. I leisurely circled around the fountain taking in the amazing architecture designs of the Monteleone's grand lobby. The fountain splashed a continuous melody of dancing water and I made a silent wish. Calm, poised, and relaxed, he waited for me to look up from my bubbling distraction. Once again my heart beat skipped to its own fluttering bounce when my eyes met his. Just colored marble tiles apart, we examined one another from head to toe. We were a step up, make that several steps up from our casual attire that we'd been sporting all week. My cowboy dressed for 'best of show' tonight. A white dress shirt, sleeves cuffed and a bolo for a tie. The hotel laundry, I'm sure pressed it for him, so crisp looking. His jeans, black, well pressed too, he ended it all with his traditional boots. Another snake skin pair by the pattern. They looked brand new, not a scuff on them. The man had more boots than I had heels with me. Eye catching to me, Nic's coal black hair, all the thickness tied loosely back in a ponytail. No hat to hide it under tonight. Would it be inappropriate to tell a man he's beautiful? The view my eyes held, I enjoyed every inch of him.

"Hi." My personal eye candy wrapped his arms around my waist.

Over the crispness of his pressed shirt, my hands roamed freely along his shoulders. My fingers rested behind his neck, playing with his loose tail of hair. I loved the smell of him. Better yet, I loved the way he kissed me and expected to be kissed back.

Nic's hands skimmed over the lace of my dress feeling all I had to offer. "You're beautiful," he murmured in my ear.

"You clean up nice." A little self guidance by my own hands, I let my fingers trickle back over his arms.

"Smell pretty too, Aubrey." Nic's hands found my cleverly tucked and stuffed curves that I carefully packed into my dress. "Ole Bones told me about this little place down off of St. Charles, not far from here. You ok to walk in those shoes?" He eyed the length of my exposed legs. First time he'd seen them without the covering of my causal blue jeans.

"I'm fine to walk. No more than a block or two...then you'll be carrying me." Nervous? Yes, the man made my heart beat, my blood pulsed. "You said Bones told you about this place?"

"The man is a food hound." On his guided arm, we headed in the direction of St. Charles under the rays of the fading sunset. "When I told him you're an executive chef, he about went nuts. Wanted to know when I was goin' to take him ta that fancy restaurant you cook for."

"You'd come to Ohio?" My eyes sparkled in hopeful delight.

"For you? Yes." There Nic went again, dropping small hints that spoke to my heart.

"Bones, he's taken a liking to you." Nic smiled and stopped me to take in a window display of vintage jewelry. "You like Italian?"

"Yes. One of my favorites. I love the smells of basil, garlic and olive oil simmering together. Wait..." My tone of voice changed, I got all serious on Nic. "I don't have shuck, suck, or eat'm raw tonight? I get real silverware?" The last of my comments had Nic's eyebrows rising and a mischievous grin crossing his weathered face.

"Aubrey, the look on your face when you let that oyster slide down your throat." Another bolt of his laughter sent me laughing. "Had my doubts about you woman."

"But I did it. I ate it. Or should I say 'sucked it.' Even ate more of those slimy, awful things with you." My nose wrinkled my lips into a cringe.

"You survived oyster suckin' night just fine Aubrey." He winked at me.

I may have survived oyster sucking, shucking night, but tonight was all up in the air. I'd hoped our casual stroll, with window shopping, would help knock the edge of nerves out of me. *Please let me be relaxed with him, I moaned silently to myself.*

"Antonio's. Ready to be the food critic that you are?" Nic asked as we stepped into the side street bistro.

As the wonderful aroma of basil, garlic, and fresh bread welcomed the senses, my mind tumbled into Italy. White linen tablecloths accented by a vase of fresh red roses were centered on each table top. Romantic candles, soft lighting, and a hint of Italian music set the ambiance into play. For our private dining experience we were escorted to a table in the front corner. As quick as the maitre' de seated us, he reappeared, with a bottle of Cabernet Sauvignon. Uncorked, sampled by Nic, the wine spilled into our glasses. Warm from the oven, fresh loaves of hard crusted Italian bread never seemed to end.

"You like eggplant?" I asked after the waiter had left with our orders.

"My mom. She made the best eggplant parmesan you'd ever had." Nic smiled at the memory. "None of us can even come close to duplicating her recipe."

"Want me to give it a try?" I did have bragging rights when it came to culinary delights. "Do you have her original recipe?"

"Parts and bits of it. She never wrote anything down. All stored up here." Nic tapped at his forehead with a finger.

"That's bad. I do the same thing. They're always scolding me at work for not writing notes." Nic poured another glass of wine for us while we waited for dinner. "You know I can make you mine. Freeze it and ship it out to you." My tasteful offer made him grin. "All I have to do is freeze it separate. Breaded eggplant in one container, sauce in another, you put it together. It should get to you fine."

"You can do that?"

"I can and I will." My simple words made our hearts melt.

A procession of waiters dressed in the signature black and white attire appeared to serve our meal. Of course Nic wanted the critic's review, bite after bite. Couldn't pick apart a single morsel; I had nothing but praise for this wonderful Italian bistro.

Nic kept me fascinated with his love for the ranch and open land as we enjoyed our evening. My mind completely toppled by his description of the magnitude of acres he owned. My little apartment, lost in the city street lights, didn't even make a dent to the wide open land he loved.

"Your review, Chef Aubrey." Nic asked as we left the bistro.

"I'm singing the highest of praise. Would I ever love to get into their kitchen to see what they've got hidden back there."

"Up for a little stroll round Jackson Square?" Nic grinned. He knew how I loved the French Quarter.

"Taro card or palm reading?" I suggested, snuggling in on his arm, as a full moon blossomed over the streets of New Orleans.

"Neither. Don't believe in that stuff."

"I do." I leaned into him kissing his cheek as we walked.

The nightlife radiated under the full moon. Jackson Square had thinned out except for the remaining taro card readers, palm readers, and other fun and colorful people. Our evening stroll ended on a park bench by the boardwalk. Another round of swapping family stories was enjoyed in the evening night air.

Beams of moonlight shimmered between the buildings as Nic walked me back to my hotel. Our conversation had dwindled during the walk. The evening turned colder than I had expected, even with Gina's shawl, I found myself snuggling closer to Nic.

"We're here again." I mumbled. I didn't want the night to end.

"Aubrey, I..." Nic's words were failing as fast as mine.

"Did you want to get a cup of coffee...or..." my voice trailed to the end. How did I ask a man up to my room for the evening?

"Aubrey...I haven't spent a night with a woman in a long, long time." Nic's honesty impressed me.

"Great. I mean. No, I meant..." A nervous laughter twisted between us. "I haven't been with anyone either, been...probably years." I felt the blush rush over me. My scarlet shade really glowed in the moonlight.

"You should get inside. I can feel your goose bumps." Nic rubbed his hands over the shawl covering my arms.

"Nic." My forehead touched his. I let my nose gently glide over his. "Nic, I'd...I'd be happy just to sleep in your arms."

"You'd be ok, just sleeping next to me?" The tension in Nic's voice released.

"I know, strange. That's me. But, yes. Will you," I tugged at the bolo around his neck, "Will you stay the night with me?" My voice, it didn't hiccup. No breaking. No cracking. My shadow of confidence shimmered for once.

"I could do that for you Aubrey." Nic's voice steady and his lips closed on mine.

The opening elevator door kindly reminded me we'd arrived on the fourteenth floor.

"My room. We're...um...we're at the other end of the hallway." Nic's hand slipped around mine for a comforting support. I fumbled in my purse to find the notorious keycard, "I love these key cards, if I could ever get them to work on the first try."

My silk shawl slipped off a shoulder and trailed down my back as we approached room 1414. I let the card play between my fingers as we stopped in front of the door. I tried once, twice and the door won't open.

"Aubrey, flip the card over." Nic held his laughter back.

"Thanks." I gave up and just handed him the card. Lickety-split the door magically unlocked for him.

"Home away from home." Jokingly I spit out. I couldn't find words, a sentence, or any conversation.

"Your place is a lot nicer than mine and Bones. Ya never want to room with two bachelors." Nic seemed as nervous as me.

"Did you want coffee, or wine, or..." I started to ask.

"No. No, save the coffee for morning." Nic suggested loosening his bolo. "Where's your friend, Gina?"

"Out...Catting around. She'll surface about midmorning." I nervously laid my purse and Gina's shawl on the dresser. "I've got to wash my face. Makeup...I...it drives me nuts." I left Nic standing alone in my hotel room. Not that it was a huge suite or anything, but I really needed to get myself regrouped and the bathroom would work.

"Oh crap. It's been way too long, this, this, I hope this isn't a mistake." I barely mumbled at my reflection in the mirror. My hands kept busy with the soap scrubbing over my skin.

"You look good with or without all that stuff." Nic's voice and body stood right behind me in the bathroom. He handed me a towel. "This isn't a mistake."

I padded my face dry and grabbed my bottle of nighttime moisturizer. "Little nervous. I'm fine, really. Just need to smear this on and..."

Nic's hands squeezed deeply into my hips turning me to face him. His lips applied directly to mine. I don't remember reading that on the bottle of moisturizer...anywhere.

"Just wanted to warn you."

"Warn me about what." My blood pulsed thudding in my ears. Nic had me backed against the vanity. He had to sample one more kiss.

"I sleep in my underwear. What about you?"

"Oh for god sake, Nic." I slapped him with the towel. "A tank and shorts. Get out of here so I can change." My heart pounded, while I shoved him out of the bathroom.

The fourteenth floor featured a great view of other buildings and a courtyard. I never bothered to drawl the drapes when we turned the lights out last night. Barely the break of dawn, a warm glow of sunshine pressed on my face. Contentedly, I found myself still wrapped securely in Nic's arms. His even tempered snoring softly purred in the quiet morning. He felt so comfortable to me, as if we'd slept this way for over twenty years or more. I always loved the so called 'spooning' position of cuddled sleep. Both my hands managed to weave through his fingers with his arm curled closely to my chest. His leg tossed carelessly over mine. Slightly stirring, he released my hands stretching his arm out over me. Last night, I got a little shock when the clothes dropped off. Well not all of them. Nic's arms, chest, and back were covered in brightly colored tattoos. My fingers gently traced over the impressive artwork on his sleeping body. Thought I'd be treated to viewing a farmer's tan. Nope, my rancher had pure Apache blood dripping in his veins. My ivory German skin glowed next to his. This moment for me, just couldn't be more perfect. Nic stayed the night with me, wanting nothing more than to let me sleep in his arms. Still lost in my perfection of an evening, I never heard the humming of the keycard in the door. The handle clicked and turned before I could say a word. Gina emerged from her night of romping over Bourbon Street.

"Aubrey. OH MY GOD." Perplexed. Speechless only for a minute. Then her mind raced for words. "Holy shit girl. You rode the cowboy."

Nothing like having a loud mouth best friend with piss poor manners. Even worse, her timing sucked. She definitely woke Nic from his lost land of dreams and stole my happiness right out from under me.

"Mornin' Gina." Nic looked at her puzzled.

Gina's top, half buttoned. Draped over one arm, her knee high boots. Her short spiked hair completely matted to her scalp. Gina's beautiful artwork of colorful eye shadows reduced to nothing more than a raccoon's mask of black. Lipstick, gone, most likely sucked off in the heat of passion.

"Gina." I sat up letting the sheet fall off me. "What happened to you?"

"Me? You're in bed with the cowboy. Explain why you've got clothes on?" She inquired with beady eyes wanting an explanation.

Nic slowly rubbed my back, his fingers lightly pinching my shoulders. His bare but tattooed chest exposed for Gina's hung over eyes. I glanced back to him, he certainly didn't hide his shit eating grin.

"Mornin' sweetie." Nic sat up running a mouth full of kisses over my shoulder. "Nice to see you've survived another trip on Bourbon Street there Gina." He tossed the covers back getting out of bed not caring if he was dressed or not.

Gina's mouth slobbered when Nic paraded past her in his black tight fitting boxers.

"Sorry Gina, no threesomes. I'm only into Aubrey." As the bathroom door shut, I heard him chuckle.

"Oh my god. Aubrey." Gina's mouth flapped open, then shut at least a dozen times. "He spent the night? No threesome? Shit, I'm really missing out. Dish. Details. Tell me, is he as good as that body brags?"

"Yes. No. Stop it." I rubbed my forehead. No coffee and too many questions. "I asked him to spend the night with me. Just spend the night. That's all." I didn't know if I should be pissed off at her or not. A lecture from a woman who collects men for the total enjoyment of having sex with them would be way out of line. She flopped on the bed where Nic had been holding me.

"Just spent the night?" Gina nudged me in the ribs. "Not bad. I'm impressed. But why do you still have...um...your clothes on? Shouldn't I have found you buck naked?" Gina cracked up, wiping remnants of makeup from her eyes. "Shouldn't I've walked in on you riding him? You know screaming. Begging for more?"

"Gina. We just slept next to each other. He held me in his arms while I slept. It would've lasted longer but you came back." I smiled, picking at the limp spikes in her hair.

"Flippin' amazing. The man is a cowboy God." Gina rolled back on the pillow as the bathroom door clicked open.

"Told ya Gina, I don't do threesomes." Nic nodded for Gina to move her tattered appearance out of his way. "Think she'd prefer my arms around her than yours."

"Hey no sweat. Coffee. I'll get coffee. Ya want some of those Bennie things Aubrey?" Gina asked making it obvious how she was enjoying the view of Nic's backside. "Nice tats man."

"Gina...Go." I commanded sharply pointing toward the door.

Smeared eye shadow and half buttoned clothes Gina bolted for the door.

"How'd I do?" Nic folded me back into his arms.

"Wonderful. You floored her with the word 'threesome.' Totally shell shocked her. When you got out of bed, thought she'd nearly hang her tongue to the floor." Nose to nose with him, I didn't even care about morning breath. My tongue slipped from my mouth licking his lips. A little surprised, he fell on top of me, cushioned by a pile of pillows his full weight covered my body.

"Breakfast." Gina announced loudly, walking back into the room. "Geez, get off her already. She needs her morning feeding." Gina sat two cups of coffee and a bag of pastries on the nightstand. "I'm hitting the shower. Ya should've seen how the doorman glared at me. Do I look like some hooker or what? Don't answer that." She reflected back in the mirror.

"Coffee." Nic rolled off me and handed back a cup of liquid wakeup. "I can't survive without the black gold."

"Coffee's good. Gets me through most anything." I grinned sipping the steaming cup.

"What about the wine?" Nic asked, sitting on the side of the bed.

Slowly I slid in behind him reaching for my hairbrush on the nightstand. I pulled the band off his hair and gently started to brush his poker straight tresses. My one leg dangled by his.

"I like this grey streak you've got going. Braid or tail?" I asked letting Nic's hand massage my leg.

"Pick one." He sipped his coffee. "Aubrey, this can work you know."

"How? You're going back to the ranch. I'm going back to the city." I pulled tighter at his braid.

"This whole long distance relationship thing, Aubrey..." Nic paused pulsing at my kneecap with his fingers. "You up for a phone, computers, fax machines, high tech relationship."

"You're on Mountain time, two hours behind Eastern. When I'm done cooking, you'd be done 'slapping' those hogs of yours. We could meet up every night for a date over the phone." I said tying the end of his braid securely.

Nic's shoulder found its way into my chest as he faced me, "Aubrey, just marry me? Come back with me? Come to Wyoming with me? You'll love it there, I promise."

"Nic...did you just ask me to marry you?" Stunned, I managed not to go pale. I didn't faint either. For a split second my ears rang with chiming wedding bells.

"Yes Aubrey. Marry me." Nic repeated himself to me.

"I'll marry you." I whispered, very sure of myself.

My eyes stared with security into my future husband's eyes. Never in all my life did I feel this comfortable with a snap decision. I let my arms wrap around Nic's chest, my head rested peacefully on his shoulder. He gathered my hands kissing my fingers tips. Connected, contentment, even love, I felt it all with him. Needless to say we didn't hear Gina's shower finish. The bathroom door flung up and a toweled Gina strolled out.

"You two still…oh…oh….one of those moments…I'll be in the bathroom." With dignified grace Gina excused herself back to the bathroom.

Chapter 5

A Wedding

My hands shook while I applied the last of my plum mascara. Not from fear, maybe a little, mostly from the uncertainty. My life, always black and white, everything planned to a tee.

"You're really going to do this?" The woman facing me with worried eyes in the mirror asked. "What do I have to lose?" I answered her back.

A light rapping on the hotel door guided me back before the reflection in the mirror could sway me to her side. I glanced at my watch. Punctual as always. Nic tapped again.

"Hi." I stepped back from the open door.

"Morning," his quick kiss of reassurance landed on my lips, "You ready?"

"Yeah. I think so." Nerves, they displayed themselves with a colorful force.

Nic handed me a paper box with a cellophane peep window. A wrist corsage, red roses and babies breath tucked neatly in tissue paper stared back at me.

"Mom always said a bride…she needs flowers on her wedding day." His fingers slipped over his nervous lips, "You look beautiful Aubrey. Purple's your color."

"Thanks." I'd never seen him so nervous. "Funny, Gram says something like that too." I held up a single red rose, waiting to pin it on his white cotton dress shirt. "I think I would've loved your mom." My hands trembled trying not to stab him with the pin.

"Aubrey, I'm not into fancy jewelry. Just picked this up at a pawn shop. Promise, I'll get ya…"

"They're perfect." I interrupted Nic. My hands slid under his holding the blue velvet box, "I never got into wearing rings...cooking." With a smile, I snapped the little box shut on the silver bands kissing him. "I'm ready."

"If you. If you want to wait..." Nic kept a hold of my hands.

"No. I don't want to wait," My eyes, steadily held on his, "I'm sure. You...you're not backing out on me?"

"No. No, just needed to hear you say that." Nic's happier sigh filled the empty space between us.

My mind kept running without me as we walked hand in hand out of the Monteleone. With a fast inventory tracking in my head, I counted: purse, wallet, driver license, clean lacey bra and panty set on the body with a hint of light perfume. I specifically ducked out to the Wal Greens next door and bought a few scented candles. A splash of romance for the hotel room when we returned.

Only a little after nine, the cab ride took less than fifteen minutes. Our wedding chapel, nothing more than an old stately southern home, which doubled as the office of the Justice of the Peace. Eighteen minutes early for our nine thirty appointment. An appointment I'd be keeping for the rest of my life. Nic's hand pushed on the small of my back as we entered the red brick building. Early meant you take a seat and wait.

"Never thought I'd get married." I played with the edge of my purse.

"Never?" Nic asked rather relaxed.

"After hitting the thirty-five mile stone mark, oh, that's coming close to ten years ago," I shifted on the wooded bench next to him. "I just gave up on the whole girly 'fu fu' wedding. Just put it in a box. Put it on a shelf and closed the closet door."

"I've been waiting for you," Nic boldly announced, running his finger down my jittery arm.

Astounded, my only reply, "Thought you didn't believe in all that hocus pocus stuff?"

"Nic and Aubrey," A robust African American woman called out our names in a thick southern drawl. "I'm Judge Phyllis Combs. It's my pleasure to unite you in marriage today." She held the heavy wood door open, pointing down the long hallway. "Such a beautiful Monday morning, I'd like to officiate this union in our courtyard."

Judge Comb's choice in an outdoor wedding fit perfectly. A small garden of flowers still erupting with summer blooms accented the greenery. Vines willowed along the inner brick building walls and surround the trees. The center of the courtyard, tied together all the charm with a cascading water fall.

Judge Combs added her two cents on the view of marriage. "Let me offer up a little advice. You two look sensible. Just remember," she handed us our marriage certificate and a five by seven card, "Remember to kiss often. Hug daily. Forgive one another. And love each other forever. You can overcome all obstacles, just trust in each other. Words to live by, my good children."

Judge Combs, no older than us, handed back our cell phones, she also served as the photographer. With a few simple 'I do's,' we did. A thin band of silver circled my left ring finger. In a picture postcard setting, Nic and I married. The city girl officially became the wife of the Wyoming rancher.

"Allison is going to be so disappointed." I told Nic while dialing her number.

"Dad's not. He can't wait to meet you," Nic grinned dialing also, "Dad you get the pic's?"

Finally, Allison picked up the phone. She answered on the third ring, but to me, it seemed like a life time.

"Allison. Allison are you sitting down?" I impatiently tried not scream into the receiver.

"Yeah, I'm at your place. Mr. Perfect is curled in my lap. What are you so wound up over?"

"Allison…Nic and I just got married. Like five minutes ago." My vibration of excitement blew my sister away.

"Married? You married the cowboy?" She screamed back overjoyed.

"Hold on he wants to talk to you." I handed my phone to Nic taking his to greet my new father-in-law.

My father-in-law instructed me to call him Dad or Charlie, with the warmest welcome I'd ever received. Surprised, shocked, I'd never been so welcomed by a total stranger into his family. Nic must have been boasting about me all week. Charlie, or Dad, had a great perspective of me.

"Your sister, she's beyond thrilled." Nic said handing back my phone.

"Charlie, no wait Dad," I grinned at Nic, "seems to know an awful lot about me."

"You tell Gina yet?"

"No." My answer hit flat toned. "Not going to tell her till we get home. For Gina, the word 'marriage' cross cuts her soul in deep pain. I don't want to spoil the day."

"Breakfast?" He asked as I tucked our marriage license and little quote card with words to live by in my purse.

"I'm starving. Sex after you feed me." I caught what I just said to my new husband. My mouth dropped. I shocked us both. Didn't mean for it to come out so, so…

"I have to feed you before I bed you?" His lips curled, with a devilish grin.

"Bed me?" I whispered still trying to recover from myself. "Are you going to throw me in a pile of hay and…"

"Yep. Wait till I get you home." He took my hand kissing my fingers. "Aubrey I love the way you just say it right out."

We'd only spent one night sleeping in each others arms. Reality hit me…I've only known this man for five days, this; the sixth, and I married him. Nic slipped his arms around my waist; quick to pick up on the panic dancing in my eyes. My head rested on his chest. His even breathing called to me to calm, but his heart stepped a few beats faster.

"Nic…I'm just a little scared." I molded into him like the vine wrapping around the trees in the courtyard.

"Makes two of us." He kissed the top of my head not afraid to share his feelings with me. "Breakfast?"

I just nodded my head 'yes' letting Nic lead me out onto the busy street. We shared our wedding breakfast at an open air quaint French café instead of our usual hole-in-the-wall diners. Black wrought iron fencing surrounded the terrace of the dining area where we were seated. The sun shone brightly dancing between the tree branches. Greeted with two cups of coffee by a purpled haired waiter, we asked him to snap a few photos for us.

"I like his hair. Practically matches my outfit."

Nic raised an eyebrow to me.

"Really, I think I'll get high lights that color."

"Please don't." Nic started, "Let me guess, pancakes, two or three?"

"Pancakes. Probably just one." I giggled.

"You better take three; you're going to need the energy."

Instantly I blushed liked the virgin bride I wasn't. "You've never seen me on a sugar rush." I retorted trying to save face.

"Aubrey," Nic fingered his own wedding band. "You know I'm expecting you to move to Wyoming."

"I know, I think that goes without saying." I laced my fingers in his touching his band of silver.

"I'm not into this long distance, you here, me there stuff. I need you with me." Nic didn't order. And he didn't beg.

"I didn't expect you to give up your ranch and move to the city. But I'm going to need a little time to pack up. Get my stuff moved..." My own words closed tightly in my throat. "My job. Cooking, it's everything to me. Oh god...I'm going to have to quit my job."

"Aubrey. Aubrey look at me." A rough texture of fingertips lifted my chin, meeting his eyes.

"Nic, I've been a chef for nearly twenty years. I've lived in a city all my life." My new husband just got a sweet look at my minor panic attacks.

"We'll get adjusted honey." He pulled the end of a stray curl, smoothing my emotional outbreak. "After you get to Wyoming, get settled in, look for something. Part time, I hope. Biggest city's, about a three hour drive."

"Part time. That could work." My world collided with my standards. Never give up your dream. Did I? I'm a well-known chef. I could pick up a position just about in any city I wanted.

"Aubrey, you ok?" Nic's voice clouded with concern.

"Um, yeah. Panic's over. Fine. I'm fine." Talking to ones self, did help with reason.

"You get home, drop the bomb on everyone. Then how 'bout I come in a week or so. Want to check out this family of yours." Nic's offer rang like notes on a music sheet to me.

I managed to sip my coffee without drooling all over myself. "My family, oh you're in for a treat." My plate of pancakes, with ample maple syrup and butter, slid in front of me. Nic he was straight up eggs, bacon and toast. That's easy to fix I thought.

"Nic, I can't lie. I'm excited. Thrilled beyond words. But I'm scared to death. Are you sure you're willing to put up with my madness for the rest of your life."

"Wouldn't of asked ya if I didn't think I could handle you and all your girlyness for life. Besides, remember how you came up and asked me to dance?" Nic gave me a wink adding hot sauce to his eggs.

Hot sauce? The man ate that crap on everything. I'll have to fix that, I made another mental note about my new hubby.

"Yeah. Thought you were going to bop me for pulling your hair." I took a bite of the fluffy sugar coated pancakes.

"Aubrey, none of us missed what Gina yelled when we walked in that place. But then you were right there behind me, waiting, more like ready to run." Nic and I laughed remembering our first night's impressions. "I knew right then I wasn't going home without you."

My head spun slowly absorbing his words, he knew, he knew that night.

"Eat up, little lady. I'm going to teach ya how to ride." Nic grinned. His eyes glittered watching how many shades of pinkish red I could turn.

"You mean a horse, right?" With shades of pink rolling down my pale skin, I teasingly asked.

The smell of lavender filled the hotel room as we entered. "I like candles." A small whisper appeared to be my voice. My nerves got the best of me. I couldn't even peel the wrapper from the candle.

"Candles. Nice. I like them." Nic lit one with his lighter. "Aubrey. Who ya callin'?" He asked kicking off his boots.

"Shhh." I put my finger over his lips trying to silence him. "Hey Gina, it's me. Listen, can you not come back to the room for about..." Nic held up two fingers, then shaking his head held up both hands as I interpreted ten hours. "Just give me about two hours. Yeah. Yeah, I'll explain everything. Yes. Yes he's here. Later Gina, later."

My eyes rolled, while I tossed the phone on the night stand. "Gina wants details."

"Two hours? You think I'll be done with you in two hours?" Nic pulled off his shirt, unzipping his jeans.

"Come here Mrs. Ravenwood." With a hand, he teasingly motioned for me to join him.

There was something wrong with my feet, they won't budge. Nic's hair fell over his shoulder brushing the top of his chest. Muscles. How did I ever miss those broad shoulders and thick, defined biceps? Oh wait, my fog of a fantasy captured my attention again. Nic's tattoo's played my mind into mush. If I thought his tattoos distracted me, I was kidding myself. His jeans, fly wide open, those sexy boxers peeking out teasing me, I never knew a man could look so incredibly yummy.

"Aubrey, you going to make me come in get you?" He toyed with me, enjoying how I slowly came back from my dreamland.

My head kept shaking back and forth. Words, they disappeared or got stuck with my feet. "Nic…" I swear I just wiped drool off my lips.

We were only steps away from each other. An arms reach, well for Nic I would be. Finally my feet gave in and I took steps flipping my heels off. For once in my life I'm glad I took Gina's advice and forfeited the panty hose. My finger tips outlined and brushed lightly over the artwork displayed on his body. Willingly, he waited for me to find a comfortable ending to my little game of sensory touching. Nic slowly felt around my waist, tickling the curves I have growing. Gently he felt his way through the silk material, letting his hands free the zipper of my skirt that was bonded to me. A little yank, a little tug, shifting from side to side, and my skirt tumbled to the floor. My hidden curves would all soon be felt and seen by my new husband. My skirt crumpled around my ankles. My first notion, pick it up. Smooth it out. Don't want it to wrinkle. Instead, I stepped on it. Took my toes and inched it away from me while my hands roamed freely back over Nic's bare chest.

Our heads whipped simultaneously toward the heavy banging on the door. "Housekeeping." A little grey haired maid let herself in. "Oh, good heavens. I'm so sorry. You, you…you need to put the sign on the door."

She staggered backwards yanking the 'Do Not Disturb' sign from the back of the door slamming it shut behind her. In the mist of laughter, my sweater disappeared over my head. I fell back on the bed showing off nothing but my soft rose colored bra and matching lace panties. Glad I'd dressed for the occasion. My legs dangled between Nic's, slyly rubbing my toe up the inseam of his jeans. Jeans…gone. Boxers…no more. Nothing separated us except my lacey underwear. Nic's naked body straddled over me, letting his long hair bunch on my chest.

"So your girlfriend Gina, she wanted details did she? You kiss and tell, Aubrey?

"No." My breath slipped away as Nic's hand released the hook on my bra.

"You just tell her you got your first riding lesson." Nic lips closed locking around mine.

Chapter 6

Going Home

    Nic attempted to kiss me goodbye and leave three times. I shut the door behind him for the third and final time; still kissing him till my lips ached. He'd promised to be back in time to join me for the airport. I clutched him closer, pulling him harder into my towel wrapped body. Nic barely got himself dressed after our little steamy shower together.
    "Aubrey, I've got…" My tongue licked at his lips, "I've got to get packed so I can get back here."
    Enticing him, I stepped back, dropping my towel. "Jesus god woman, you play dirty."
    "So make it fast cowboy." A little aggressive even for me, I grabbed his belt buckle playfully guiding him back over to the bed.
    "This is no 'wham bam thank ya ma'am, I'll see ya in an hour." Nic hustled out the door after another satisfying romp on the bed.
    I let him escape without protest, this time. "Gina." I smacked my forehead. I learned some great Italian hand moves from her. "Crap. Crap. Crap. She's going to want me to dish every single thing."
    Not everything, some things I'd be keeping to myself. The room totally ransacked, pillows tossed, the covers barely clung to the mattress. Quickly I started to straighten the room; no way did I feel the need to dish details. Nic and I both had late afternoon flights. He'd planned on being back here by three. One rumpled bed made tidy again, I sat there staring at my wedding band, I'm married. In one short morning, we married, enjoyed our little wedding breakfast, and did a fast bed romping honeymoon. What, all in less than five hours? That's got to be a world's record. The door clicked open; Gina hesitantly came in as I packed.

"Is it safe? Any naked cowboys banging the hell out of you Aubrey?" She crowed at me.

"No, my naked cowboy went to pack his stuff. He'll be back about three. Offered to take us to the airport. So I said yes." My smile, even for Gina, was a little too dreamy.

"Aubrey, you take a ride on that man or what?" Gina smirked, while flinging her belongings into a suitcase.

"Yeah. Something like that." I hoped my jubilant grin didn't sell me out.

Gina had me skirting around all her questions about the dirty deed as she liked to call it. Nicely put, she seemed happy with all my answers, or just preoccupied by her ringing phone. Packed and ready to go, Gina gabbed nonstop to her new lover. Even the short ride in the elevator couldn't separate them.

For good luck I tossed a penny in the fountain where Nic and I had met for our dates.

"You're such a wisher." Gina commented in her rude tone and went to check out.

"You've got everything?" A hug from Nic circled me.

"All but you." My whole body swayed under his embrace.

"You tell her yet?" He nodded over towards Gina.

"No. Conversation for the plane ride home. Does Bones know?"

"Oh yeah. He's bustin' a gut to get over here and squeeze the stuffing out of you." Nic joked.

Security check point became the most dreaded, depressing moment of my life. Separation approached way too fast. We won't be seeing each other for two possibly three weeks.

"Nic, can't you come to Ohio? Please." I begged, burying my face into his plaid covered shoulder. I never begged a man in my entire life. But Nic, I'd beg him for another night, any day.

"As soon as you land, call me." He circled my face in his hands.

Promise made with protest, "But you'll be in the air when we land."

"I've been gone from the ranch too long. Dad can only handle it for so many days. First thing, I'll get arrangements made to come to Ohio. Then you're coming home."

"Do you think your dad will come too?" I bartered for more time with him. "Ask him for me." Nic learned fast, tears came with the package of me.

"Miss Aubrey." Bones waited. "Congratulations. Got yourself a fine man. Can't wait for you to join us." Bones, who'd ever thought he'd be as soft as he was round. Nic was right; ole Bones nearly squeezed the stuffing out of me.

"Aubrey." Nic reached for my hand. "You needed more than just a plain silver band." He slipped an eloquent ruby and diamond ring next to the silver band on my finger.

"Oh. Oh, Nic…when did…oh my gosh. Thank you."

"Found it when we were out bumming in those antique shops. Thought you needed it." Nic held my hand out for a better look. "Get Gina. Get to your flight. Call me." He ordered kissing me goodbye.

For the moment I'm glad Gina didn't think I existed. Gab, gab, gab on her cell phone. Seems man number three captured her heart, or just her body, who knows? I nudged Gina pointing to flight schedule. Nic waited till we topped the escalator. My honeymoon ended for now as I waved goodbye to the man in the black suede hat.

My window seat didn't offer the view I wanted back. Silly me, I wanted my husband. I wanted a real wedding night, not just a couple of hours. I sulked in the seat next to Gina, wishing I could turn my cell phone on and see all our pictures.

"He had a silver wedding band on Aubrey." Gina loathed cheating men. All three marriages, the rat finks cheated on her.

"I know Gina. I know." I tried shushing her, keeping our conversation to just us in the tight quarters of the airplane.

"Aubrey. Wedding band. Dumb ass, married. Hello." She snapped at me.

"Yes Gina. I get it. He's married." My smirk, my shit eating grin, it was so hard to keep from her.

"He used you and you let him." In total disgust, Gina tossed her hands up to the air. "You know, I was liking him. What a fuck head." Gina's choice of phases caused the woman seated in the row next to us to have whiplash.

"Gina, keep your voice down." I tried to tell her. "Let me explain."

"Explain? Really, Aubrey? The ass probably has like ten little ranch brats and a big ole fat wife. He's married. I can't believe he's married." She spouted under hushed breath.

"He's married to me, Gina." With pleasure I shoved my wedding rings in her face.

"Oh good god, Aubrey. What the hell did you do?" Gina slumped in her seat.

I enjoyed the show; first Gina's face slowly drained itself from all blood. A lot of coughing, sputtering and her lips forming words, but her voice won't hack them up.

"We got married this morning. Justice of the peace. I got lots of pictures on my phone. Can you talk yet?" I asked ringing for the stewardess.

"Could I have two, no, better make it three, bottles of whiskey please?" I handed her my credit card to charge the beverage to bring Gina back to life. "Seven-up, too, please."

"She alright?" The stewardess asked.

"She'll be fine. Her brain is trying to focus. I'm sure the whiskey will snap her back to reality." I smiled as the stewardess hurried to fill the order.

"I called Allison, she's tickled. I even talked to Nic's dad. He sounds so warm, I hope he likes me. I've got so much to get done before I leave."

Gina grabbed my arm. Her 'man eating' red nails dug deep into my flesh. "Leave? You're leaving? You're going out to that unknown, dirty I don't know what kind of place." She smacked herself hard in the forehead. "You can't leave me."

"Do you think three is going to be enough for her?" The stewardess returned with Gina's feel good beverage.

"I just broke the news to her that I got married and I'm moving to Wyoming to be with my husband." I beamed; I'm a blushing bride sitting in coach.

"Oh congratulations, honey. How wonderful." At least the stewardess seemed happy for me.

"Stop that. It's not wonderful. It's not great. What the hell are you thinking Aubrey?" Gina sobbed as people started staring.

"Gina, honey, take a drink. You'll be ok. You can come visit anytime." In a motherly way I patted her back. "You know, you might like the wide open wilderness.

"There's freakin' cow's out there. And dirt. Do they even have indoor plumbing?" Gina downed her first drink.

"Wait a minute. Is that why you called me this morning? You two were getting it on? Weren't you?" She mixed herself another drink.

I started blushing. All shades of red popped out from behind my little lilac wedding outfit I wore home. "Gina," My snickering erupted into a blast of giggling. "You'd be so proud of me. I got my first riding lesson from a cowboy."

Chapter 7

Nic's Arrival Home

The elder Ravenwood man waited for his son and ole Bones at the small turning carousel inside the Buffalo, Wyoming, airport. The evening skies had cleared to a crisp coolness as Nic and Bones walked in off the tarmac. Charlie Ravenwood hugged his son. He handed both men warmer coats, a third jacket remained draped over his arm. A new weather front brought in an early September cool down.

The first words out of Charlie's mouth, "Where's the new Mrs.? Thought she was a comin' home with ya." Disappointment surrounded the fading smile on his face.

"Put her on a plane back to Ohio. She needs to tie up her life there before she can start one with me here." Nic pulled his bag off the running carousel with a huff. "Told her I'd fly back in a week or so. Meet the family and all. Dad, you'll be going with me."

"What if she don't want to come, Nic? Then watch ya going ta do?" Bones asked the impossible question packing a wad of snuff into his gum. Bones worried that the new Mrs. Ravenwood would back out on the marriage.

"She'll come. Or I'll go back and bring her out here." Decision made, Nic headed out the double doors to the parking lot.

"I couldn't believe it when ya called, son. Ya married yourself a Yankee girl from Ohio. She's a chef. No, an executive chef to boot." Charlie led them to the waiting truck.

A week's worth of mail left Charlie's hands and into his passenger's. When wedding conversation hit a low, the mail would fill in for the three hour ride back to the ranch. Charlie wondered in silence, did his son do the right thing? Too fast? Too soon? Should've gotten to know her better. Not many women coming from city life could handle the long days on a ranch. As he started the truck, Charlie eased his mind remembering his boy followed right in his steps. Charlie had met Nic's mother, Ruthie, at the county fair. Asked her to marry him that night, of all places in the horse barn, she was only twenty. Forty-two years of marriage, Charlie glanced at his son smiling.

"Something on your mind dad?" Nic asked reading over the latest livestock report. "Spit it out man."

"Things will be alright son. Just wanted to let ya know...I like the sound of Aubrey's voice." His dad's voice hushed and low, he turned the truck to the highway. "Just thinkin' of your mama."

Nic glanced toward his father, "Think she would of liked her dad."

"You knock her up or somethin'?" Bones leaned forward between the two men. "You know, ya don't have to get married, cause, well ya know." Description of words just wasn't in Bones nature.

"No, Bones, I didn't knock her up." Nic shook his head holding back his laughter. "Well at least, don't think I did. Guess I'll have ta ask her when I call. Ah crap, it's midnight there." Nic tapped the clock on the dashboard. "She's two hour ahead of us."

"Call her anyways. Let her know you landed. You know, polite and all." Old Bones did have a heart.

From his shirt pocket, Nic pulled out his cell phone. Sure enough Aubrey's number lit the screen. "Hum, she listened to me." He dialed her number back. After several rings her sleepy voice flooded the line to him.

"Hello."

"Hey beautiful."

"Nic, it's you."

"Sorry. Didn't mean to wake ya. Got in 'bout half hour ago. Everything ok there?"

"Yeah, yeah no problems. Got here fine. I told Gina on the plane. Wish you could have been there. She's a riot." Aubrey stroked her cat's silky fur. "When are you coming to Ohio? I miss you."

"Soon honey. Give me a week or so, then I'll be out." Nic could hear the sigh of disappointment in her voice. "Love ya, I'll talk to ya tomorrow."

"Love you, too." Aubrey whispered sleepily.

Talk between the three men turned to the happenings of the past week. Ranch life, who did what and who didn't do what. By the time they'd reach the house, it would be close to midnight. The house, Nic's thoughts ran rampant. He couldn't bring Aubrey into a run-down, unmaintained ranch house. The old home place had taken second fiddle after his mom passed away four years ago.

"Dad, we got to do something about the house." Nic started.

"Already been thinkin' about that. Three things a woman needs." He started using hand motions while driving as he spoke. "One," he held up a finger. "She needs an up ta date bathroom, clean one at that. Two, you better do something about that bedroom of yours. Can't bring a new bride in ta that rat hole. Gut it and get some pretty sheets and stuff. Your mama always liked that girly fluffy stuff. And don't be say nothin' to her about sleepin' pink flowered sheets.

"Got it dad." Nic laughed. "Mom made you sleep in pink flowered sheets?"

"Women, they love that, what do ya call it?" Charlie racked his brains searching for the word.

"Word's feminine, Charlie. Women you know, they like feminine, girl stuff." Bones spoke up from the backseat.

"Feminine, huh Bones? So what's number three?" Nic waited for his dad's response.

Charlie held three fingers up, "Oh yes. And third, this wife of yours, she's a gourmet cook, Nic. All that fancy stuff, like I see on them there cookin' shows. How the hell are we going to fix that old kitchen up for her?"

"You two, you're up shit creek. No paddle to save ya, neither one of your hides." Bones added his two cents toward the womanly conversations, laughing harder.

Chapter 8

Breaking The News

"What the hell do you mean you got married?" My brother Phil twitched nervously in his shoes with his mouth bounding to his knees.

Phil threw his glasses on the kitchen counter slapping his hands over his bugged out eyes. Brutally, Phil rubbed at his eyes. I really thought he was going to yank them out of their sockets. Dee, his wife, rushed to his side reminding him about his fake illnesses. The heart condition, kidney condition, brain tumor, the list went on and on for my hypochondriac of a brother.

"You can't be serious? You just married some hill jack? And…and you're moving to Idaho?" Phil finally finished his brutal assault to his eyes.

"Phil, darling, calm down. She said Wyoming. Isn't that it Aubrey? Wyoming?" Dee snatched the paper bag from my hand so Phil could practice his breathing. "It's a mistake. Right, Aubrey? You're getting an annulment? Right?"

"Mistake? I think not. I'm married. Yes, I'm moving to Wyoming to live on a fifty thousand acre ranch as soon as I can get organized. Ok, within two months, if not sooner." The ruby on my hand, I dangled it under Dee's nose making her slobber with jealousy. "Guess you're going to have to find someone else to be your errand girl, there, Phil. Better listen to Dee and sit yourself down."

"How could you just make a snap decision and marry some stranger? What? You knew him for a day and you jumped in his pants?" Dee whispered in her sultry let me try to show you who's boss voice.

"Ha, you're a trip, Dee. No I didn't get his pants off him till after we got married. Seriously, since when were you so interested in my sex life?" I let my shoulders chuckle with laughter at Dee's expense.

"But, but, Aubrey, you married a total stranger. That's…it's just wrong. I'll phone Hal. You know my lawyer friend, the one you should really be dating. He'll get you out of this mess." My brother Phil stood there with his high tech phone. He desperately thumbed down the address book.

"Put the phone down, Phil. It's done. My choice. I'm married and I'm staying that way." I felt my anger creeping up the back of my neck. Someone was going to get hurt and really soon.

"You didn't even ask us…" Dee shut her mouth as if I slapped her.

"Since when do I need you two's permission to do anything with a man?" Steam boiled hot under my collar.

"You're leaving us…I don't understand why…how could you?" Phil stammered out the words as if I punched him in the gut.

"Grow up, Phil. You're fifty-one years old. Get a freakin' life. You've mooched, begged, and sucked me dry. You and Dee Dee kitten here even tried to move into my little apartment a few times. You're a cheap ass. You're all on your own, brother dear." I hissed, letting it all out and it felt great.

A tad bit stunned, Phil had to get his feet under him before he could attack me again.

"You…you just jumped into this. Like you always do with all your so called love relationships or whatever you call them." Kitten Dee Dee stood behind him pretending to be Phil's defense cheerleader.

"You're still nagging about my sex life?" The word 'sex' had Phil up in twitches again. You didn't dare say the dirty word 'sex' out loud to my god fearing brother and his wife.

"You just wait. I'm telling Gram. She'll, she'll make you leave that dirty ranch hand, thing, or whatever he is." In award winning form, Phil stumbled for the kitchen chair by his side. He should have taken it when Dee tried to get him to sit down the first time.

"Listen up you stupid moron…" My premenopausal mood swing hit in full force. My hand clinched around the dish towel, I envisioned squeezing Phil's neck like the towel in my hands.

"What I'd miss?" Gram and Allison let themselves into my apartment.

"You have a key?" Soft little kitten voice Dee asked, stunned.

"Gram, oh Grammy, did you hear the disgrace Aubrey brought to our family?" Phil played his 'oh, pitiful me' role to a hilt.

"Ha. Beat ya to it. Told her right after I called Allison. Um, yeah that's right, Monday. After I said I do's with Nic." Laughter, it saved me. "Ha...looks like you're last on the totem pole again."

"Yes, Phil, we all know that Aubrey got married. Got a picture of him? Allison says he's one hot dish. Let me see this boy." Gram pushed past Phil, who stood there with open waiting arms to be comforted.

Huddled like a football squad, everyone waited for my computer to boot up. All our wedding photos taken by the justice of the peace, had been downloaded from our phones. Nic had even sent me pictures of my future home to share with my family.

"Ok. Ok. Here he is." I danced in my office chair like some sixteen year old getting a love note by e-mail. Even Dee crept in for a peek at my new husband.

"Oh, Aubrey. He's beautiful. Look at that hair. No, eyes. Oh my, nice body under those clothes, huh sweetie?" Gram, she said it like it was. "He's Indian."

"You married an Indian?" rang Phil's voice from the kitchen table.

"He's Apache." I ran my fingers over the screen of the computer wishing I had him here.

"Where's my Bible? We need to pray for Aubrey's soul. God help her, she's gone astray. She married a savage. Dee get over here." Phil found his soapbox of faith...again.

From under Phil's nose, Allison stole the conversation back. "See I told ya, Gram. Look at her. You should of seen the way he looked at her when she asked him to dance." Allison took Gram in her arms twirling her around. "If you didn't believe in love at first sight, you did that night."

"You asked him to dance?" Gram patted my back while we clicked through my wedding pictures.

"Well...yes. Harry Connick, Jr. was playing; we all know I love my Harry. Plus after a few glasses of wine, Gina and Allison egged me on. You should of seen the chick he shot down. Blonde, boobs out to here," I did the hand gesture out in front of my own chest, "turned her flat down. But he said yes to me." Oh yeah, gloating felt good.

With all the giggling girl talk going on, we forgot about Phil and his dramatic display of saving my soul from my new savage of a husband. He tucked his tail between his legs and pussyfooted over to where we girls were ogling my dreamy husband.

"That's him?" Phil pointed at the screen curling his lip into a sneer.

"Yeah, Phil. He's your new brother-in-law. Get used to it. He'll be here in two weeks to help Aubrey move." Allison so loved to push Phil's buttons.

"Phil, you just better suck it up and put your big boy pants on. This cowboy ain't going to take any of your shit." Gram slapped him on the back nearly knocking him to the floor. "What'cha going to do now, Phil? You done did sucked me and Allison dry. Looks like the Aubrey gravy train is heading west." Gram kept her sternness without cracking a line on her wrinkled face.

Ugly truth be told, my brother and his wife had their hand out for any greasing they could steal. Sob story after sob story would be twisted to benefit their greedy needs. I'm sure someone from their church would be calling to give me a thrashing lecture over the choice I've made. It wasn't the first time Phil had sicked one of the congregation members on me. And I'd lay money on it, it won't be the last. The sting of my punch along with Gram and Allison not falling into the Phil and Dee Dee trap, no doubt left them agitated. Their meal ticket is skipping town for a rancher from Wyoming.

"What about your assets? Did you protect yourself?" Finances, Phil would love to have his sticky mitts into my personal affairs.

"Of course she protected herself the first time they had sex." Gram smarted off smugly. "Oh. Sorry, wrong assets. Yep, he looks like he's got good assets honey." Gram patted me on top of the head like the good little girl she knew I was.

"Let's correct that sentence with a big red marker Phil. Yeah, I got a lot stashed away. Think about it Phil. I just married a man who has fifty thousand acres of land. Cattle, purebred horses, and the livestock list goes on. The man I married didn't even ask for a prenuptial agreement. He wants me, you ass, not my money." Dressing Phil in my sarcasm felt good, and fueled me.

"You know, I'll call the courts. Claim you insane. You know I can do it." Thinking wasn't one of Phil's better attributes. He thought he'd won the upper hand. A little scare tactic he learned from the one prelaw class he'd taken. "You're mental. Any court and judge will side with me."

"Mental. Because I got married? Here, here's Nic number. Why don't ya take it up with my new hubby? He's got lawyers that will eat you alive." With gritted teeth my smile reflected in Phil's coke bottle glasses. "If you can't share in my happiness, don't let the door hit your egotistical ass on the way out."

"Dee. Dee I'm leaving." Phil bellowed for her. "Why are you still looking at that damn Indian?" My poor apartment door, yanked opened, and ricocheted off the wall, all from Phil's anger.

Dee stood up from the computer where she and Allison had been flipping over all the pictures Nic had sent me.

"Congratulations. I hope you have many years of happiness Aubrey. You deserve someone good."

She hugged me. Dee just hugged me and said something kind to me. Gram, Allison and I had just been blindsided. Dee never went against what Phil said. "Seriously, Aubrey, I mean it."

"Dee. Where are you?" My brother stormed into my open apartment, punching the innocent door again. "We're not done, Aubrey Hunter. You'll see. I'll come after you. Make you come home. You owe me. You need to take care of us."

"Phil Hunter…shut your mouth." Dee screamed nearly blowing out her lungs. "You know nothing about this man and you should be supportive of your sister. What kind of a Christian are you?" Dee in her want-to-be fashion model swagger left Phil standing in the doorway with gooey egg dripping on his face.

Idle threats chimed from Phil as he followed Dee down the hallway. His dictatorship had left the building.

Gram shut my battered apartment door. The three of us, our eyes silently bounced from one to the other waiting, wondering what the hell just happened.

"Did Dee just hug me?" Shocked, I asked. "Did she really say congratulations?"

"Looks like all that praying paid off for her. She did more than grow a set of balls; the girl's got a Vajayjay for sure." Gram filled our wine glasses. "To you my dear and Nic, and to Dee for finding her voice." We drank to Gram's toast. "Serious note." Gram inspected the bottle of wine and refilled our glasses. "Good wine, but, I'm not underestimating you. Not pulling a Phil here. You're a levelheaded strong willed woman, Aubrey."

"Gram this isn't like you to tap dance around. Spill it."

"You're a respected chef. You worked hard for where you're at. I'm…"

"Gram, I'm forty-four years old. Look at me; I've got the world by the tail. Got it all. Hell, I'm even an award winning chef. You think I'm taking a step down marrying a rancher?"

"Aubrey, no. Not at all. None of us have seen you…for lack of better words, so head over heels in love. But my issue here is, are you giving up your dream?"

"No, Gram. I'm just enriching my dream. I admit this isn't going to be easy. City girl to country life, scary. It's not like I can't find another job. Nic and I've already discussed it. I like the idea of part time. I'm comfortable with my choice." My little reassurance eased the worry lines on Gram's face.

Chapter 9

Welcome To Cleveland

"So, when's hubby get in?" Gina, not known for keeping her voice down, announced.

Steadily, I worked over a chunk of salmon. My apricot honey walnut glaze drizzled all around it. "Shush, I haven't dropped the bomb on Maria yet." Gently, I laid the salmon on the sizzling grill.

"You haven't told her? Oh, this is going to be ripe. Ya selling ring side seats?" Gina snickered. "She's going to shit. Let alone you're married, but you're leaving her. What will she do without her prized number one chef?"

"She still has you, oh golden one." I got a small jab in on Gina as I checked the grilling salmon. "I planned on telling her Sunday night. You know, at the big reception Gram's having for me and Nic."

"Oh, you're cruel. No, you're a chicken. Bock, bock, bock." Gina spread her arms out, making them wing shaped. Her head bobbed back and forth pecking like a chicken. She strutted around the kitchen clucking at me.

"You know, Nic said they just whap the chicken's heads right off. They run around headless spewin' blood all over." My hands erupted like a fountain. "I wouldn't be clucking near him, bet he'd mistake you for a chicken."

Gina stopped mid strut. "They kill their own chickens?"

I rolled my lips tight, nodding my head yes. I picked up the butcher knife next to me. The head of lettuce, decapitated, right in half and Gina screamed.

"Aubrey, don't. I don't want to hear anymore of Nic's head chopping stories. He's kidding right?" She picked up the two halves of lettuce, molding them back together as if they had once been breathing.

"Gram's going all out on this shindig of hers." I switched gears easing Gina's mind back to our way of civilization. "Did I tell ya, Nic's dad is coming too? I hope he won't mind sleeping on the sofa bed."

"His dad? Really? His dad is coming? You're going to meet his dad?" Gina poked me. She'd always loved and still is in good standing with all three ex-husband's parents.

"Yeah we talk on the phone almost every day. Sometimes his dad just calls me to say Hi."

"You're in. If the guy's father likes you, you've got it made." Gina played in the corn muffin batter. "What about his mother? You've never mentioned her."

"Ruthie, she passed away a few years ago. Nic didn't say much, just he misses her." I wiped my hands on my apron. "I didn't press for details. He said she'd been sick for a while."

Business was slow; a Tuesday evening trademark. Just a handful of us ran the kitchen. Even the owners took Tuesday night off, unless we had a big affair. Gram had made all the arrangements with Maria for the private party on Sunday night. She made sure to remind Maria that Gina and I would not be the chef of choice for the gala. Come this Sunday, Maria's perfect chef would shatter her world like dishes crashing on the tile. She always said I'd never leave her. The lady's going to need her top shelf bottle of rum, for sure.

For me, taking a Friday or Saturday night off was next to impossible. Even if I asked in advance, I usually got denied. I pulled one of my brother's numbers, all week I faked a dreaded sickness. Each day I looked worse, so tired, just dragging myself around. Thursday, I even wore a surgical mask, to help fake my sickness. I got sent home early when Maria found me bent over the sink looking as if I were going to heave my cookies.

Amazingly my nutty plan really worked to a tee. Nic and his dad were arriving Friday afternoon and I had my whole weekend free and clear to celebrate with my new husband. Husband. When I said it out loud, I tensed. I really have a husband. Now that was something new for my vocabulary. But calling myself

Mrs. Aubrey Ravenwood, and yes I took his last name only to be hyphenate for work, it sent me into stitches of giggles.

My apartment became a battle zone of specifically marked boxes. The once decorative entryway, now stacked high in cardboard cases, waited for the moving service. Mr. Perfect, my seven year old Siamese cat, occupied the top of the piled boxes. Somewhere, he'd found a dirty black shoe lace, the tip missing. Most likely chewed off by his little needlepoint teeth. All the laces in my shoes were accounted for. My crazy fur ball left his dirty shoe lace fall between the boxes reminding me of a snake dangling, waiting to strike. Nic said he had a barn full of cats, but I certainly hoped he didn't think Mr. Perfect would be attending the wild side of barn life. My cat belonged with me, curled and cuddled in my new home. In good spirit, I teased Nic about his furry competition.

Nothing like hitting Friday rush hour driving though Cleveland, and trying to get to the airport. My temper flared at idiot drivers.

"It's September, just rain out there people. Just drive." I wailed at no one in particular.

Two weeks of waiting. Two weeks worth of e-mails and phone calls. All I wanted, my husband. A little nervous about meeting "Dad" as he often reminded me to call him. I'm not sure who I talked to most Nic or his dad. Finally, the exit for Cleveland Hopkins airport appeared in my view.

"Who's calling me now?" My phone buzzed like a bee sitting in the change holder. "Allison." So happy it was her and not work.

"Hey. Gram and I are at your apartment. I'm cooking." She laughed so hard I thought she'd wet herself. Everyone knew who the cook of the family was...me.

"You mean you're warming up in the micro?" I laughed with her.

Gram swiped the phone, "Are you there yet?" I could hear the microwave beeping in the background.

"Just found a parking spot. Heading in to get my cowboy." I clicked off the engine.

"Well, go rustle them up and get him on back here cowgirl." Gram's way of blessing me, over the phone.

Delta Flight 372 arrived and I headed directly to baggage claim. Who needed escalators? They only slowed you down. I bounced down the steps like a kangaroo in a hop off match. The baggage claim floor packed with rush hour people. The airport seemed never to sleep. I darted in and out of people, bags, and kids in strollers until I found the Delta turn style. A hat, black suede, next to him another hat, same brand, I think. From the back I gathered my view of father and son. Yep, the traditional cowboy boots, jeans, flannels, must be a prerequisite for being a rancher, flannel shirts. Two braids one jet black, sliver streak twisted in. But Dads, all silver, shiny, just the ends bared a tip of inky black hair. Nic pulled off two bags from the carousel chatting with his dad.

"She said she'd find us here," he scanned the crowd. "Aubrey."

My feet double stepped, I flew into his open arms like a waiting bird. My hug, the hug I was sent home with. To hold onto until we met again, this was real. My berry wine lip gloss smeared Nic's lips smudging back at mine. I wrapped my legs around his waist like a monkey hugging a tree. His hands cradled around my bottom side, his fingers sinking in, supporting my wrap around style hug.

"Ahh, kids, um people are looking." A gentle deep voice came from behind me.

A solid hand rubbed my back as I slid off Nic turning to face my new father-in-law.

"Ya got any of that pretty lip stick left for me, girly?" Charlie Ravenwood held his hands out waiting for his hug.

This time I didn't jump like I did for Nic. A little hesitant, I embraced a hug that came from a bear. He swung me in a full circle, dropping me right back where he'd picked me up from.

"Easy on her, dad. Don't break her." Nic stepped up behind me. "Dad, let me be the first to introduce you to my wife."

"So, you're the little filly who stole my son's heart are ya." He grinned, teeth perfectly straight, holding both my hands.

"Hi, Dad." I hugged him again. I stopped trying to dry my eyes. Emotions, I still couldn't control them.

"Tears. Aubrey you're crying." Nic pulled me back into him.

"I know. I'm just so happy. You're here." Swallowed by massive arms I rested my head on his chest. "Get used to it; I forgot to tell ya, I'm an emotional basket case."

"Already figured that one out, Aubrey."

The drive through downtown at least didn't wreak the havoc it did for me getting to the airport. My Escape was a huge vehicle to me, nothing like the trucks Nic and his dad drove around the ranch. Right on schedule, I swung into my parking garage tunneling down under the apartment building. I whipped into a parking spot close to the elevator, happy to get it.

"Here let me take that." I grabbed Charlie's carry-on while Nic grabbed the other two bags. "I live on the fourth floor. Got a pretty nice view of the city from here. Charlie..."

"Call me dad, honey." Nic's dad insisted.

"Dad." I giggled as the elevator climbed to the forth floor. "My apartment is only a one bedroom; I hope you don't mind sleeping on the pullout sofa."

"No mind, honey. Just you two keep the racket down in the bedroom. Don't want to hear Nic screamin' and hollarin' all night."

"Dad." My high pitched whine blended evenly with Nic's deep bass of laughter.

"Here we are. Number 413. This is home." I turned the key in the lock. "Please don't mind all the boxes, I've been packing."

I ushered my husband and father-in-law past nine large boxes, taped, marked, and ready to be shipped to the West, my new home.

"Good gracious, girly. Nic, we're going to have to build a new wing onto the house just for Aubrey and all her things." Charlie pushed his way into my living room.

"Packing. I like the sight of that." Nic kissed me crowding into my small foyer.

"They're here." Allison and Gram appeared from my tiny kitchen.

"Nic, you remember my sister Allison. This is my Gram, Angela." It never failed me, I sucked at introducing people. "Gram, this is Nic."

Dreamy eyed, filled with over-the-top excitement, my mind was only on Nic.

Gram's eyebrows raised, her smile deepened. "But who's this fine gentlemen?"

My Gram, she had her own charisma. I needed to take a few lessons from her.

"Oh my gosh, I'm so sorry. Dad, Charlie." I took another breath, "This is Nic's dad, Charlie."

Simple introductions could be unbelievably frustrating to me. The oven buzzer summoned me to the kitchen. Allison had followed all my directions for heating tonight's dinner. The kitchen, my home, I could finally relax. Walnut crusted lamb chops, fresh asparagus with toasted almonds, and a dash of lemon juice and nothing better than lobster mashed potatoes would soon be served.

"Aubrey, you need any help?" Nic filed into an empty spot in my kitchen.

"Does your dad drink wine?" I glanced at him while touching up the glaze on the lamb. "There's a bottle of Merlot and Pinot Noir chilled in the refrigerator."

"Aubrey. What the hell is that staring at me?"

I whirled around to see Mr. Perfect perched on the tip top of the refrigerator. Each step Nic took, Mr. Perfect growled at him. Nic had his hand on the door when a paw flung out smacking his hair.

"Mr. Perfect. What a bad kitty. Shame." I grabbed him before Nic could. Thank goodness he had come to me declawed. "Where's your manners?" A little smack to the cat's bottom side and I was repaid with a growl, a hiss, and swiping of a tail to my arm. "He's usually very friendly. I don't know why he's being so ornery." I apologized to Nic for my cat's bad cat-attitude.

"Cat. You named your cat, Mr. Perfect?" Still not amused with my cat, Nic finally retrieved the wine.

"He's a shelter cat. The name came with him. I rescued him about four years ago." I smoothed the cat's fur down. "He's really very nice."

"You plan on bringin' it with ya when you move?" A little disgust hinged in Nic's voice.

"Yes." I stood up for my cat. "He's my furry little man." A little batting of my eyelashes won points with Nic.

I put my problem cat down and shoed him out of the kitchen. "Go mingle with the other guests."

"You cook like this all the time?" Nic popped the cork on the wine.

"Only when I have company. Usually bring something home from work or I'm a sucker for peanut butter and banana sandwiches. Ever had them grilled?"

"Thought you only ate stuff like that when you're pregnant?" Nic grinned while taking the wine and two dishes heading for the table.

I ignored his comment, knowing at forty-four a baby would be a slim chance. The lamb smelled heavenly as I placed it in the center of the dinner table.

"Aubrey, honey, I've come up with a great plan." Gram's eyes twinkled.

"A plan for what Gram?" I asked, passing the lamb to Charlie.

"Well, I've invited Charlie to stay over at my house. You know I got all those rooms. It'll give you kids a little more honeymoon time. Alone." Gram smiled.

Did Gram just wink at Charlie? Not even half an hour and she stole my father-in-law right out from under me.

"I'll bring him with me on Sunday evening to the reception." Gram patted Charlie's hand.

"Gram, you hussy." Allison loved getting pot shots in. "What would the Reverend Phil Hunter say? You're taking the father of Aubrey's savage lover into your home. Have you no shame, woman?"

"Savage lover?" Nic's fork dangled from his finger tips at me.

I choked on a mouthful of potatoes. Gram spit her wine out in her napkin as the three of us nearly broke the walls down with laughter. Nic and his father stiffened, a smile of confusion drifted back and forth between them.

"Who's the Reverend Phil Hunter? Is he related to you ladies?" With concern Charlie asked.

"Ya didn't tell'em did ya, Nic?" I sobered up the laughter.

"Nope." Nic buttered his biscuit. "Savage huh, woman? Want ta play, Aubrey?"

My eyes lit, grinning from ear to ear, I would've gone with him. But what do I do with my company?

"Pay no mind to these girls, Charlie." Gram ended our fun. "Phil is their brother, my grandson. He's not a Reverend. Just likes to think he's a good church going person." Gram got all diplomatic on us.

"Poking fun at Phil will have to wait till Sunday." Allison added with a sarcastic grin.

"They're coming?" I nearly gagged on another mouthful of potatoes.

"Yes, Dee Dee said they'd be there." Gram smiled so innocently.

"Want to skip town while you still can?" I asked Nic.

"Can't wait to meet my new brother-in-law. If he gives me crap, I'll hog tie him, and use him for a centerpiece." Nic didn't flinch an eye. Didn't crack a smile. He just kept eating.

"Is he serious?" Allison mouthed in a whisper to me.

I shrugged my shoulders, peeking at Nic while he ate.

"Pass the potatoes and yes, I'm serious." Nic thanked Allison.

Coffee and pie would be placed on the waiting list. I overstuffed all my guests with dinner. The dishwasher hummed along as Allison and I put pots and pans away. Nic motioned out toward the living room. Mr. Perfect climbed into Charlie's lap as Gram kept the evening conversation rolling.

"I'm done and I'm heading home." Allison kissed me. "Don't stay up too late; remember you're sick with the flu or something like that."

"Nic, you think your dad will be ok staying with Gram?" I wondered while Gram charmed the pants off of his dad.

"She better be careful, Dad moves in fast." Nic chuckled massaging my shoulders.

"I take it, it runs in the family." Not meaning any sarcasm, I winked at Nic.

"Well you two need some, you know, alone time. Don't need us old duffers keeping ya up any longer." Gram smiled slyly. She was smitten with Nic's dad, already.

"Need help with your bag, Dad?" Nic asked. "How 'bout this?" Nic pulled a little square foil package out of his back pocket.

"Neither son. Got everything covered. Call you in the mornin'." Charlie batted Nic's hand out of his way, opening the door for Gram. "Thanks for dinner, sweetie." Another hug, but this one was for me and not Gram.

"I don't think we'll be seeing Dad for a few days." Nic shut the door behind them.

"Tell me about it. Think Gram is keeping him for the whole weekend. Heard her say she wants to take him to her bridge club and show off her granddaughter's new father-in-law." I cracked up laughing leading Nic back to the living room.

Chapter 10

A Real Wedding Night

Utter exhaustion exhaled itself from my body. A warm tingle danced in my veins. I'd finally gotten my way, alone time with Nic.

My old sofa cushioned my flopping fall, "They're gone. You're all mine." Nic folded his rugged body around mine. "You know I need your help here." I pointed around my emptying living room. "Furniture. You like? Don't like. Should I pack certain...?" Two of Nic's fingers secured my babbling lips shut.

"Aubrey, no more talking. We'll figure out furniture...moving later." Nic's tongue circled my lips, his teeth nibbling down my neck. "I've waited nearly three weeks to get my hands back on these curves."

With double weight occupancy poured to the max, my old sleeper sofa held up to the end. An occasional spring sang out a twist of pain, reminding me of a more comfortable place to be.

"My bedroom...it's...it's down the hall." One hand yanked at Nic's shirt tails. The other fumbled, pointing towards the hall. "You're going to look so pretty in my purple flowered sheets."

"Flowered sheets? Oh no. Not yet. They'll wait Aubrey. They'll wait." Nic had a little force behind the way he pulled me from the sofa to my feet. "Shower. I want you, naked, soapy, in a steaming shower. Now Aubrey."

"Wait." I blurted, halting him.

"Aubrey. I'm not into playin' chase ya down. Don't run away from me." Nic moved into the kitchen behind me. "Woman, what the hell are you digging around for?"

"Candles." I held up and collected every candle I owned.

"Candles? That'll work." Nic took a handful of candles from my arms and followed me down the hall.

The match flared as I tried to light the bundle of colorful candles. An aroma of chocolate, fruit, and floral filled into the glowing bathroom. Carefully I arranged my flaming scents. Preferably, I'd like our honeymoon blazing, not a burn it to the ground kind. A spray of heating water misted behind the pulled shower curtain. I didn't hear him shut the door, didn't even notice he'd turned the lights out. An amazing glow flickered on the bathroom walls.

"Coconut body wash ok by you?" I flashed him a sly grin.

Nic's shirt, missing in action already. My half naked husband and his display of tattoos grinned at me. Coconut body wash, forgotten. On automatic pull, my fingers outlined, freely running over his colorful artwork.

"Never met a woman so intrigued by my tattoos Aubrey." Easily, Nic loosened my hair from its tied ponytail.

Aggressiveness wasn't in me. But I thought what the heck, give it a try. Maybe even surprise him. I reached for his belt buckle. A simple buckle, but I struggled till Nic's hands covered mine.

"I got it." Nic finished letting me rub my hands over his chest again.

"Zippers, buckles, simple for a guy, I guess." I've got problems with my own clothes and here I am trying to undress Nic.

"Aubrey. You're shaking." A teasing tone and Nic's jeans fell to the floor.

Shirt, jeans, those sexy boxers I love to see him in, all on the bathroom floor. Nic ran his finger along the crochet neckline of my sweater.

"It...um...buttons down the back." I pointed over my shoulder helplessly.

"I noticed." Nic's hands guided me in a semicircle facing the shower curtain.

Quickly, I pulled the tail of my hair off my back letting my hands fall, reaching for his bare thighs. Nervously my fingers kneaded into his thick and warm bare skin. One by one he unbuttoned the delicate pearl buttons of my angora sweater. For a man with large callused hands that handled animals all day, he was amazingly gentle. My sweater slipped over my arms. I caught it sliding out of my jeans tossing the duo over to Nic's pile of clothes. Purposely, I had shopped for sexier underwear. My choice of lingerie exposed any and all of my fleshy curves.

"Nice. Very nice." Nic's hands cupped over my lace bra.

I leaned back into his chest letting Nic follow the road map of designer curves on my body. A simple snap and all the effort of shopping for something sexy ended up on the ground, piled high with the rest of denim and lace. Someway I managed to step out of the lacy underwear before Nic turned me back to face him.

"Nic."

"Humm?" His lips, warm, sliding over my bare shoulder.

"The shower. Can we get in?" My reach, I batted several times trying to open the shower curtain.

A thumping and wailing meow came from behind the closed door, an untimely distraction.

"Don't tell me? The cat?" Nic glared at the back of the bathroom door. Present mood nearly blasted down the drain.

"The cat. Just open the door. He won't bug us. Promise." I pulled on Nic's hand, nodding towards the rush of running water.

"You and your damn cat." Mr. Perfect hit another ultimate sour note with Nic in only a few hours.

"Please Nic, he won't be in the way. He doesn't like closed doors. Please."

The steam of the shower wrapped around me as I stepped in. Slowly I let the creamy body wash slip over my wet body motioning for Nic to join me. Door open, one cat content, and I hoped to make my new husband even happier.

Chapter 11

Who's At My Door, Now?

"Seriously?" My miffed mumble didn't even disturb Nic's slumber. "Who'd be nervy enough to be knocking?"

A wish I'd hoped for this morning, being aroused by my husband. Not the person rat-a-tat-tapping on my apartment door at eight thirty in the morning. Nic didn't even budge when I shifted his arm from around me.

He rolled to his back, "Oh my gosh they really do, do that," I mumbled wrapping up in my housecoat. "Great I've got one boy that licks his harry balls, and the big boy, who's in my bed, scratches them in his sleep."

And to think I laughed at Gina when she told me such a tale. Mr. Perfect finished his morning grooming and curled up on Nic's chest. Kept in a timed rhythm came the snoring and purring of the men in my life. The tapping persisted. Lightly, but longer, I prayed it wasn't my brother. No, second thought, if was his holiness, he'd be beating on the door screaming. Best thing the landlady ever installed, peep holes. Every apartment door got one along with a double chained bolt and lock system. After a double take I rubbed the sleep from my eyes. Again I peered through the peep hole. Dee, my 'goody two shoe' sister-n-law stood on the opposite side of the door. Between tapping, shifting from one foot to another foot nervously, she managed to hang on to a cake.

"Dee. I'm a little surprised here." I backed up letting her step in beside me and my hall of boxes.

"I'm sorry, I should've called. But, well you know. I was in the area." Dee, she couldn't lie to save herself.

"Phil doesn't know you're here, does he?" I took the cake from her trembling hands.

"No. Swear to me you won't tell him." Dee batted pleading eyes at me.

"Not to worry, never told Phil anything about your stop bys. All secrets are safe here, Dee." Cat grin, I know, but I won't sell her out. "Come on, I'll put a pot of coffee on."

Dee neatly hung her jacket on the chair and sat down at my café style of a kitchen table. With each perk of the coffee pot, Dee kept twisting her neck. Round and round, constantly she looked over her shoulder.

"Where is he?" She glanced around my living room this time.

"Nic? He's in bed yet." I sat two plates and a knife out in front of her.

"Oh. Did I? I'm so sorry. I should go, let you get..." Dee stuttered getting redder in the face.

"Dee, Nic's out cold yet. Snoring away with Mr. Perfect tucked on his chest." I sliced the chocolate zucchini cake she had brought. "Did you come by to meet him?"

"No." She sighed, lying, she just couldn't. "Well, yes. I wanted to come to dinner last night. Gram called, invited us. You know Phil, he blew another gasket. The excitement this time, heart palpitations. Plus, he had me sitting in the emergency room, again, for the whole night. Not a damn thing wrong with him."

I rolled my eyes. No secrets to Phil's fake illnesses. "Got some leftovers, lamb chops. Want to take them home?" I offered with a consolation smile.

"Not for Phil, I won't. I'll take one for me. I love your cooking."

"Dee, what's bugging you? You're a wreck. Like the glue that usually holds you together just melted. Give." Coffee poured, I sat down with her.

"Nothing." Dee circled her cup banging the spoon on the edge. "Aubrey, Phil forbids me to come to your reception party Sunday night. Said he didn't want no part of you marrying that...bre" Dee stopped her words. "Sorry. I won't call your husband that. You realize Phil faked the whole illness so we couldn't come to dinner too.

"Dee, I'm sorry. But you know how your husband is," just what I needed at eight thirty-something in the morning.

"If it isn't Phil Hunter's way it's the way highway." Dee and I chanted in unison.

Dee twitched and jumped at every sound made by my apartment building. "Dee, what's going on?"

"I've got to…I've just got to tell someone. Those church people, I can't confide in them. Aubrey, I'm leaving Phil." She nearly passed out waiting for my reaction.

Wow. Stern words. Actually to the point. Did it really come out of Dee's mouth? I didn't even think she could speak for herself without Phil telling her how.

"You're really going to leave him?" I asked pouring more coffee and shoving another piece of cake her way. "Or are you just pacifying yourself?"

"Thank you," Not missing a beat, Dee dove into her second piece of cake. "Yes, yes I am leaving. I've been soul searching. Thinking, reflecting. Even made that, you know, write two columns. Put the good here, bad there and guess what?"

"The bad, it out weighed the good?" I noticed the light bulbs in Dee's head just flipped on.

"Yes. I've sat back and done nothing. Nothing, but be by his side, defending him. I've done everything the Good Book tells me to. And for what? I'm miserable. I'm not happy. He's sucked me into his black hole of Phil Hunter's, do as I say, don't do as I do. The highway is looking very inviting these days."

"Wow." I sat back in my chair. "I need more cake."

"Another piece." Dee pointed to her plate.

Dee really did grow a Vajayjay as Gram put it the other night.

"I look at Allison right in the prime of life. And her husband is snapped away from her. But she went on. She's still a happy person even though she lost the love of her life. Then you go to a convention. Meet a man and marry him, just five days later. Look at you; you're glowing. I was with your brother for two years before we married. I didn't glow then and he sure the hell hasn't made me glow in years."

Dee just gagged me literally. I scrambled for my coffee to wash down the bite of cake I choked on. Dee and Phil were strictly a no talk of romance, sex, or even kissing in public kind of couple.

"Dee, how long have you been harboring these feelings?" I asked. "You're cake is really good." Correction, I gave her the chocolate zucchini cake recipe.

"It's been burning inside me for a few, no over a, going on nearly a year. I've tried Aubrey. Really, I have." Dee moped in her coffee. "Stupidly, I asked him to go for counseling. You know a little marriage "R&R" retreat with the church. Shot me down flat. Told me I had the problem."

"Humm, like I haven't heard that before Dee." I started another pot of coffee for us.

"I ran into his ex-wife, Millie, over at Lowe's the other day. She's happy Aubrey. She doesn't look all tired and worn out like I do. It really started me thinking. I deserve better than someone who is nothing more than a two faced, double standard, mouth piece for a church. The way Phil goes on, you'd think he was the minister." Dee folded her hands waiting for me to close my mouth and say something.

"You got a plan? Got your self somewhere to go? My apartment will be free by the end of next month." I just offered her my digs; well I won't be needing it anymore.

"I could move in here? Just pick up where you left off? What was that?" Dee jumped in her chair flying around looking back into the living room.

"Nic's up. Relax, you'll love him."

"Aubrey?" Nic rounded the corner into the kitchen, buck naked, holding Mr. Perfect under his arm.

"Oh! Oh, my heavens." Dee squealed shielding her eyes with a napkin.

"Nic. Oh, my gosh. Here." I tossed him the dishtowel, not knowing who to laugh at first.

Nic dropped the cat to catch the towel, "Sorry didn't know we had company," smirking, he headed his naked self back to the bedroom.

"Aubrey is he gone?" Dee's entire chair shook as she kept her eyes closed.

"Your eyes are safe. Nic went to put some clothes on. Drink your coffee, Dee." I laughed at my sister-in-laws reddening face. She out blushed me by miles.

"He's, he's so, oh those pictures didn't do him justice, did they?" Dee rubbed her hands together nervously.

"Mornin' ladies. Really sorry. Thought it was just me and Aubrey and Fuss Nuts here." Nic patted the cat on the head, a little too rough.

"Nic, I'd like you to meet my sister-in-law, Dee. She's soon to be Phil's ex-wife." I gave Dee an encouraging smile, reassuring her to just go for it.

"Oh, I should really be going. You two just don't need me hanging around." As if someone glued Dee's butt to the chair, she didn't budge.

"Don't rush off on my account. Need my morning smoke. Stay, finish your visit." Nic grabbed his jacket off the back of my chair.

"Here, fresh coffee." I poured him a huge mug stepping over to the door with him.

"She alright?" He asked kissing me.

"She'll recover after another cup of coffee. Not used to seeing a hot naked Indian man and all those tattoos." I couldn't help it; I smacked my hubby's jean covered butt.

He threw his jacket on over his shirtless chest. Didn't zip it. No boots, bare feet, and kissed me while running his cigar under my nose. "Be back in a few."

"Dee, you ok?" I joined her back at the table.

"See what I mean. I don't even get that. Not even a kiss anymore." Dee sulked while slumping in her chair.

"I always wondered what you saw in him, Dee. You realize Phil will play the sympathy card on you. He'll beg you to stay. If you're really going to leave, cut the strings, don't look back." I felt like a newspaper advice column all of a sudden.

"I really like the idea of moving into your place Aubrey. You've always made me feel welcome, even when I wasn't the nicest to you." Dee patted my hand.

"I'll let Rosie know you're interested. She's a great landlady. Plus, I'm not taking some of my furniture. Place will be half furnished for you." For once in my life I got a sister-in-law to be friends with and I'm moving away.

"How long is Nic here? Did you say his dad came with him too?" Dee stuffed another bite of cake in her mouth.

"They're leaving on Tuesday. Gram took Charlie, Nic's dad back to her house. They wanted to give us some alone time." I did the little quotes in the air with my fingers making Dee giggle.

"You're really moving out West with him?"

"Yeah Dee, I'm really moving West. You can come see me." I meant the offer I made.

"Are you going to look for a restaurant out there to work in?"

"Not at first. Nearest big town, about a hundred miles away." I frowned.

"I better get a move on." Dee fidgeted in her seat. "Thanks Aubrey. You know I'll be there Sunday." Dee finally started to relax.

"Hey now, don't be stealing my thunder by announcing you're leaving Phil." I giggled.

"No. No, I would never." Dee nearly jumped out of her skin as the door clicked open. "I should really be going."

"Why?" Nic filled out the archway of the kitchen door nicely. "Have breakfast with us." He looked down at the half eaten cake and back to us. "Vultures attack that cake?"

"Nope. Just had a little accident," I sheepishly grinned at Nic. "It kept falling onto our plates."

Before Dee left, I stuffed a shopping bag with dinner from last night for her, and hopefully sent her on her way to a new life without Phil.

"Let me guess, eggs, bacon and toast?" I started pulling ingredients from the refrigerator. "Did you talk to your dad yet?"

"No and No." Nic grinned.

"No you didn't talk to your dad and no you don't want breakfast? You feelin' ok?" I asked all confused, wondering why he looked at me grinning.

Nic yanked on the belt to my housecoat. "Breakfast can wait."

Instantly he tossed me over his shoulder. My hands grabbing for anything in my upside down sight. The back of his pants worked as I mocked kicking and screaming.

"You're going to hurt yourself." I screamed, again latching onto the pockets of his jeans.

Next landing, my bed with a thump. I narrowly missed the headboard, landing on the safety of the pillows. In the midst of disrobing me, Nic's cell phone rang on the nightstand.

"You better answer it." I slipped my tongue over his lips.
"No."
"What if it's your dad?" I ran my fingers over his tight butt cheeks.
"Fine." He swiped the phone up reading the caller ID. "Old man, this better be good." I could hear Nic's dad laughing on the other side.
"Ya breakin' your new little "Filly in?" Nic fell on top of me so I could hear their conversation.
"Yeah dad, I'm ridein' my wife. What the hell do you want?" Nic's annoyed impatient voice rippled over the phone line to his dad.
"Just wanted to say good morning to my pretty little daughter-in-law, ya savage."
"I'll have her call ya when I'm done brutalizing her." Nic clicked the phone off, then turned it completely off. "Damn old man. Surprised he didn't do that last night, too."
"Nic Honey. Shut up and service me." I loved his long dark hair. It made me greedy for running my fingers through it. Better yet, great for making him come to where I wanted to play with him.

Chapter 12

Mr. Perfect

Mr. Perfect maintained his guard perch high on top of the packed boxes. I'm sure my smart-assed Siamese cat, waiting with fish breath, contemplated on how he'd be taking Nic out. The tattered black shoe lace flossed around his fangs. He arched his back in a Halloween cat pose, and waited for Nic's return. Another new finding about my husband, he believed in starting his day with coffee. Strong and black, accompany that with his morning cigar. Nicotine and caffeine jump started Nic's day. That's a habit I'd have to get used to. He never once smelled or reeked like a chimney in the five days we spent together in New Orleans.

The door handle rattled, Nic and a half empty cup of coffee filled the cramped entrance way. He tossed his coat next to Mr. Perfect who batted a paw at the intrusion. From where I sat in the kitchen detailing my 'to do list' I could see Nic put both hands up on the box where Mr. Perfect had planted himself for attack.

"Listen up ya 'nut-less' wonder of a cat, I'm the man in her life now. Don't be thinkin' after ya wash your de-nutted balls you can just crawl up on my chest and sleep. Don't be wiggling between us. She's mine. Got that clear, Fuzz Butt?" The man of the ranch laid down the law to Mr. Perfect. "What kind of a cat are you? Ya let her take ya out and look--she got your balls whacked off. Didn't she? Made ya a damn pussy boy, didn't she?" Mr. Perfect flopped to his back letting Nic rub his tummy. "Won't last a day with my barn cats would ya?" The cat purred, rolling side to side tangling itself in the shoelace. "You play your cards right, might let ya keep your pansy ass in the house with ole Toby."

"You some kind of a cat whisperer now?" I asked, taking his coffee cup in for a refill.

"Just havin' a little man to pussy talk. Wanted to make sure your animal understands who's boss." Nic turned his back to Mr. Perfect.

Immediately the cat pawed and batted at Nic's loose hair. I handed him another cup of coffee as Mr. Perfect draped himself over Nic's shoulder.

"So who's the pussy now?" I gloated at seeing how Mr. Perfect had won him over. "You never said you had a dog."

"Toby?" Nic sat down at the table with a cat riding his shoulders and looked over my notes. "Had ole Toby for about fifteen years. Damn good bloodhound. Finally brought him inside. Just stays in the kitchen, sleeps most of the day."

"A dog? A dog in the house?" Nic looked at me like I lost a few more marbles.

"He's no bother. Shouldn't worry yourself over it." Nic pointed to my list. "What's all this?"

"Changing the subject?"

"Yep." He tapped the piece of paper again.

"Everything I need to get done in a month." I answered him still miffed about the dog.

"Quit your job yet?" He leaned back in the chair knowing I hadn't.

"Sunday night. I'll break the news at our little dinner reception." I rolled my eyes knowing this would be a night to remember.

"Aubrey?"

"I'm ok. It's just…" I lost my nerve.

"Just what?" Nic waited me out.

How do I tell my husband I've never depended on a man for anything. "I don't want to offend you…" My voice squeaked like the mouse I wasn't.

"Say it." Nic waited for me to muster up the courage to speak what he'd been reading in my mind.

I shrugged taking a deep breath, "I've never depended on a man to take care of me." In the silence of the kitchen, you could hear me swallow the massive lump in my throat. Nice and slowly my eyes inched up to meet his.

"You won't have to ask for anything. Whatever you need, you'll have it." Nic crossed his arm over his chest, but not annoyed with me.

"Nic, I'm not used to asking someone for something. I'm so used to just doing for myself." I put a little backbone into that line.

His chair landed back on all four legs with a thud, and he leaned over the table. "Get used to it."

"Nic," I sighed, "I don't want to have to come ask you for twenty bucks when I want to buy something. I don't want to ask you for grocery money. I've taken care of me for a long, long time. It's going to be hard for me to get used to not having a job too."

Nic pulled his wallet from his back pocket. Next, three shiny credit cards were laid out in front of me. Master Card, Visa, and Discover. "You won't have to ask. Already took care of it. You're on every account the ranch has, plus more."

"Nic, what did you do?" My eyes bounced from the plastic cards up to him.

"You're worried about getting a job? Aubrey, there isn't a decent place to eat for miles. A drive to town is a good hour. You've got me, Dad, Bones and, if you want, the ranch hands to cook for."

"I can have my own little restaurant, right there at the house." My little 'independent me' mood swing just swung back to happy.

"Change your name yet?" Nic pointed to the line of cards. All printed Aubrey M. Ravenwood glossed up at me.

"Yes. All but my driver's license. Figured I'd wait till I got to Wyoming to get a new one. You even got them with my middle initial." I tapped at the plastic cash. "I planned on hyphenating when I'm looking for a chef position."

"Don't have a problem with that. When the news got out, word spread like wild fire that I got married. So nearly the whole county knows your name, just not that pretty face of yours…yet."

"Nic, I don't know what to say?" Personally, I had my own set of credit cards, Nic just doubled me up.

"Lets get this list of yours done, woman. You can thank me later." Nic had a way of just fondling my knee and I melted.

Chapter 13

A Classic Hunter Family Wedding Reception

"You're not dressed?" Nic noticed my pouting protest.

"I don't want to go. It's just a disaster waiting to happen." Mr. Perfect wound around my hand, comforting me.

I hated parties. Hated them even more when I knew I'd be half the center of attention. Good for me, Nic, he'd be on display too. Still wrapped securely in my bath towel, I wouldn't inch off the bed.

"Tell me, Aubrey, you worried about this brother of yours? Or the fact you haven't told your boss you got married and you're leavin' her?" Nic questioned me from the doorway.

"Both." I sighed. "How'd you get so good at reading me?" I threw the towel from my hair at him.

Nic's instincts scared me. The man easily read my emotions like a well loved recipe. Unfortunately, he'd left me fumbling around trying to figure out what makes him tick. Slowly I dragged myself to my feet. To Gram, this reception was a huge deal.

"Nic," I held up my lilac sweater and skirt to him, "too summery?"

"You're asking me?" Nic, he had the whole fashion thing down pat. Nice jeans, pressed shirt, clean boots. How flipping simple could it be. "I like ya in that outfit Aubrey." His simple smile eased my nerves.

Not wanting to disappoint Gram, I painted on my happiest of faces. There would be a show down between one of the said parties. Of course, I'd be smack dab in the middle of it.

Sunday night and parking with no game in town was a complete breeze. Who needed valet parking when you had a spot next to the front door? Nic and I stood on the sidewalk, our reflections looming in the glass doors. A big white sign hung in the side window "CLOSED: PRIVATE PARTY." I've walked through these doors for years. Now it would soon be my former place of employment.

"Ready?" Nic asked and reached for the door.

"No." Surprisingly, I pulled back from him.

"Aubrey, come on. Things will be fine." Little did Nic realize we were about to enter a hornet's nest.

"Can't we just make a run for it? Let's go hide back in my apartment. Sex any way you want. All night long." I bit my lip rocking back and forth in my heels.

"Nice offer. Like this little erotic side to you, Aubrey." Nic tried to soothe my never ending nervous attack.

"Erotic? Ok, I'm game." Nic's hand caught my elbow pulling me towards the open door. "Sure you won't reconsider?"

"Tempting. But no." He whisked me inside; Maria had been waiting for us.

"Aubrey, darling, you're here. No one will breathe a word about this little gala. I know it has something to do with you."

Maria, the most rigorous, torture-minded boss, I'd ever worked for. But her heart, simply pure gold. High society defined Maria with impeccable taste and grace.

"Aubrey, who's this?" Maria eyed Nic over as she kissed me on the cheek in her French style greeting.

Before I could utter one happy word like my husband to her, Gina stepped in.

"Where'd you get this beef cake?" She winked at Nic. "Another escort, Aubrey?"

Bless her heart, Gina kept my secret. By the grin on her face I'd be owing her big time as she sidetracked Maria back to the kitchen.

"Maria, she doesn't know yet." A cleansing breath released a little of my tension. "Oh, this is going to be fun."

"They're here." Gram now controlled the small group of people. "Everyone gather round. Could I have your attention please?" On the side of a water glass, Gram clicked the knife. "I know you've all been waiting to know what this little dinner party is about."

"We know already." The unfriendly echo of Phil's voice interrupted Gram.

"Phil this isn't about you tonight." Gram shot him down, oh yeah. "As I was saying, I'd like to be the first to introduce Aubrey and Nic Ravenwood. They got married a few weeks ago."

"You did what?" A high pitch wail screamed from Maria's lips. "You didn't even tell me. How could you keep something so precious from me?"

"Need the bottle there, Maria?" Gina handed her a bottle of top shelf rum. "It'll help what else Aubrey's going to share." Gina's way of getting revenge for me for leaving.

"What? What are you going to tell me? Tell me now." Maria poured a glass of straight rum, over two fingers high and chucked it down.

"No, let me tell you what she did." Phil stood up from his backseat table.

"Sit down." Allison wacked him in the chest with her purse. "Shut your damn mouth, you ass."

My kid sister, the youngest and littlest, packed a wallop with a purse. Phil doubled down in his seat and Dee smiled, pretending to comfort him.

"Aubrey? Ok, I got it. You're married. But what else didn't you tell me?" Maria took another hit of her drink. "Honey, if you're expecting, we can work something out."

"Pregnant? Did you knock me up already?" I innocently asked Nic with batting eyelashes.

"Think ya'd know that before me." Nic played along. "Just to put everyone's mind to rest, Aubrey's not pregnant...yet. I come from a good line of producing Stallions. Sure I'll be able to get the job done." Nic didn't miss a beat, didn't even crack a smile.

"Must you discuss your intimate affairs in front of us?" Phil's mouth was up and running. "You just up and marry some cowboy out of nowhere. So yeah, everyone thinks you're knocked up." Phil finally got in his long awaited dig.

"Phil, that's enough." Gram's powder soft voice echoed like a roaring lioness.

Phil, he couldn't hold back, "Did ya tell lover boy all about the men you had relations with over the years? How about those little flings you had? Running around with Gina like some tramp."

"Let me guess, brother Phil?" Nic rolled his eyes.

"In his prime. Up on his soapbox ready to preach to us." I clung to Nic's arm.

"Humm, nasty situation you've caused here sonny boy." The deep steady voice of Charlie weighed in. "What these two done in the past, is the past. The present, the future, that's all that matters."

"See why I didn't want to come." I whispered to Nic.

"Thank you Charlie. Philip, I did not bring you up to be so nastily rude." Gram's glare, eyes squinted, lip creased tight. Ass kicking time Gram's way and directed right at my brother.

Saved by the grace of Allison, she handed us a glass of champagne. "Everyone, I'd like to give a toast to my sister and her new husband, Nic, and welcome him and Charlie, Nic's father to our family. Some of us are thrilled and wish you the best."

A small ringing of glasses clicked together settling the turbulence of a rocky dinner party.

"Dinner will be served and no, not prepared by Aubrey, but Gina. So everyone take your seats please." Allison ushered us to the center table.

"Gina, you're a guest. What happened?" I pulled at her sleeve wanting her to sit with us.

"You want a crap chef or someone who can kick your butt in the kitchen?" Gina hugged me. "My pleasure to make the wedding dinner for my best friend."

Gina and I rivaled with each other when it came to cooking. One would constantly try to out do the other and she did it tonight. Beef tenderloin wrapped in bacon, smothered in onions and mushrooms, and then topped with blue cheese. Gina actually stole one of my creations. Acorn squash, in its shell, stuffed with an herb dressing and topped with roasted garlic accompanied the main dish. I could hardly wait for what she had planned for dessert.

"Maria, I guess now is a good enough time to tell you." She sat directly opposite me at the dinner table. "I'm giving you my two weeks notice."

Her fork dropped from her hand, "What do you mean two weeks notice?"

"Just what I said, Maria. I'm leaving." Nic eased back in his chair, arm draped around my shoulder. "End of month I'll be moving to Wyoming with Nic."

Maria said nothing; she looked down her narrow nose, over her silver jeweled glasses. Confusion, hurt, and then daggers shot from her eyes hitting my heart. "I need a cigarette."

"Good." Nic replied. "Need a smoke myself. Shall we?" He motioned for Maria to join him.

"Could this night get any worse?" Hopelessly, I sighed. Before Nic escorted Maria to the door, he ran his fingers along my jaw and swooped in for a kiss.

"She's going to eat him alive." Gina whispered sitting down in Nic's empty seat.

"She don't know my boy." Charlie leaned over me grinning at Gina.

The smoke break, short. Way too short. I don't think Nic even had a chance to enjoy his cigar.

"Would ya look at that smug ass grin on Nic's mug?" Gina said as they crossed the room together. "I would bet, definitely put money on it, he put her in her place."

"I think dessert would be great right about now. Don't you think Gina?" She took my hint. Gina leaped from her chair concealing her own smug smile.

A comfort settled over me, having Nic to the left of me and his dad close on the right side of me. A good guarded feeling. I felt safe from the yet to come fallout with Maria. She'd already sucked down half the bottle of rum, straight, no chaser. Phil dragging Dee by the hand, bee lined in our direction. The next disaster, waiting in the wings, just flew in, seating themselves across the table from us. Chest puffed like he was some Sherman tank rolling in to eliminate the enemy, Phil straightened his posture trying to be intimidating.

"Let me formally introduce you to my brother, Phil, and his wife, Dee." I don't know were I got the strength, but I found it. "Phil, Dee Dee, my husband Nic, and my father-in-law, Charlie.

Dee extended her hand to Nic, "So nice to finally meet you." Her smile relaxed knowing her secret was secure. Nic and I pretended she'd never laid eyes on his naked buff body.
"Mr. Ravenwood, you're getting a fine daughter-in-law."

"So you're a ranch hand." Phil snorted, nudging Dee so hard she nearly fell off her chair.

Nic held his hand out to shake Phil's. "No. No, I'm not a ranch hand. I'm the owner. We've got fifty thousand acres of wide open land."

Gram, seeing the storm brewing saved Charlie from any fallout of a verbal war, asking him to join her for a cocktail. Lucky save, wish I was joining them.

"What kind of animals do you have on your farm, Nic?" Dee tested out her new found independence.

"It's a ranch for Christ sake, woman. Didn't you hear the man?" Phil snapped her head off, but Dee didn't cower.

"You know, Phil, good woman are hard to come by. You should cherish the one you have." Nic pulled me tightly next to him. "Dee, to answer your question, we have just about every animal you'd find on a farm, but in larger quantities."

"So that's all you do is ranch?" Phil banged at the question. "Anyone can saddle a horse and herd cows. No sweat. Bet I could show you a few tips on that fancy ranch of yours." Phil pushed back in his chair cracking his knuckles.

"There's a lot more to ranching than you think, Phil. Why I'm going to have Aubrey trained to clean out horse stalls and slop the hogs." Nic slipped a small lock of loose hair behind my ear, kissing me again.

"Slap the hogs? Oh I don't think so Mister." Jokingly, I complained back helping myself to another of Nic's kisses.

"I don't believe this." Phil's nasal voice grew louder. "You just can't come riding in on some sunset and take her from us. She's got responsibilities to us. Right, Dee?"

Nic held his hand up to Dee, signaling her not to answer. "Phil, Aubrey is my wife now. The only responsibilities we have would be to each other. You're welcome to visit your sister any time in Wyoming. Why, with your boasting experience, I could always use another hand."

Bells, whistles, and red steam boiled out Phil's necktie shirt. The Sherman tank steamed ready to blow any second. A riveting slam from Phil's hand to the table top silenced the room.

"You're not taking her." Phil's chair flew out from under him in his standing rage. "Aubrey you go with this dirty, filthy breed, you're going to burn in hell."

I grabbed for Nic's arm, while he rose to meet Phil's stand off. Calmly, I pulled myself to my feet, standing next to my husband.

"You know, brother dear, if I'm going to hell, there will be a chair right next to me for you." My brother's favorite pastime was to sentence everyone to hell who didn't play ball with him.

"Philip Hunter. Who in the good lord's name do you think you are?" Dee pounced on him, striking with all ten claws. "Look at the horrible, hateful man you've become. Why can't you be happy for your sister and her new husband?"

"Where leaving. Now, Dee." Spit blew from Phil's slobbering mouth as he reached for Dee's arm.

"Don't you touch me. You can leave if you want. I'm staying." Dee crossed her arms over her skinny frame daring Phil to say another word. "Your chair. Pick it up." Head held high, Dee escorted him to the other side of the room.

"That had to feel good." I nearly applauded Dee for finally asserting herself. "I'm sure I'll be transferring my apartment lease over to her."

"Was that the same woman who sat in the kitchen yesterday?" Nic asked, shaking his head.

"Yep it is. Ya still want to stay married to me now that you've seen the best of my family?" Crap, what if he said no? I won't blame him for tearing out of here and hopping the next flight back to Wyoming.

"Got a problem being married to a, what did he call me again?" Nic found humor in my disastrous family.

"A dirty filthy breed. Kind of got a thing for ya there cowboy." My head fell on Nic's shoulder. "Can we go now?"

"Cake. It's time to cut the cake." Like a school teacher, Gram clapped her hands rounding us together.

Finally, a reprieve from all the madness. A three layer wedding cake rolled out from behind the kitchen doors. Gina excelled in the dessert specialties. She handcrafted each flower, petal, and scallop of frosting. Fresh roses of white, pink, and purple cascaded from the top layer.

"Up here, you two." Gram waved. "Nic honey, haven't a clue of what kind of cake you like. As for Aubrey, white with butter cream frosting." Gram turned back to Nic, "I suggest you remember that, Nic."

Allison, the professional photographer of this messed up family, caught all the candid shots of this bizarre and stressful dinner party. If I knew my sister, she'd be putting together an unforgettable wedding album for us.

"Listen." I nudged Nic. "No one's attacking either of us." Sugar, there really was something to be said about its calming affects.

"Aubrey." Maria offered me a cup of coffee. Only woman I know who can drink her coffee stronger than Nic, "Let's chat."

So much for my peaceful sugar rush. Maria laced her arm around mine making sure I couldn't escape her. We sat at the end of the table, alone.

"After that scene with your brother, let me tell ya, sobered my piss poor attitude right up." Maria shook her head. "Thought for sure Nic was going to punch his lights out."

"Pretty impressed with Dee. Never thought I'd see her slap the golden child around like that." Maria's brewed coffee tasted perfect. "I wanted so badly to…"

Hands waving in front of me, Maria stopped me. "Aubrey, I'm hurt. I can't believe you didn't say a word to me. And Gina…Gina knew."

"I know, I'm sorry, Maria. I can't take another verbal beating. Phil's been riding my ass ever since he found out. I had to tell Gina. She caught us in bed together." We both laughed clunking our heads together. "Then she thought he was married, but she didn't know it was to me. To shut her up on the plane, I had to tell her."

"Got to admit, I just wanted to kill you. You kicked me right in the gut, girl. You've been mine. You make the restaurant what it is. Put us on the map. All these years, you've been mine." Maria sighed shaking her head, sipping the coffee in her delicate hands. "My little cigarette break with your hubby, the man is to the point. Laid it all out; black and white, no mincing words. The man's got a degree in agriculture and business management, and veterinary science or something like that. How'd you find one that's smart and so damn good looking?"

"Isn't he beautiful?" I giggled. "Can you say men are beautiful?'

"You're making me miss my Harold, God rest his soul." Again Maria's hands shot up to heaven blowing a kiss to her late husband. "Wish his ugly mug still walked this earth. He would've loved tonight, been proud of ya too. Just wish that man of yours wasn't taken ya so far away from me." Maria's smile faded.

"Oh Maria. I know, I know I'm giving up a lot for that one single word called 'love.' All for a man." I glanced back to Nic, now sitting with shutterbug Allison and her fancy cameras. "I can't ask him to give up his ranch. The man would feel like a caged animal here in the city."

"Aubrey, if it doesn't work, and I'm not sayin' it won't, you come back here. Promise me." Maria clasped her hands around mine.

"Promise, but I'll only be back to visit. Maybe stop by, make a dish or two." Darn tears, they won't stop running, so much for my face full of makeup.

I tapped at my watch. Did it stop? "Only eight thirty." I tapped it again. In just a few hours I'd been sucked dry of every emotion I lived with. Joyful, happy, sadness, and I want to kick my brother's ass. Did that count as an emotion?

Charlie pulled the chair out beside me. "How ya doing, girly?"

"Better. Maria's ok, sad, but ok. Dipshit in the corner, there's no making peace with him. How are you and Gram getting along?" I poked Charlie in the ribs with my elbow.

"Any chance your Gram will come out west with you?" Charlie grinned; his eyes followed Gram's swaying hips as she walked over to Nic and Allison.

"Dad. That's my grandma. You're hitting on my gram?"

Charlie grinned at my teasing. "Fine woman, your gram. Reminds me of my late wife." Charlie sat straight in his chair, smiling his heart out to Gram.

Gina bustled through the doorway carrying a wicker basket filled with pink and purple wrapped presents. "A wedding reception won't be one without cake…and gifts."

"Gifts?" I questioned her with raised eyebrows.

"We girls, Gram, Allison, me, even Dee, did a little shopping." I didn't like the smirk on Gina's glowing lips.

"Gina, this…it wasn't necessary. Thank you." I knew what shopping meant for them. A few clicks made computer shopping a breeze. A few stops at the some lingerie stores and it was all wrapped pretty and put in this basket.

"Aubrey, honey why don't you open it?" Unsuspecting Nic asked, not knowing what those four were capable of.

"Sure, honey, come help me." I played the game teasing him.

"No. No don't open them here." Dee shouted nervously. "Take it home, you know you'll have more fun."

Poor Dee, her faced flushed pink. Phil's went red and I poured myself another glass of well deserved wine. I'd kept my happy drinking on a leash. Helped to keep my verbal skills in check too, but it was time to end this evening.

"Gram, everyone, I'd like to thank you for a wonderful wedding reception. It had all the highs and low's expected for this family. I held up my glass to toast Gram for all her efforts. "Right now, I'd just really like to take my husband back to my little apartment and find out what's all wrapped up in this basket."

Chapter 14

A Basket Full Of?

Half past ten chimed on my replica grandfather clock as we made our way in. The usual greeted us, cardboard boxes stacked to the ceiling. The moving truck scheduled for tomorrow afternoon would take the bulk of my life possessions. One day left before Nic returned to ranch life and we'd be spending it packing more of the decorative brown boxes.

"Memorable, don't you think?" I laid my coat over a box and went to feed Mr. Perfect. "All wedding receptions should have such the height of drama."

"It was good, Aubrey. Nice evening. Well, for the most part." Nic could see the strain of my brother's actions flare on me. "Nice of your Gram, she went all out." Nic followed me into the cramped kitchen. "Your brother's an ass, Aubrey."

"Really? Personally I thought you two bonded nicely." My creative words of sarcasm met with an evil glare from Nic. "Now do you believe me?"

"Totally fuc.., never meet anyone as screwed up as him." Nic poured me a glass of wine, and then cracked a beer for himself. "Aubrey I'm tellin' ya now. Put'n my foot down. No way in hell is he ever going to come live with us."

My crackle of laughter sent Mr. Perfect flying out the kitchen door. "I promise. That will never, ever, ever, happen. I can't imagine Phil even wanting to visit."

"Dad had himself a good time. Sure likes Gram. A lot." Nic grinned handing me the wine. "I won't mind if the rest of your family came for a visit. Even Gina, she'd be alright. Just got to keep off the ranch hands."

"Your dad is making it with my gram." I blurted out.

"Making it?" My interpretation took Nic off guard. "You think?"

"You didn't notice how he eyed her all night? Gram's a beautiful woman. Well ok, I know there was a lot going on concerning you and me. But seriously you didn't pick up on their little flirtation?" Wicker basket and wine glass in hand, I headed for the sofa.

"Dad? My dad? You really think he's getting it on with your gram?" Nic plopped down beside me kicking his boots off. "Damn, the ole man still got it."

"Talk about moving fast. See ya learned something from your dad." I slapped Nic's knee laughing at how forward the Ravenwood men really are. "Do you know your dad even asked Gram if she would consider moving out West with me?" I handed Nic a pretty little package. "You first."

"He did? And you thought I moved fast, woman." Nic peeled the paper off reading aloud the prize inside, "Edible Massage Lubricant, Butter Rum flavor." His finger skimmed down the front of my sweater as a grin filled his entire face. "Think I really like the women in your family."

"They didn't?" I tore into the next present. "They did." I held up a bottle of strawberry "edible" shower gel. "Do you know what they did?" I gasped pretending to be horrified.

"Why don't ya tell me Aubrey." Nic handed me my glass of wine. "Drink a little more. Help relax you."

"Relax me? Needed this a few hours ago." I huffed, sipping the wine. "My sister, sister-in-law, and best friend, oh my god and Gram too. Do you know what's in here?" I pointed to the basket with about two dozen more presents to open, frowning. "They filled it with dirty. Naughty. Tacky. Filthy….you better start opening. We're going to use everyone one of these." I tossed Nic another gift and we let the ripping of paper commence.

****

The smell of coffee tickled my nose. "Nic?" Sleepily I reached for him, his place beside me, cold and empty. Mr. Perfect curled purring on Nic's pillow. "Where's your new daddy?" I scratched the cat's head crawling to the side of the bed. The massage so called taste good lotion sat open on the night stand.

"Let me tell you." I picked up the bottle snapping the lid shut, "You've got a nasty morning after taste. Coffee. I need coffee."

Nic's jacket was here, but he wasn't. My apartment was completely empty all but Mr. Perfect and me. Then again with all these boxes anyone could hide in here for a week and I wouldn't know it. I figured he stepped out for a smoke 'til my house phone rang.

"Morning Aubrey." Nic's smooth voice floated from the other end. "Find your coffee?"

"Nic...where are you?" I didn't mean to blast his ear in surprised panic.

"I'm having a very nice breakfast with Dad and..."

"And who Nic?" I pounced again. And he laughed, laughed right in my ear.

"Your brother Phil should be here. Yep right on time."

"Nic. No. Don't do it." I shouted into the receiver.

"It's all good, honey. Won't take me long to put things in perspective for him. Be back in an hour."

"I've married a crazy man." My grumpiness didn't even help.

"Love you too, Aubrey. Now say goodbye and go drink your coffee." The epitome of calmness oozed from Nic's voice.

"Breakfast with my brother? He's nuts." I sounded off to a buzzing dial tone, "What is he up to?"

My nose followed the coffee aroma trail. Nic really made me coffee before he left. For breakfast, a steaming cup of coffee joined by a slice of left over wedding cake. Nic, I'd give him a surprise of my own. Got myself all sugared up with a caffeine buzz. That's what he gets for dumping me for a breakfast date with Phil. Me, my coffee, and the sweet treat of cake stopped by the living room sofa to sulk.

"Can you believe Nic picked Phil over me for breakfast?" Another bite of cake delivered into my mouth as Mr. Perfect listened to my rant. "They're leaving tomorrow. Tomorrow. And he picks Phil. There's got to be more to this." Again a heaping forkful of cake made its way to my lips.

I couldn't stop dwelling on it as I stuffed my face with cake, washing it down with a second cup of coffee. In Nic's absence, I managed to dress myself. Eat more cake. Pack more boxes, and drink the pot of coffee. Energy level exceeding hyper, my body and mind fully wired. Nearly all my cookware had been packed when I heard the cat hissing about something.

"What the hell got up your nut-less ass?" Nic matched the unpleasant greeting.

I appeared in the hall as my boys boxed it out, "What are you two doing?" Mr. Perfect took another swipe at Nic's hand. "Stop teasing him. Give him back his filthy shoe lace, would you." Hand on hip; I shook my head at them both, "Well?"

"Well what?" Nic smirked taking another blow from a padded paw.

"Stop smirking at me. Tell me why you and Dad met Phil for breakfast." Ok, I demanded an answer.

"Little touchy aren't we Aubrey?"

"I've sugared and caffeine myself up into one splitting frenzy. So spill it, mister."

"Think I like you better on a couple glasses of wine." Teasingly Nic played with my hyper space mood. "Any coffee left?"

"Yeah. Come on, tell me what happened." Begging, you'd think it would have worked.

"Nothing." Nic kissed my pouting lips reaching for the dripping pot.

"Nothing? What do you mean nothing?" Getting ticked while on a sugar rush isn't a good way to start the day.

Nic leaned back on the sink, "I thought if I explained to Phil what kind of life we'd be spending together, he'd ease up. You know, bein' friendly. Trying to be a nice brother-in-law. Just trying to put Phil's mind at rest."

"There's your first mistake. Phil and mind in the same sentence." I frowned at Nic. "So what happened?"

"Just thought if he knew where his sister would be moving to. Showed him pictures of the ranch, the house, the cattle, the horses, the land. You've got to admit, it's beautiful there, Aubrey." Nic had no idea of the disappointment he'd set himself up for until now. "He looked at everything I showed him. Didn't say one word. Nothing. Just kept eating."

"Free meal. You paid, didn't you?" Nice gesture from my new husband.

Nic just grinned and continued. "That doesn't matter to me. I wanted to try to reach him. Let him see how much I love you. Idiot thinks I knocked you up."

"Still? I hate that. Why can't two people get married because they love each other?" My mouth spouted off. "Let me guess. He kept eating, letting it go in one ear and out the other." I bobbed my head from shoulder to shoulder.

"Aubrey, I've been around a lot of unhappy men, but your brother, he's about a belligerent cuss."

"Did he make a scene in the restaurant?" I cringed and hung on to the back of the kitchen chair.

"Told me straight out he don't like my kind." Smugly Nic laughed. "Said he refused to accept the fact that you married a dirty breed."

"Oh shit." I slipped down into the kitchen chair. "Please tell me he didn't?"

"Dad, he left the table. Don't blame him. I just wanted to...." Nic smacked his fist hard into his opposite hand.

"Oh Nic, I'm so sorry." I whispered blown away by Phil's hatefulness. I knew Phil scraped the bottom, but this went beyond low. "If it's any consolation, I really appreciate that you tried. I've learned over the years, people like Phil are just meant to be miserable. No matter how hard you try."

"He kept mouthing off how you owed him. You owe him money or something?" Nic asked getting us another cup of coffee. "If ya do, no problem. Tell me how much and I'll pay the son of a bitch off."

"Generous of you, Nic. But that's not how it is. If anyone owes money, it's Phil. Owes me, Allison and Gram," I closed my eyes shaking my head, "the sum...staggering. I'll never see a dime of what I've loaned him. None of us will."

"What's with the whole you owe him thing then?"

"Owe him?" I laughed with cattiness. "Phil believes that Allison and I owe him, for succeeding in life. I make a very nice piece of change being a chef, I'm known."

"Let me get this straight, cause you got some money he thinks he's entitled to it?" Nic asked confused.

"Basically, yes. Phil's worked several jobs, couldn't keep them. Between his know-it-all attitude and religious views, he got himself canned plenty of times. I think he's got it right in this job. He's management you know."

Nic rolled his eyes, "I still don't get it Aubrey. Why do you owe him?"

"Allison and I, we always bailed him out. I even paid for his divorce. Yeah, I know, smart of me. After his divorce, he got really abusive with us. The verbal confrontations…horrifying and the guilt trips he'd lay on us. Too much to handle. After he remarried, he got worse. Became two different people. To Dee and her family, he's the greatest. But all his anger still hits us. With Dee came the whole church thing, she's extremely active in her church. But Phil took it to a whole new meaning. We joke calling him the Reverend Phil Hunter. I believe you've seen that." My coffee somehow comforted me. I took another long drink before finishing. "It's really sad to see someone you once loved and hung out with turn into something like that. If Phil isn't happy with your life, he'll do anything and everything to bring you down."

"Ya hit that on the head, Aubrey. Was he always like this?"

"No. Well, I could've just been blind to it when I was younger. Didn't start realizing it 'til I got out on my own. Started seeing the world through my own eyes. Sorry, not a pretty perfect family picture now is it?"

"Aubrey I'm sorry. I…I don't know what to say." Poor Nic he really was at a loss for words.

"Thank you." I just smiled at Nic. "Phil just handed me a new freedom."

"Freedom? For?"

"You stood up for me. No one has ever dared to face Phil down."

"Your brother is nothing compared to the guys I've taken on in my life." Nic laughed, even petting his competition, Mr. Perfect.

Chapter 15

A Goodbye For Now

With little patience, I waited while Nic and Dad checked in at the Delta counter. Our four days slipped away quickly. Nervously, I rolled my wedding band around my finger. Only four weeks to go. Then it would be my turn to say goodbye to everyone.

"Not again, Aubrey." Nic wiped a tear from my slightly swollen eyes.

"Get used to it, son. Women have an emotional attachment bigger than the universe." Charlie chuckled, pushing Nic aside. "I'll see you end of next month, little lady. Don't be makin' me come back to fetch ya."

"No. I promise I won't, Dad." Another bear hug from Charlie and he excused himself, saying he needed a magazine.

"You do that a lot, Aubrey?"

"Do what a lot?"

"This crying stuff." Nic and I took our time walking toward the security check point.

"Yes. I'm female, remember?" I shot him a look of how could you forget that. "So get used to the mood swings." Easily my head rested on his shoulder. "I'll be ok. Really."

"Doubt that woman."

I clung to Nic, like Mr. Perfect clung to that damn shoelace.

"Call ya as soon as we get in. Promise me you won't go home and sugar yourself up again." Nic tried to lighten the mood.

"Can't promise that. Good news, the movers are coming this afternoon. You got a huge shipment of me coming your way."

"Kiss her goodbye already. I want another hug." Charlie reminded us time ticked on.

The wall helped to support me as I watched Nic and Dad wait their turn. Boots, hats, belts, carryon's all piled on the conveyor belt of the security check point. Nic and Dad redressed and waved a final goodbye to me. Car keys in hand, I moped towards the parking garage.

"Ahh." The buzz, then ringing of my phone scared me. I prayed it wasn't work. No way would I be going in. They got me for two weeks starting tomorrow. My mood lightened seeing the number glow on my phone.

"I know you're not in Wyoming yet, mister."

"Thought I'd at least walk ya to your car." Nic's voice cheered me.

"You should've boarded by now."

"Yep. Waitin' for the old man to sit himself down." I could hear Dad's muffled voice but couldn't make it out. "Four weeks woman. You make it that long?"

"No. But I'll manage." My sigh echoed over the line. "I'll be there. Promise."

"Aubrey, I got to hang up. Love ya, honey."

Chapter 16

Just A Chat

"City's nice to visit. Don't know how that girl can stand to live in it. Too much noise. Be glad to get back home." Charlie settled his old bones into the seat. "Son, we got ta do something with that house. Aubrey steps foot in that place, she'll be back on a plane screamin'."

"Yep, been thinkin' that over, Dad." Nic looked over at his father wondering how they let the ranch house find its way into a sad, run down mess. "Going to have to gut the kitchen. Completely gut it. I'm talkin' down to the bare frame. I'm havin' Aubrey send out pictures of what she'd like to have."

"Good. Good. That's a good start. She's one fine cook. Needs herself a fine kitchen. Good heavens, what about that bathroom? Lord, son, your mother, she'd die all over if she'd see what we did to her home." Charlie swiped his hand over his face. "Ruthie took pride in our home." After Nic's mother died, the beauty of their home died with her.

"I know Dad, I know. Bathroom will be a hell of a lot easier to fix than the kitchen. Won't take but a few days. Don't think we'll have to gut it. Coat of paint, fix the tile floor, she'll love that claw foot tub." Nic silently grinned to himself. Still playing in his mind, a morning shower. Nic's own fingers tingled remembering the feel of Aubrey's wet naked body under the steamy water.

"We've got a month to gut out the kitchen and restore the bathroom." Charlie interrupted Nic's fantasy.

"What's next, Dad? You've been married. What else do I need to have ready for her?"

"You clean that bedroom up of yours, yet?" Charlie knew his son kept little to nothing in his room. Dresser, bed that summed it up. "Why Aubrey, she had her little apartment all dolled up. She's all girl, son. Surprise her. Get some of them pretty sheets. Like I told ya before, your mother had me sleepin' in all those fancy dancy girl colors. Didn't hurt me one bit. Made the woman happy. Besides when the lights are out, ya just don't care what your sleepin' on." Charlie chuckled out loud.

"Little late for a man-to-man talk, don't ya think, Dad?"

"Better be stopping at the Wal-Mart before we get home." Charlie suggested.

"Wal-mart it is. Ya think I should get a new bed and mattress?" Nic and his dad exchanged glances.

"Mattress for sure. Don't want to bring your new bride home to a bed you did…you know…with other women." Charlie muffled a loud chuckle. "I noticed Aubrey likes old furniture. She had some nice pieces in her place. You know, I put the bed your mom and I slept in up in the attic."

"You still got that? I remember bouncing like a jack rabbit on that bed when mom would be cleaning the upstairs. Bet Aubrey would love it. Wait a minute, Mimi…bet I can recruit Mimi to help?"

"Mimi, sure sure. She'd be good at that. Shoot her one of those e-mails." Charlie tapped on Nic's computer.

"I'll give her a list. Now there's a woman who loves to shop." Nic waited for the computer to finish booting up. Four days away from the ranch, meant triple the paperwork. "You handle all the demolition, Dad?"

"I'll get Bones and the boys. We'll have that house perfect for the new Mrs. Ravenwood. It'll make your momma's spirit so proud. So proud."

Chapter 17

Phil

A sledge hammer style thud hit my apartment door. Like a migraine beating on my brain, it kept hammering. Thump, thump, thump. Only one person thumped a door with that much nonmusical skill.

"It's open." I yelled, straddled over another taped box.

A clumping of footsteps stopped in the foyer. "Where are you?"

Did I know my music scales or what? Pegged that one. Brother Phil dropped by for an unannounced visit. "Ya can't miss me, Phil. Place is next to empty. Living room."

The tape screeched over another box while sour puss looked around to seat himself. The furniture Dee didn't need, I'd donated to the Battered Woman's Shelter. Only a few stray pieces were left and covered with boxes.

"You don't even have a kitchen table." Phil remarked holding up the wall.

"Nope. It's at Nic's." I stood up tape gun in hand. "What do ya need?" Loaded question, I know. Felt pretty tough, had a tape gun in my hand. I could always tape his mouth shut. I caught myself snickering at a puzzled Phil. He never got my humor.

"Couple beers left. Care to join me?" I pushed past him into my not so tiny kitchen. Finally I could turn around in here.

"You know, I don't drink." He snapped like I committed a huge sin. I waited for the lecture. "Yeah, I'll have one with you."

"Good." Not surprised, I knew he was a closet drinker. I popped the top and handed it to him. "Just to let ya know, my check book is closed. Or is this a social call?"

"Why do you think I always want something?" Phil snapped defensively.

"You need a moment to reflect on that statement there, Phil?" Just not in the mood for games with the big bro.

"You're really going?" Phil tried to pretend my slam wasn't true.

"Yep." I passed by him back to the living room.

"What if I said I'd miss you?" He slurped at the beer.

"I'd question that, but believe you. Nic have something to do with this? Or did reality bite your ass?" I took a squat on the floor pointing for him to do the same.

Phil slid down the wall till his butt hit the floor. "No. No, your breed of a husband didn't have anything to do with it."

"Call my husband that again and I'll personally toss your ass out of here."

Point taken, Phil grumbled under his breath. He sat there staring at me, "I don't like him, Aubrey."

"Good. He feels the same about you. You better not have come here to give me some burn in hell sermon like you tried at our reception." My glare mixed with my words piped Phil down before he could start.

"You're leaving. Allison's talkin' about another job. I don't have anyone, Aubrey." Talk about sulking in your beer, Phil played it up.

"Really, Phil?" I couldn't help myself. "You drive people away screaming, Phil. You give no one a chance unless they're kissing your ass. It's all about what you can get. Milk'em dry and ring'em out till they bleed. And you sit there and wonder why you have no one."

"Yeah, I, Dee left me, Aubrey." The room fell into silence. Phil sat quietly waiting for me to gloat in his face. Sadly enough, it's the only way to get his attention.

"I know, Phil. She'd been thinking about it for a long, long while." Would have been easy to fling the digs at him, but I know how it hurts.

"She told you?" Phil didn't take surprise well. "When did she tell you?"

"You really didn't see it coming did you?" I thought to myself, Dee's a great person when she's not kissing your ass. Should've said it; rub that salt in the open wound. He'd done it to me if he'd have the chance. "Did you even know we had breakfast, lunches together?" I have to stop hitting him with the surprises.

"She did? When? She never, I didn't know." He looked at his half empty bottle.

"Phil, she told me you won't even do the church marriage counseling thing with her. She was reaching out to you." I picked my words carefully; I wanted so badly to let my sarcasm flow. "She told me she was leaving you the weekend Nic and his dad came in."

"Why didn't you tell me?" Phil's tone, a little snotty for someone in need, I thought.

"What and spoil all her fun?" Just a tad of sarcasm. "You wouldn't have believed me, Phil"

"She's been packing her things, emptying out everything. Even filed for divorce." Reality really hurts when it hits you full force. "You know that too, right?"

"Yeah, I do. She took over my lease. Phil, all she wanted was you to love her."

"Right, like the cowboy loves you." Phil snapped slamming the bottle on the carpet.

"Keep that temper of yours under wraps." I flew back at him. "And yes, my cowboy loves me."

"But you're my sister. You should be on my side."

"When did you ever treat me like your sister?" The beer fizzing going down my throat felt good.

"I'll never see you again, will I?" Could it be a change of heart coming from Phil?

"I'll be back to visit. You could always come to Wyoming to visit me." Nice of me to offer. I could just hear how Nic would respond when I told him.

"Yeah, like your cowboy lover would welcome me with open arms."

"I believe he tried to do that. Breakfast, remember?" I smiled finishing my beer getting up off the floor. I opened my mouth again, but a huge burp echoed off the empty walls.

"Real lady-like Aubrey." Phil's comment rolled off me.

"Ya know, we should've tried this chatting thing with beer a few years ago. Things could've been different." I walked Phil to the door not feeling any guilt.

"This is it? Goodbye?" Phil looked like I hit him with a two by four.

"It's goodbye. You can always call me. Write me. Even e-mail me, I'll answer you. You're still my brother, but the bond, it never existed." Painful I know, but truthful.

"Yeah, I get it. Not like you and Allison." Phil flung open the door, halting under the arch. "Guess this is goodbye. Will you call me when you get settled?"

"Sure thing." I opened my arms in a half hug like pose. Waited, and he left.

The doorway vacated, I could make out each of Phil's devastated footsteps stopping at the elevator.

I stepped into the hall, "Take care of yourself," I called after him.

In return, just a hand wave goodbye and the doors on the elevator slid shut, with a deafening slam. The door clicked behind me, everything seemed to echo in my empty apartment. The only seat available, Mr. Perfect sat on the window seat, sunning himself.

"You're going to have lots of windows to do that in pretty soon, little guy."

From the street below, Phil stood on the sidewalk looking up towards my apartment. Odd. How very odd of him. He's never tried this hard in his life to be a brother to me or even a friend. My cat curled in one arm, I waved to Phil. As if he needed that one last look of me, afraid of his own words that he'd never see me again. I lingered in the window a little longer. Not sure why he still stood there. He finally gave me one last wave.

I dumped Mr. Perfect on a box with his black shoelace. He'd chewed the other tip of the lace off too.

"You're a strange cat aren't you? Strange, strange was what just happened here." Conversation with my cat, I did it a lot. "I guess if everyone I'd known just up and left me, I'd be feeling pretty depressed too."

Another chapter in my never ending crazy family life closed. But a small part of me hoped that the door didn't slam. Just an inch left open for Phil and maybe his change of heart. Another box zapped with tape and added to the mover's pile. I just kept plugging along. This was it. The last of my belongings loaded up and would be sent out to Nic tomorrow. Lucky me, I'd be living on bare necessities for the next two days. Still had the land line, my cell phone that drives me nuts, and my laptop hooked to Dee's printer. My one bedroom apartment in the old redbrick building looked naked and cold. Soon it would flourish with love again as Dee's new life was just beginning.

Chapter 18

Kitchen Talk

My last remaining shipment went out the door with the two "You Pack It, We Move It" husky-built men. Everything I owned; boxed, taped, labeled, and shipped to Nic and my future home, the ranch. One last bag, half packed, sat on the lone chair in the empty living room. Dee showed up at a perfect time, while the movers were here they helped bring a few of her things up. My laptop now occupied Dee's kitchen table and chairs, plus she so sweetly left me her coffee pot. Nice trade for all the stuff I was leaving behind. We all knew this chef won't part with her favorite cookware and utensils. All recipes and herbs left with me. Food wise, Dee had a fully stocked kitchen awaiting her.

Mr. Perfect went flying off the printer when it warmed up next to me. I had been waiting for Nic's latest pictures of my new kitchen to download for printing. One of the first six glossy prints started its descent to the paper rack.

Picture number one, the teaser, showered me with the beauty of the stately ranch house. A large picture window gleamed under the cover of the full front porch. Tucked at the end of the porch, a swing with a view of an open meadow waited for company. A canopy of oak trees shaded the snowy white ranch house. Lush green grass outlined a stone walkway to the front steps. My mind was held captive by the first picture. I had a yard, real grass, and flower beds. Big waving trees and a porch with a swing, instantly I fell in love with my new home. My excitement grew as the printer kicked out picture number two.

"Oh. My. Gosh. Oh no. No, this can't be true?" My excitement frizzled picking up picture number two. Stunned and horrified I handled each one as it flowed out. "You've got to be kidding me." That was an understatement.

But Nic didn't warn me that this beautiful home held a very deep, dark, and dirty secret, and I held it in my hand. Hubby was to have e-mailed me the photos of my newly remodeled kitchen.

Picture number two, the kitchen, and I say this loosely. "Good gravy how could you even boil water on that age old stove?" Completely black with grease, or did the stove look as if it had caught fire and burned? I couldn't tell.

Picture number three didn't ease my mind in the least. The sink, one huge sink, piled high with dirty dishes and a note taped on the bottom of a pan read: "Honey these are for you." Oh, so not funny. I pulled the chair out and planted myself down to see what picture showed up next.

Photo number four. "Please humor me, please be better." Nope. Saying please didn't get me anywhere. Red checked wall paper ripped and peeling from the not so sunshiny yellow paint that it once covered.

Number five rolled out, my husband in front of an ice box as old if not older than my own grandmother. Horrified, I shuffled over each picture while number six waited for my hand to pick it up. Number six, Nic, Dad and a few of the "hands" all stood in a completely gutted kitchen smiling as if they'd done me the greatest favor. Cigars and cigarettes hung out of a few of those smiling mugs. Nothing left; no cupboards, no appliances, no paint, no wallpaper, just a huge overhead light, casting a glow on the ceiling beams and the bare sides of the house.

When he told me to send him pictures of what I'd like my kitchen to look like, I went wild. In between packing and fulfilling my last two weeks of work, I become a regular at Lowe's and Home Depot. I took on the roll of shutter bug in the kitchen department, snapping pictures of several samples of tile for the floor, to style of sinks, to what kind of stove I wished to cook on. I snapped off several pictures of lighting fixtures and sent samples of paint colors. Nic knew if I was going to be happy, I needed a working, functioning kitchen. He even promised me, his domestic goddess, a laundry room. No more 'Laundromat.' He may be the head of the ranch, but the kitchen…my domain. I create a world of happiness there with food.

Deep in my thoughts, the old wall phone rang, nearly scaring me out of the chair. He knew I liked talking on the land line better than my cell.

"So...what do you think?" came the cheery voice of my beloved.

"What do I think? Please tell me the rest of the house doesn't look like this?" I cringed trying not to cry. "Is the bathroom that bad, too?"

"You'll see when you get here." His chuckle didn't relieve me.

"Nic, I'm serious. You're making me panic." I got all edgy with him.

"I told ya the old place needed some fixin' up. You worry too much, woman."

"Bathroom, you didn't even send me a picture of it."

"Aubrey, who's in charge here?" Nic's laughter hinted with sarcasm.

"I am. Don't forget it, mister." And I didn't laugh.

"Here's a clue, kitchen...it's done. Bathroom...finished, our bedroom...you're doing it. I'm done with all this girly crap."

"Seriously? Don't play with me, Nic."

"I can't wait for you to get out here so I can play with you." He interrupted me.

"Nic. Focus. Details, I need details." I hit my happy place just hearing the kitchen and bathroom were done and I got to decorate our bedroom.

"Details. Ok, first, I'm going to haul your ass up the stairs, rip all your clothes off and throw you down on the bed."

"Nic, no. I meant the kitchen." I floated back to earth.

"Your sister taking you to the airport?" I always loved the way he changed the subject on me, but I tried to go with it.

"Yeah, not sure if Gina and Gram are coming. Allison has a meeting in Denver, so we can fly together. I'm worried about Mr. Perfect flying."

"I hate your cat, Aubrey." Nic's voice went flat. "Can't Gina or Allison take it?"

"Did you get rid of that bloodhound, dog, animal of yours?" Hard not to ignore a man who hates your cat. "The vet gave me some pills for him. Said he should sleep the whole flight."

"Double the dose," Nic snorted, "Need to make sure Fuzz Nuts stays asleep."

"You are just down right mean, Nic Ravenwood." Smugly, I added.

"Honey, call me when you leave Cleveland. Make sure you call when you transfer in Denver." Nic did it again, subject changed. Better get used to that. "Just leave me a message if I don't pick up."

"Ok." Ok, that's all I could say. "I'll see ya tomorrow evening."

"I'll be waiting for ya sweetie." Nic was quiet, "You're going to love it here, Aubrey. Love ya."

"Love ya, too." The phone went silent and my stomach knotted.

The clock on the stove showed eleven forty-eight. Nearly midnight, good reason why I was tired, I closed up the laptop, turned my few lights off and crawled into my bed. Mr. Perfect padded gently up the covers next to me.

"Well partner, this is it. In less than twenty four hours we'll be in our new home." With my cat's soft purring, I drifted into sleep.

Like the last curtain call at the theater, my old life as I knew it closed. The lights diming away. On the horizon, a new future. Hopefully a bright and beautiful future. When did I get so philosophical with myself?

My reflection flashed back at me in the bathroom mirror as I brushed my teeth. Auburn red hair, touches of grey patterning and setting up permanent residence on my head. Smile lines greeted me back, when I slathered my, swear by Olay, facial cream all over my skin. "Not bad for forty-four." I said to Mr. Perfect, who chose to continue his own grooming, in the bathroom of course. My few remaining personal items from the bathroom, I collected, bagged, and dumped in the suitcase.

"I feel too sad for eight in the morning." The coffee pot and I were buddies. Lately, I shared all my dark deep feelings with it. "Wonder if Nic's up?"

Click of a switch and my laptop warmed up. Mountain Time, that's two hours behind us. I reached for the phone. "Well look at that, I've got mail." Not sure why I was talking out loud to myself so much. Nerves, just nerves. "Yeah, mail from Nic."

Mr. Perfect's head swung round when I said Nic's name again. "Don't worry boy, I won't let him put you out in that old nasty smelly barn." My cat landed on the table next to my laptop as if he planned on reading the e-mail with me. "Not much guy, daddy's already in the barn doing his ranch stuff. I'm really going to have to pay closer attention to what all he does."

The time of day traveled along without me. Why I needed more time, why I wanted to stay? Who knows? Each clicking second had me making excuses for just another day here. Talked with Gram for awhile, she was already making plans to visit, think she wanted to visit Nic's dad more. Gina gave me a wine and cheese send off a few nights ago, I didn't dare call her today. We didn't say goodbye, just see ya soon. Everything packed neatly in my bag, carry on ready, cat carrier and cat drugs ready. The knock on the door had me jumping liked the scaredy-cat I seemed to be. Maybe I should be the one taking the cat's sleeping pills.

Allison poked her head in, "Hey, ya ready?" This wasn't going to be easy on either one of us.

"Yeah. I think so," My eyes wandered around my next-to-bare apartment. "Mr. Perfect gets a sleeping pill." I grabbed the cat unexpectedly by the scuff of the neck. One, two, three, pill down the hatch, kitty should hit dream land in fifteen minutes.

"How 'bout I take this stuff down for you?" Allison had my bag, "You take a minute…make sure the cat's ok." She hurried out the door, hiding her tears.

Home, my little slice of heaven. A place to retreat to when life sucked. I was leaving my secrets deep and safe in these walls. I had to walk to each room physically standing there saying goodbye. It was only a one bedroom apartment, just one last stroll. My bedroom, empty, but the memory of Nic warmed me with a smile. Living room, kitchen the hub of my apartment, every get together we all seemed to crowd into here. In the middle of the floor, Mr. Perfect had fallen over, knocked out cold by modern medicine. I scooped him up, he was all wiggly like jello and tucked him safely into his carrier.

"Sorry, guy." A blanket wrapped around him, along with that god-awful dirty shoelace. Laptop, purse, cat and one long last gaze etched into my memory. I switched off the lights, and slowly closed the door to my life in Cleveland.

Chapter 19

A Goodbye, A Hello

I felt like a real regular jet setter for as much as I'd been to the airport in the last two months. It amazed me at how simple, easy, and a breeze, even with a deranged drugged cat in tow that we got to our gate. Call me crazy, call me stupid as Nic did when I told him I bought Mr. Perfect a seat, but I wasn't about to have him so called safely loaded into the belly of a plane with the luggage. In his little carrier, looking like he just drank Gina under the table, Mr. Perfect had a seat between Allison and me. All other belongings were stowed and we waited for take off. I glanced over at Allison, whiter than a ghost, so not like her. She flew all over for her job, so why did she look so pasty?

"Allison." I barely called her name offering my hand on top of the carrier. "You sick?"

"No. Why?" Her clammy fingers wrapped around mine instantly.

Sometimes it's just easier not to say anything. Allison and I sat nearly side-by-side, nearly shoulder-to-shoulder. The plane tipped to the right, one last look at Lake Erie. The sun just thinking about setting. I'm going to miss my city. Was I second guessing myself? The usual monologue played like the credits to a movie in my head. 'You jumped into this not thinking. Why did you say yes? You gave up your life here to move cross country to Wyoming.' Then the bolt hit me, Phil's voice ringing loud and clear, 'you're going to fail.' The bouncing voice of the steward's announcements: "All electrical devices may be used at this time," snapped me out of the annoying conversation I was having with myself.

"Yes," I dived down to the seat in front of me yanking my laptop to my lap.

"Did Nic send any more pictures? Any updates on the mysterious kitchen yet? Allison asked leaning over a snoring Mr. Perfect. "How much did you give him? He's out cold."

"Most likely dreaming of how he's going to torture Nic." I laughed while we waited for the computer to boot up. "Nic won't budge on details. I even bugged his dad about it. He didn't budge either. Every single time I bring it up, change of subject, or worse." I opened to the inbox.

"Worse? What do you mean worse?" Allison's attention perked up.

"Yeah, worse." I rolled my eyes. "At the mention of the word 'kitchen,' Nic just starts sayin' how he was going to make me scream." I contorted my face into all kinds of nightmarish shapes at Allison.

"Make you scream?" Amused, Allison chuckled.

"Oh, yeah. On the kitchen table. The island. The counter top, and best of all…the washer, with it on the spin cycle.

"Washer? Spin cycle? Your husband's twisted, and missing you." Allison giggled. "You'll be lucky if that man lets you out of bed for a week."

"Allison, he said in the barn. In the barn on hay." My next expression, gagging noises.

"The barn? Like in where the animals live?" A little dismayed, Allison gagged along with me. "They have eyes Aubrey. They'll see you and Nic naked doing the nasty in their hay."

"No. No way. That's just creepy. In the barn?" I squirmed in my seat. "A barn? It's dirty out there."

"You will and you know it. Just keep your eyes closed." Great advice came forth from my sister.

"Got mail. Got mail from my stud muffin rancher." I sang dancing in my seat. "Allison, check this out."

I clicked on the picture less than an inch high. A full screen of cowboy hats, blue jeaned, flannel shirted people appeared. All but one lady, she wore jeans, but had on a very stylish sweater.

"Look there's other women there too." Relief, thought I was going to be lost in the world of cowboys.

"Aubrey look. These two, the ones with there arms around each other. What do you think they do there?" Allison tapped at the screen.

The top of the e-mail read: "Howdy from your new family." Everyone who lived on the ranch typed me a message.

"Here, here they are." I scrolled down to where the women's name appeared. June El Thompson and Mimi Fredrick. I slid the computer over closer so Allison could read with me. "June El is a horse trainer." I said out loud. "And Mimi is her partner. And not a horse training partner, partner as in couple. Wow." We slowly read over their welcoming bio:

"Hi, Aubrey. Welcome to Wyoming. I'm Mimi, Juney's partner. I work part time in town as a legal assistant at the court house. I'll show ya all the great shops here. Speaking of shopping, your hubby recruited me to help with some decorating. Hope you like it. Can't wait to taste this fabulous cooking of yours that Nic's raved about."

"Hey, Aubrey, June El here. Sure you figured out that the other two women of the ranch are well…in a partnership. Been together going on ten years. I'm Nic's horse trainer, better than any man in these parts. Been workin' for him last five years. Glad Nic found ya. Got to hear that story of how he got ya to marry him so fast. Less than a week. Amazing for him, I mean. Oh yeah we've been counting down the days till ya get here. Can't shut him the hell up about you. Welcome, ya need anything come find us."

Allison and I finished reading at the same time. "He never said a word about June El and Mimi. Let see who else we've got."

Bones, the only name I knew him by and that's the only name he typed. "Welcome to your new home, Miss Aubrey. Talk to ya in person real soon." Short, simple, and sweet, just like him.

One person caught my eye, Jimmy. No last name, just Jimmy. "I am slow. Got a condition in my head Makes me slow. I can type. Learned at school. Mr. Nic hired me last summer. I work real hard. When I do good Mr. Nic let me play games on new kitchen computer. Mr. Nic, he smiles a lot when he say your name. Jimmy

Thanks to Jimmy I just found out I had a new kitchen computer. Jimmy, I scrolled back up to the group shot. Tall boy, skinny, so skinny, but a smile as big as his heart, he couldn't have been more than eighteen or nineteen. Allison and I finished matching names and faces with my new family. Most of them were simple "Howdy and Welcomes" from this close knit ranch family. Less than twenty people including Nic and his dad kept the ranch up and running.

"Little relief to see you've got some female company to pal with." Allison smiled.

"Won't be like you and Gina, that's for sure." My eyes focused back on the couple. Mimi, a petite thin blonde. Looks like if the wind blew too hard she'd float way. But she just bubbled over in her picture. She even looked like she'd be a great prankster. June El on the other hand, wouldn't want to meet her in a dark alley. Broad shoulders, little rough around the edges, wouldn't be caught dead in a dress even if someone paid her, and she looked like she could kick some ass if anyone pushed her.

"Think they'd go in for wine and cheese parties?" I mentioned to Allison. Already I missed our girl's night of smutty gossip, cheese, and wine freely filling our glasses. "Will you send me cheese from the West Side Market?"

"Just tell me when. What about your wine collection?" Allison and I always shopped for wine together.

"I wrapped it all and sent it out." I waved my hand wishing I had a glass. "Nic's going to shit when the case of Chocolate Kiss from Viking shows up. Plus I stocked up on Soft Rose, the one from Oliver. Nic said there's a Wal-mart close, but I'm not chancing it."

"Does he know about your chocolate addiction?" Allison laughed at me.

"Yeah, he caught me. Well, saw me wolf down half a bag of Hershey mini's the night of the reception. Had to accept his cigar habit." I rolled my eyes at her.

"He smokes? Never even smelled it on him." Allison was as surprised as I was when I found out.

"Yep. Every morning. Cup of coffee and a cigar starts his day."

"Oh, you two are made for each other. You, coffee with chocolate. Nic coffee with a cigar. Really a cigar?" She crinkled her lip and asked.

"It's not as bad as I thought, he has flavored smelling ones." I shut the computer off to enjoy my face to face conversation with Allison. Who knew how long it'd be until we could be together again.

"Let me guess, next you'll be telling me it makes him smell sexy." Allison winked at me, "And you'll want to take him to the barn." One last dig with sex and the barn came out of Allison's mouth.

"You've just been hanging around Gina way too much."

"We will be arriving at Denver International Airport in approximately twenty two minutes." The steward's reminder, just another step closer to Nic.

Mr. Perfect let out a small meow, taking a stretch and returned to his curled napping spot.

"Allison, when you're done in Denver, why don't you fly up to Wyoming before you go back to Cleveland?" I hinted as the plane made its final descent.

"I've got a wedding to shoot that weekend, else I would. I can't wait to see your new digs, city girl." Allison and I quietly watched Denver come into view.

The plane touched down and I felt a million miles away from home. Or what used to be my home. Allison and I lollygagged in our seats waiting for the rest of the passengers to exit the plane. At least I didn't have to go searching the entire airport for my next gate. Same concourse just had to hoof it to the other end.

"I've got a late check in at my hotel," Allison twitched, "Your flight leaves in what, hour? Hour and a half?"

"You'll wait with me?" Crap. Tears. We promised each other we wouldn't do this stupid crying thing.

"Well someone has to help you with that cat of yours." Grateful for not having to wait alone, I needed a little of her sarcasm.

Silence again, as we walked to my gate. The only time we'd been separated from each other was our usual trips, conference, and vacations. We lived within fifteen minutes from one another and a half hour away from Gram. Always together. Always on the phone. Always, always, always. We were always within an arms reach of each other. And then I pulled the fast one, I'm the one leaving.

"Promised Nic I'd call when we got to Denver." He'd been on speed dial ever since he put his number into my phone when we were in New Orleans.

"Hi honey, we're in Denver. Allison is hanging out with me 'til my plane leaves. I'll see ya in a few hours." I tried to smile at Allison, "Had to leave a message. Guess he's in the barn or doing something outdoorsy." Neither of us could break the awkward silence of not wanting to say goodbye.

"We'll be boarding Flight 7721 to Buffalo, Wyoming in a few minutes. Any passengers needing assistance please come forward." The sweet voice of the stewardess addressed the small crowd of people waiting.

"Oh my god, Allison, this is it." I started to panic. My face twisted into sadness and my eyes snapped shut holding the swell of tears in. Tears that came and wouldn't stop. Over Mr. Perfect's peaceful sleep, Allison and I latched into such a hug that you'd have to take a butter knife to separate us.

"I don't want you to go, Aubrey." Allison sobbed, pulling apart from me. "I'm sorry I shouldn't say that. It's...we've always had each other. Now you're half way across the country."

"Come with me. Just move out here. Nic said the house is big enough." I begged my sister to change her life for me. "Promise you'll visit. Really, really soon? Call me every day. Send me e-mails. I promise I'll learn how to text message, too."

"Now boarding all passengers at this time." I didn't like that sweet voice much anymore.

"Come on, that's you and Mr. Perfect." Allison helped me collect my cat and walked me to the last spot in line.

One last hug, a long hug, and we said goodbye. Allison waited till I handed over my boarding pass and I turned giving her a wave, mouthing 'love you, sis.' Being the last person on the plane can really suck, especially after you've sat there crying in front of the waiting crowd. Thankfully my seat with the cat was close to the front. I loved the plane. So small, two rows, one side double seats, the other, a single row. Mr. Perfect and I settled in for the two hour flight.

"How's the cat doing?" The lady across the aisle nudged my arm. "I'm Polly. You heading to Buffalo too?

"Yes. Just had to say goodbye to my sister." I tried to smile and for some reason felt a little motherly peace coming from Polly. "I'm Aubrey."

"Aubrey, pretty name. Just visiting?" She inquired.

"No. No, I'm moving here. My new husband lives out here." I hoped she'd keep talking with me.

"Explains all those tears you two girls just shared." Polly handed me a tissue over the aisle. "You'll like it here. Summers are beautiful, fall even better. The winter, its cold honey, I won't kid ya. Snow up to your wing wang. We get the works here. That'll lead ya into a nice spring. God's country, ya know. Endless miles of blue sky. Looks like you'll fit right in with folks, sweetie."

"I hope I do, Polly." As I patted my swollen eyes I managed a smile. "We'd get some pretty hard winters in Cleveland, but nothing like what I'm expecting out here."

"Your cat, ya must of had him long time to pay the extra expense for a seat." Polly smiled warmly.

"I rescued Mr. Perfect from a shelter. He came with the name. Siamese cat with the attitude to back his breed. My husband said he's going to put him out with the barn cats." I chuckled. If Nic knew what was good for him, he'd learn to love Mr. Perfect.

"Let me tell ya a little something about men, honey. Been married for forty-seven years. You're not a doormat, don't take his crap either. As a new bride don't be trying to please him and lose yourself. But like that sayin' that's out there, something like love lots, hug lots, you know which one I mean, just remember to cherish each other and you'll be fine."

"Thanks Polly, best advice I've gotten so far."

I didn't know who Polly was, but I hoped she lived close by. I instantly attached myself to her for the duration of the flight. The very round woman was like a sitting history book of the new town I'd be living close too. She gave me all the background I needed to know. The best part, details of all the town's shops, diners, hotels, and when cattle would be driven down Main Street. She shared all of her views, thoughts, and life details with me over a cup of airplane coffee.

"Greetings, fellow passengers. Just a friendly welcome to Buffalo, Wyoming. The plane should be touching down in about twenty-five minutes. Tidy up your areas. I'll be through with the trash bag. And please, everyone, let's keep the noise level down. We have a sleeping cat on board today." The middle aged stewardess enjoyed her job.

"Polly, I'm so glad to have met you. I hope to see you around town soon."

"I sure hope so, girly. You get settled in. Come look me up, last name is Holiday." She patted my hand. "By the way, I own the little bake shop in town. You make sure to stop in now, ya hear me?"

"A bake shop, I'll definitely find you, Polly." The plane touched down. I've finally arrived.

Polly had the whole grandma package thing going. Sweet lady, I wanted to gobble her up and take her to the ranch with me. We chatted our way to the baggage claim together. A well weathered gray haired gentleman met her with a bouquet of roses. Their display of endless love for each other had my eyes running with moisture again. Not like I haven't been crying enough, I'm sure as soon as I lay eyes on Nic the waterworks will flow again. I'd never been in such a small airport. This place hopped as if it were rush hour in Cleveland. My cat and I wandered around the crowded baggage claim. Black, brown, white, and gray, cowboy hats dodged in and out. They all looked the same to me. I didn't care about my bags or even Mr. Perfect at this moment. I just wanted to see Nic. In the middle of the crowd making his way to me, I spotted him. I screamed like a crazed school girl over seeing her first rock star. A few ears got pierced by the pitch while I bumped my way through the thick sea of people. Cat carrier dumped to the floor with a rocking thud, me with a flying leap, and I landed in Nic's arms. People grinned, chuckled, and stared, but there was no way my lips were leaving his. Fingers laced together, I felt his callused hand and realized how much I'd missed him. Slowly, he ran the back of his hand over my cheek. His usual braided hair flowed over his shoulder allowing me to twist an end around my finger. You would have thought we just stepped back into New Orleans where we met. "Get a room." Someone muttered loudly as they walked past.

Nic ignored the helpful hint and locked his lips around mine again.

"Figured ya might need this after leaving your sister." He handed me a chocolate bar. "How many bags ya bring with ya woman?"

"Just these two," I pointed to Mr. Perfect's cage and my shoulder bag setting on top of it, "I had to check one."

"Just one?" Nic seemed surprised. "Ya sure?"

"Did all my boxes arrive?" My weary tiredness didn't slow me as I bounced around him.

"Yep, put'em in the spare bedroom. I didn't want ta touch… ya know you got a lot of girly stuff. Where do you plan on wearin' all those fancy shoes to?" Nic tried to hide his snickering grin.

"Oh, thought I'd wear them out in the chicken house or something." My life changing experience had just begun as I reached for my bag rounding the edge of the carousel.

"Got it for ya. You take that damn animal of yours." Nic hoisted the bag up while I picked up Mr. Perfect. "You OD the cat?"

"I hope not. Just gave him one pill like the vet said." Through all the commotion of traveling Mr. Perfect and his tattered shoelace stayed asleep.

Only a three-hour drive to the ranch. We'd be getting to my new home close to midnight. I wasn't adjusted to Mountain Time yet. My body clung to my time schedule of back East. It screamed "Hello it's past your bedtime, you need sleep." No way was Eastern Time going down easily to change.

"A truck? I never rode in a truck before. No little car to go zooming around in?" I swayed as if driving in and out of traffic.

"You've got so much ta learn, little lady. Trucks are a staple on a ranch, honey." My first ride in a pickup truck left Nic snorting with laughter.

Little by little the lights from the Buffalo city limits dwindled behind us. Most of our drive consisted of the freeway. Exits shot off into the black of night with empty roads that lead into what seemed like a nowhere land. I'd spot a house here and there, but nothing like the row after row housing developments back home.

"Need a stop for coffee?" Nic asked while exiting towards the Get Up and Go Truck Stop's neon blinking lights.

"And a bathroom." I added in.

After an hour and half in the truck, I needed the stretch, bathroom, and the pick me up of hot coffee.

"How much further?" I sounded like a kid riding in the backseat.

"'Bout another hour, maybe less." Nic shook his head at me. I wasn't sure if it was because I checked on the cat again, or how clueless I was to his lifestyle. "Things are pretty far apart out here, Aubrey."

"I talked to your dad yesterday; he's really happy I'm finally getting out here."

"That's all I've heard since we got back from Ohio, 'Why can't you come sooner,' haven't been able to shut the ole man up. And Bones."

"Oh how's Bones? Your dad and him, talk about a tag team on the phone. Did you know, one of them has called me nearly everyday?"

His eyebrow lifted with a slight grin. "Dad's been calling you? Bones too?"

"Um, yes," I sipped at the coffee. "Usually in the morning. When I'd ask for you, they'd say you were out in the barn. Your dad still going to stay with us, isn't he?"

"Oh yeah. The old man can't wait for you to cook for him. Dad's got his room in the house. Then sometimes he likes to go down and bunk with Bones and the other guys. He's been calling ya has he?" Nic grinned.

"I think it's sweet of him. Told me about town. There's a Wal-mart out here." My little coffee rush perked me up into an endless chatter box. "Target's over an hour drive." I frowned at Nic finding it hard to except I'd be driving over an hour to a store.

"Target, huh? Your brother warm up to the fact you married me?" Nic smirked.

"Oh my gosh." My hands went up in the air hitting nothing in the cab. "He showed up at my place. Even had a beer with me."

"Ya don't say. What'd he want?" Nic's curiosity peaked.

"I asked Phil if it was a social call or if you had something to do with it." I couldn't help the snicker; I remembered the boys' breakfast date. "He still can't get over the fact that I left his needy clutches and married you. He's got to fend for himself these days." I braked for another sip of coffee. "The big one, totally blind sided him. Dee really did file for divorce. She even took over my lease for the apartment."

"Are you shitin' me? I didn't think she'd have the guts to stand up to him. Let alone go through with it." Nic replied shocked.

"You know it was really sad. Sad, sad, sad. I walked him to the door and you know, kind of held my arms out for a hug…and he walked away. He just walked out. After he left, Mr. Perfect was sunning in the window, so I stopped to pet him."

"Aubrey, shorten the story for me." Nic so politely stopped my babbling spree. He had a way with that. Short and to the point.

"Oh fine, fine. Anyways, when I looked out the window, Phil was on the sidewalk staring up at me. I finally waved and he left. Talk about a sad person." Rejection, I'd become immune to it with Phil. So why did it still bug me? "I invited him to come out and visit."

"Sisterly of ya. Rat bastard can bunk out with the cows."
"Nic."

"Don't think you'll be hearing much from him, honey." A warm squeeze of comfort came from Nic's hand. "You're cold, woman. Where's my jacket? I brought it for you."

I crawled over the seat retrieving his brown leather jacket and slipped it around me. The smell of cigars were well embedded deep into the coat. The October night air packed a brisk punch of coldness and I enjoyed snuggling down inside Nic's jacket. Nic had turned off the highway in what seemed like hours ago, and we drove along the desolate county roads. The outline of the mountain range edged itself into the darkened sky. Totally pitch black, another thing for me to get used to. No street lights, just the gaze of the silver moon patterned over the country side.

"Time to spill it. Details. Kitchen, bathroom something please." I turned in my seat towards him, yanking on the arm of his flannel.

"Aubrey, well, honey, let me put it to you this way," He turned his head, as if he saw something hiding in the darkness out the window. "Honey there's been some setbacks. Got delayed. Cattle broke down a fence or two. Damn coyote came sniffin' around." He totally sidetracked me.

"How far done is it?" Nic pressed at my panic button.

"How about we…I'll explain it all to you in the morning."

Another sidestep from him.

"Nic how bad is it? Please just tell me?"

He slowed the truck down, turning on the left blinker. I wondered why. We hadn't passed a single car on this road and nothing followed us. I soon saw why. The headlights reflected the huge stone archway. The words "Ravenwood Ranch" arched in thick heavy wrought iron over the driveway, supported by the two massive stone pillars.

Spontaneously I grabbed at his arm again, "We're here?"

Nic stopped the truck, letting me take in the full view of the archway. "This is home, Aubrey. I really hope you like it here." Nic rubbed his thumb softly over the back of my hand, the way his face lit up saying this is home, his smile was contagious catching with mine.

The gravel road had to be over a mile or two long. Barbed wire fences reflected slightly, outlining the driveway length. In the blackness of night the images of the out buildings began to appear under a few huge illuminating lights.

Around the south side of the house, Nic parked next to three other trucks. Thankful for his coat, the bitter cold slapped at me when I opened the door. A steady quietness of the night enveloped the ranch house and surrounding buildings. A lone coyote howled out its lonely song, startling me as did the voice coming from behind me.

"Aubrey, you're here." Charlie's voice not only scared me, so did his welcoming hug.

"Dad. You waited up for us?" Surprised and happy to see Charlie, I embraced him in another hug.

"Had to make sure my girl and her cat got here. Give me this." He took the cage from my hands. "I'll take care of pussycat. Promise you'll see him in the morning. Go on you two. We'll catch up over coffee."

"Thanks Dad." I kissed Charlie goodnight stepping around the truck trying to see the house. From what my eyes could make out, it matched the only decent photo Nic had sent me. Even in the darkness, I made out the shadow of the porch swing. Coming closer to the front steps, the shimmer of a lamp sitting in the front window glowed a soft sign of welcome. Another coyote let his bark be heard as we stopped on the top step of the porch.

"It's a coyote, honey." Nic chuckled as I glued myself closer to him. "Welcome home, Aubrey."

A moaning creak from the screen door echoed in the quietness as Nic pushed open the door. Suddenly he whisked me off my feet carrying me over the threshold. My purse tumbled onto the nearest chair as we passed through what I thought was the living room. With no light to guide him, Nic headed to the steps with me in his arms.

"Nic that was my head." A door, door frame, something just collided with my head enlisting a small cry of pain from me. "Really, I can walk."

Caught by a soft landing, I flopped in the middle of a bed. I obviously figured this must be the bedroom he intended us to share. A switch clicked and a bright light blinded me for a second. I was sitting in the middle of a huge wooden bed. Just by the look of the wood, I thought it could possibly be maple and old. It had to be some family heirloom. The headboard alone stood over six feet high with a carved floral design running up both sides and then topping it. The bottom foot board, I don't know how he didn't crack any other of my body parts on it when he tossed me, stood half the height of the headboard.

"Nic, it's beautiful."

"Story is, belonged to my grandparents. They gave it to my parents when they got married." Nic smiled, "Dad said you needed it."

I fell back on the bed, head at footboard admiring the old antique. "It's totally amazing and so well preserved."

"Just don't mind the comforter. Told ya, you're finishing this room yourself." Nic tugged at the sleeve of my coat. "Got plans for you woman."

"Oh no, not till I see my kitchen." I demanded, playfully bouncing up on my knees.

"No." He unzipped the jacket, stripping it off me, tossing it to the hardwood floor.

"Will you at least show me the bathroom, because I really need to use it before you jump on me."

"I like the way you think, woman. Up for a midnight shower?" Another pull on the arm and he had me off the bed. My feet barely getting planted on the solid wood floors, he yanked me back down the hallway he carried me up. "Hold on a minute. I got ta warn ya." Nic stopped us at the closed door. "We didn't gut the bathroom, just gave it a face lift."

He switched the light on letting me push open the door and past him. A claw foot tub in enamel white became the center of my attention.

"Original?" I crawled into the empty tub fully clothed.

"Yep. Ya want to add some water?" Nic immediately started stripping off his shirt.

"No. Stop that. Just...the bed." Still standing in the tub, I pointed towards the door. "Go like fluff the pillows, I need girl time."

"What the hell is 'girl time,' woman?" Nic gave me his hand, helping me step from the tub.

"Stop calling me 'woman' and get out of the bathroom." With a playful shove, I pushed him out the open door.

"Hurry up." His voice echoed through the closed door. Nic just became the kid in a candy store, with me, his treat, hiding out in the claw foot tub.

I could hear Nic's boots striking the hardwood floors as he went back to his, no, our bedroom. Boots, he wore those things everywhere.

I scanned over the bathroom's facelift, "Please don't let him wear those clippie clumpy boots to bed."

A coat of white paint, the fumes still fresh, I could work with that. The vanity showed off itself under the mirror's light with a pretty marbled emerald green top and a simple white sink. My new bathroom could have held two of my apartment sized ones. Shoes in hand, my stocking feet slipped along the hardwood floor like a dust mop. I couldn't wait to see the rest of the house in the morning.

"Nic, can't you please show me the rest of the house?" I begged switching off the overhead light.

"Aubrey I've had two things on my mind today." Nic clicked on the night lamp beside him. "First, getting you here in one piece. Second," he held up two fingers, "Most importantly, getting you under these covers."

Nic moved quietly, let alone quickly. My shoes fell out of my hand as his hand circled behind my neck. Slowly the kiss lingered.

Layer after layer of our clothing were tossed feverishly around the floor. I slipped under the covers snuggling tight to Nic's warm naked body. My fingers threaded through his hair as I felt his hand skim my curves with a touch of roughness.

Chapter 20

My Kitchen

    My automatic alarm clock ticked inside my body, only five in the morning Mountain Time. Body clock chimed seven Eastern, and I'd over slept. Next to me a soft purr of snoring rumbled from under the thread bare quilt. I wiggled myself free from the tree trunk leg of my hubby that held me prisoner. I was really here. The sun was just breaking into the spiraling colors of an early morning dawn. My eyes focused carefully out the curtain less window beside me. Not far in the distance a mountain range back dropped the morning skyline. Something I'd never wake to in the city. I so badly wanted to wake Nic. Wanted him to show me what his mornings were like here. Mr. Perfect bounded with a spring in his step onto the bed. In pussycat perfection he padded over Nic's sleeping body to me.

    "Where did you come from?" I scratched the back of his ear. "So tell me, like your new digs? Been exploring all night haven't ya?" The cat hummed a purr louder than Nic's snoring.

    The wonderful aroma of coffee trickled upstairs to me. "Dad must be up." I grinned, carefully sliding the covers back. "Such a pretty purple print of flowers," I felt the sheets again, "They've got to be brand new. They hadn't even been put through a wash cycle yet for all the stiffness." I glanced back to Nic, who didn't even stir with my idle chatter. He'd rolled to the center of the flower patch covers with you know who tightly curled next to him.

    Clothes were tossed across the bedroom as if a tornado danced over the floor. I grabbed up his flannel shirt and wrapped myself in it.

"Perfect mini dress." I murmured quietly smoothing it over myself.

One sock found, the other one, who knows where it ended up in our mad disrobement. There was no way he was letting me sneak a peek at that kitchen last night. One foot left sockless, I stood up staring at the bed I now shared with a man. He's really my husband. Nic's hair flung carelessly over the pillow, his rugged body decorated by floral print sheets. I grinned at the soft purr of snoring rumbling from deep inside the antique bed. The glow of honeymoon sex still glimmered over my heated body. I toyed with the inkling thought of arousing him. Nic snored on as my body's time clock honed in on the Eastern Time zone. I slipped quietly from our bedroom and padded down the oak staircase.

"Coffee." There is was again, the whimsical smell of coffee. "Dad? You around here?" I stopped at the bottom of the stairs, the living room to the right of me. Just me and the empty first floor.

Hardwood floors lined this entire house from top to bottom. "My furniture." I whispered aloud. Nic had taken the few pieces I sent out and arranged them in the living room. My nose couldn't take it anymore and started me following the scent of coffee again. I wandered to the left and stepped inside an empty dining room. No formal table and chairs, no hutch filled with china. All four walls covered in a rich floral pink and rose wall paper. An empty cherry fireplace occupied the far wall, a huge mirror hung above it.

"Excellent dining room, sure hope Nic left this for me to furnish." Captured again by the aroma of coffee I followed my nose. "Where is my kitchen?"

I had to be getting close. Out through another doorway and I stepped into my heaven. My kitchen, perfectly designed from all the pictures, pamphlets and color swatches I had sent to Nic. A fresh ray of morning sunshine welcomed me into my place of domestic creation. An indoor garden box built right into the bay window, put there especially for me to grow my herbs. My one bare foot soaked up the coolness of the black slate tile on the floor. The kitchen counters inlaid with shiny black granite, beveled and grooved were silky to the touch. Every cupboard painted white, accented with copper handles. A double oven built into the wall right at my height shined in chrome; the dishwasher and refrigerator all coordinated. A wall of stainless steel appliances couldn't be complete without a six burner gas stove. My number one pick, the rustic candelabra of lights. Black wrought iron with at least twenty globed candle lights hung over the island and a smaller version over the kitchen sink. Four high back wrought iron chairs lined the opposite side of the center stage island. A groaning coffee pot called to me and I whipped open a cupboard door to find my dishes neatly stacked as if I lived here all my life. I bounced along from door to door swinging them open. All of my heavenly kitchen possessions were to be found. He had organized and placed all of my accessories according to my specific needs without even knowing where I needed everything. Easily I found my huge coffee mugs. I slopped coffee on the counter hearing Nic's voice behind me as I poured out two cups.

"Just couldn't wait could ya?" He yawned reaching for me with one hand and coffee with the other. "Meet your expectations?"

"Unbelievable. Amazing. I can't believe you did all this for me." I giggled slipping out of his reach running my hands over the smooth countertops as I walked along admiring all the handiwork. "A real breakfast nook." I giggled again. "Do you realize my whole little apartment could fit inside this kitchen?"

"Everything you need to cook with should be in here somewhere." Nic leaned his bare back side up against the counter.

"Aren't you cold?" I couldn't help wondering why he walked the house naked as I ventured back to him.

"Nope." A fast grab by Nic's hands and he lifted me on top of the counter.

"Oh. That's cold." The tail of his flannel didn't cover my bare butt hitting the granite countertop.

"Told ya I'd make ya scream on your new countertop." He teased with a grin, slowly kissing me.

Nic's naked body slipped between my dangling legs. Warm hands climbed up and under the flannel shirt that robed me. "Nic, really on the counter?" I quickly unbuttoned the flannel, "I've never…" He closed my worried words with a teasing kiss. The soft shirt tumbled from my shoulders and bunched at my wrists. My breast tingled brushing over his bare chest. Lost in a wave of desire I continued to slip kisses up and down his neck. In the midst of our heated countertop passion, something started to lick my foot with a warm slobbery tongue.

"What the hell is that?" I shoved Nic back, screaming. The huge brown floppy eared dog used its wet tongue to floss between my sockless toes.

"Toby." Yelled a voice I knew well. "Damn it dog, where the hell are ya?" Bones hustled in through the back entrance of the kitchen. "Good god. Nic. Aubrey. What the hell are you two doing?" Bones stopped dead in his tracks. An instant red flushed his round face.

I buried my head and matching red face into Nic's chest. Thanking him for yanking the shirt back up and over my shoulders so fast.

"Mornin' there, Bones." Nic shielded me while I peeked over his shoulder.

"I, I, just came in for coffee. Damn animal of yours flew in beside me. Miss Aubrey, I am so sorry." Bones took on another shade of red, averting his eyes to the kitchen tile.

"Good morning Bones." I managed a smile from behind the cover of Nic's body.

"For god's sake Nic, get your ugly ass covered." Bones mouthed off, stomping out the way he came, forgetting his coffee and the dog.

Nic howled with a wild laughter, but for me it wasn't too funny. "Nic that's not funny. What if we'd been…you know." I let my eyes plead with him in worry.

"What if? You mean what if I'd been bangin' the hell out of ya on the countertop." His laughter ran rampant. "Keep it to the bedroom make ya feel better?" He brushed my hair from my eyes.

"I don't know…that island looks mighty tempting." Instantly I blushed. "I can't believe I just said that. Bedroom would be better. But seriously Nic, what is that?" I pointed to the slobbery lop eared thing sitting on the floor. Its tail pounded out a rhythmic thump on the floor.

"Toby. Come here boy." The dog obeyed, sitting at his feet. "My old bloodhound I told ya about."

"It stays in the house? A dog? A dog that stays in the kitchen?" I never had a dog and really didn't want one either.

"Yeah honey. He's no bother, just follows ya around. He's a good boy." Nic tried to ease me with a smile while ruffling the fur over Toby's big head.

"Does the word C-A-T," I spelled it out sarcastically to him, "mean anything to you?" At this point, I think even Toby understood what I spelled out.

"Your nut-less wonder will be fine. He can jump, can't he?" Nic joked at my expense. "Now get your bare little ass up those steps woman, I'm not done with you."

"Don't you, like, have barn work to do?" I sneered at the dog as I slipped from the countertop. "Nic, why is your mutt following us?"

"Aubrey, Aubrey, Aubrey, Toby likes to watch."

Dear Allison,

You just won't believe it. Me the city girl out here living in God's country. That's what I get for marrying a rancher. On the old county road I travel down to my new home, my daily tour guide becomes the endless brilliant blue sky with a back drop of snow capped mountains. Dotted white puffy clouds are bunched under the canopy of the blue skyline. It's the kind of clouds we used to see hanging loosely between the high-rises.

Remember we thought country life with fresh air was walking in the city park? The mountain air is so fresh, so clean and it bites with crispness. It's like biting into an apple at Harvey's Open Air Market right in the dead of the city. Well not all air is so clean and crisp around here. There's a cow barn, with cows, real cows. They moo a greeting of hello and bat their big brown eyes at me every time I'm near them. But the stench that reeks from it on a hot sunny day, it would have me believing I was walking past the construction workers port-a-potty on Fifth and Vine. It stinks.

There are barns and coops for all kinds of animals here. The chicken coop is one of my favorites. All painted bright white, fastened together with some kind of silver like wire with tiny stop sign like holes and then attached to the thin lumber structure. The fluffy chickens even have a little fenced in playground of their own.

I've got a hot date with hubby out in the barn, something about horse care 101. Wish me luck.

There's so much more to tell you, I can't wait for you to come visit. What's your shoe size? I need to get you a pair of mud boots, still learning the "lingo" here. Details to follow.

Love and miss you,

Aubrey ☺

Chapter 21

Life Begins In Wyoming

Allison and I had taken to writing real letters to each other. The kind where you put ink to paper, put it in an envelope, and slap a stamp on it. Quick important stuff, we called, e-mailed back and forth like mad, and I learned the text message system. In no time, the calendar reflected I'd been here for two weeks. To me, it was like getting on the carousel at the fair, going round and round, trying to remember everyone's name, and everything they expected out of me, the rancher's wife. I found a list of "chores" on what my new friends decided should be my responsibilities. Several different hand writings, dirt smeared smudged fingerprints topped the note. In at number one, cooking. But I'd been given the chore of chicken care, compliments of Mimi. Her job at the courthouse had turned into a full time position. How bad could it be? Seriously? Well, the chicken coop looked so pretty, the so called delicate little birds just strutted around their caged in yard. But those vicious, fluffy feathered pecking birds, I could've used my bare hands to wring their scrawny necks. What was I thinking? Egg collecting, daily, morning only. Who the heck made up that schedule? Bull shit. I was assaulted by the feathered bitches and pecked at until I went screaming from the coop. June El found me sitting on the back steps nursing my bloody peck marks.

"Hey." June El approached me from the side yard. "Looks like you and the chickens had a pretty darn good fight." She stifled her laughter mildly. "Mimi, she's happy to dump the pampered chicken squad on you."

"Pampered chicken squad? More like feathered bitches. Thank

Mimi for the nice warm and fuzzy welcome." I cracked a smile. "I've never wanted to grab an animal by its neck and just shake it."

June El laughed right out in my face. "You ain't as prissy as Nic likes to think."

"He thinks I'm a prissy?" I huffed a little disappointed. "We'll see how prissy he thinks I am." I bolted up off the steps, wanting to show my husband what a prissy panted chick I was.

"Sit down. Man likes you that way. Compliment, ya know. Let me look at those marks." June El grabbed for my arm. "Never seen a man so in love like him, Aubrey. You've curbed that ass kickin' temper of his." She turned my arm over looking at the bites.

"Temper?" I asked. "I've never seen his temper. Seen him annoyed, but temper? Do tell." I smiled eagerly motioning her to follow me into the house.

"Holy shit, woman." June El didn't lack in words either. "Wowie, girl. They weren't kidding when they said they gutted the place."

"I'm in love with my kitchen. Every chef's dream." I washed my bloody peck marks off in the sink. "So what other tips can you give me about ranch land?"

"Aubrey, ya hear any yelling and it don't sound like someone's getting' killed, stay your ground."

"Stay my ground?" I asked, not sure of what it meant.

"Means stay put, city girl." June El liked calling me a city girl. "Someone's getting their ass chewed up. Some days it's impossible to get work done around here with all the testosterone colliding."

"Sounds so much better than the temperamental prissy chefs I worked with. They'd have full outright hissy fits. Right in the middle of the kitchen." I smiled whirling my head in a sarcastic circle.

"Not these boys. They'll be beatin' on each other. Next breath, best of friends." June El sipped at the iced tea I handed her.

"Ok, how do I say it? Guess I have to bite the bullet. How the hell do I get the eggs from my pampered feathered bitches?" My question had me even laughing at myself.

"Mimi, she'd just grab one up. Toss it to the floor. Collect up the eggs. Ya show it who's boss." As if she had an invisible chicken in her hands, June El gestured all the motions of grabbing, tossing, and collecting.

"Show 'em who's boss," in mid air I repeated the hand motions. "Got it."

June El laughed hysterically at me. Well, why not? City girl in the chicken coop, it did sound pretty darn funny.

"Nic says you're a wine drinker." June El pointed to my collection of wine bottles lying in the rack.

"Yes. I love a sweet red. Enjoy cooking with a zinging white. What about you and Mimi? You two interested in some wine and cheese get togethers?" True, I was desperate for company.

"Excellent, the boys have poker night; we could have our girls' night." June El's face lit up. "Let's set up for Saturday. Unless you and Nic got plans.

"No, he hasn't said anything. Tell me more about poker night?" I asked.

"The boys who don't go into town on Saturday night sit around drinking, scratching, and losing money to each other." June El shook her head in disgust.

"Nic plays poker too?" I tested the waters with my new friend asking for a little more information on my husband.

"Let me tell ya, that husband of yours is a smooth poker player. Cleans the table on them, but end of the night, he gives the dumb asses their money back. Personally, I'd rather kick back with some wine. This little party of yours sounds good. Mimi will love it. She's like you, all up and up girly…you know prissy."

"Better watch it Juney Bug. You hang with me, I'll be turning you into a prissy panted girly, girly too." A click of iced tea glasses rang with a friendship forged.

For a rough and tough broad, the other ranch hands called her worse; June El had a softer side. I made friends instantly with her and Mimi, both taking me under their wings.

Dear Allison,

Life on the ranch is demanding for a clueless city girl. My brood of lady chickens and I have come to an understanding...I'm the boss. My so called "chore" list has been scratched completely. Nic howled like the damn coyote that screams every night when he read over it. Seems the "boys" just wanted to poke fun at me. But I've been designated dinner cook. Not too bad of a job, don't you think? I make extra and take it down to the bunk house. It's amazing at how appreciative this group of men are. Not one of them complains if a vegetable is out of place on the plate. Let me tell you about my latest little accident. Nic finally got me to come into the horse barn. It's not that bad, really, the place is practically spotless. Just these massive beasts in their stalls. Nic kept trying to tell me about this horse named Emerald Bay, who had a foot problem. Wait, scratch that, she has an injured hoof. While he was tending to her "hoof" I perched myself up on this fence thing, not even four feet off the ground. Even Nic said I'd be safe sitting there while he worked on the horse. She's a gorgeous animal, but Allison, I'm scared to death of her. Remember that sitting thing, I'd be safe, total lie. All I did was twist around to see what the noise was behind me and I flipped backwards off the fence, cracking my head on the cement and landing on my left shoulder. Don't worry it gets better, I knocked myself out cold. Relax, relax, there's no concussion, just a lump on the head and a bruised shoulder with a bruised ego. Funny part, when I woke up, Nic had me stretched out on the living room sofa, ice bag dripping down my face and some strange man looking me over. I found Nic and Charlie right away, but I didn't know who and why this man was touching me. Real simple, he's the town doctor. Can you believe the doctor makes house calls? All in all, I'm fine, survived my first mishap in the barn. I'm sure there'll be more to follow. Nic wants me to learn how to ride this horse called Emerald Bay. I'm not so sure about riding a horse, bet it will be a trip into the emergency room for sure. I really miss you Allison, wish you could be here. Maybe over the holidays you and Gram can come out.

Love you, Aubrey ☺

Chapter 22

A Greasing

I glanced at the wall clock, "Five thirty," I muttered aloud and turned the burner to simmer. "Nic's never late for dinner. Usually hits the backdoor by this time. I wonder what's keeping him?"

I'd gotten a little braver over the past week or so and started wandering around all the barns. Mimi had taken to walking with me, so it became a great way for me to investigate all these buildings of animals. The horse barn, my usual stopping place, and where I normally found Nic. When I opened the side door, an odd warmth of moisture circled in the darkness and the smell of fresh hay greeted me. Closed up tightly for the evening, not finding Nic, I locked the door on my way out. Fast to learn, lesson one, you always close and secure the doors to the barns. One last guess, the equipment barn, never had the urge to checkout all the farm tractors. These metal monsters had hugeness to them. I'd only seen such machines at the county fair. A family of John Deere green farm equipment lined the inside of the building. Parked like cars in a lot, each piece of equipment had its own stall like the horses did. Neatness, order, and somewhat clean all rolled up in this massive garage structure.

"Nic?" A light over his workbench gave his hiding place away. "You back there?"

"Aubrey. Ya steppin' outside that comfort zone of yours?" Nic called back to me.

"Where are you?" Slowly, I inspected the silent monster machines in the sea of green as I followed the sound of his voice.

"Workshop. Just walk straight down, you'll find me." His voice muffled from the cigar hanging out of his mouth.

The click of my tapping foot steps acknowledged my presence as I rounded the corner to him. "Now don't you look pretty? We goin' somewhere? Dang, tell me I didn't forget?" With a wink, Nic ogled over my slim fit jeans and rosy pink sweater.

"No…just felt the need to look girly." I sat down on the stool he nodded his head towards. "Told ya I'd wear my fancy little shoes to one of your barn yards."

"Damn." Frustrated, Nic yelled working on something greasy in his hands. "Dinner? Sorry honey, I wanted to get this thing apart and loaded before I came in."

The thing in his hand oozed with black thick grease up to his elbows. "Nic, what is that thing?"

"Grease gun. Take my cigar for me." He wiggled his smoking habit in his teeth at me.

Carefully, I tiptoed over to him, trying not to step in the piles of black shiny goo splattered around him. "Lean," I ordered plucking the cigar out of his mouth. Side stepping him and his mess, I started backing away. "You got an ash tray around?"

"On the work bench." His hand wrapped firmly around the grease gun, he torqued with all his might. Forcibly he twisted it back and forth in his hands until "POP--Son of a bitch." The words flew from his mouth.

"Nooooooo!" Nic's pissed off rant met my blood curdling scream.

"Oh shit--Aubrey…"

A deafening silence followed my pathetic scream. My eyes glued to Nic's in horror. His smoldering cigar tumbled from my fingers, hitting the floor sizzling in a pile of goo. Like a video playing on the slowest speed my eyes viewed the horror of what splattered the entire front of my body.

"Nic! What the hell did you do to me?"

"Aubrey. Honey, don't move." Nic grabbed a greasy rag off the workbench. "Here let me…" One swipe of his hand with the rag smeared the grease deeper into what used to be my favorite pink sweater. "Oh shit. Honey, it was an accident. I never had one of my grease guns explode like this."

"Accident? Look at me Nic," Another one of my screams wailed at him. "I'm covered in black greasy goo. You just ruined my sweater. My jeans. Even my shoes." Gobs and lines of the black goo dotted my face, clung to my hair, and smeared its way down my sweater. Splotches landed with a hit and miss pattern over my jeans and one last gob fell inside my shoe.

"Aubrey. I'm so sorry." Without thinking, Nic reached for me with grease covered hands.

"Don't touch me." I batted his greasy hands from my arms. Two huge greasy hand prints remained on the sleeves of my sweater. "Nic, you're making it worse. Stop touching me." Like a child whose favorite toy had been broken, my bottom lip quivered, and tears rolled over the grease marks on my face.

"Don't cry Aubrey, I've got stuff to clean you up with." In a panic, Nic grabbed an unlabeled silver can from the shelf. He whipped out a clean rag from the drawer soaking it with the smelly liquid. "Here. Let me just…" He swiped it over my sweater as gently as he could. Another huge smear landed over my breast.

"It's ruined." With an attempt to push Nic away, the sting of fresh tears burned in my eyes as he held onto my wrist trying to find someway to comfort me.

"Aubrey. I'm so sorry honey. We can Google pink sweaters, find ya a new one." His panic on 'what the hell do I do now' grew faster than my tears.

"Nic, Gram got me this. I can't replace it."

It was an accident, I knew that. The grease gun didn't have a mind of its own, it exploded on its own freewill. The mess happened to me, my pink sweater, and pretty little flats. I shoved Nic away again, and yanked my wrist free of his grip.

"You look mighty sexy all grease covered there, Aubrey." An ornery grin flashed on Nic's face as he whisked a blob of grease from my nose. "Come here. You'll wash up."

"You're laughing at me?" A little thing called 'humiliation' snapped in me. "How could…"

First it was the chickens, then I knocked myself out falling off the fence, and now I was attacked by an exploding grease gun. My only solution, turn tail and run. I ran out of the barn hearing Nic's strained voice yelling how sorry he was.

I didn't walk. I ran, hitting the back door harder than I ever heard Nic slam it. Charlie dropped the lid on the skillet. He'd been caught red handed sampling dinner, when I appeared frazzled, out of breath, and sobbing.

"Good heavens, child, what the hell happened to you?" Spoon still in hand, Charlie's arms motioned around me, trying to find a place to put them for a hug without getting greased.

"Barn…cigar…sweater…dinner…grease…exploded. Now look at me." A babble of words tumbled out between all my tears, not making one bit of scene to Charlie.

"Aubrey." The backdoor slammed open with Nic yelling for me.

"No. Don't you touch me. You laughed at me." Nic, never one to listen, grabbed me anyway.

"What the hell did you do to her?" Charlie barked.

"Damn grease gun exploded on me."

"On you." I shouted, slapping Nic on the shoulder. "I'm the one wearing the damn grease." One shove of disapproval and I escaped his so called hug of comfort and made a mad dash for the upstairs bathroom.

Securely, I clicked the lock on the bathroom door. Yeah, I knew if Nic wanted in, he'd pop the door above the lock with one good smack and it would spring free. I stripped out of my clothes in need of a hot shower, anything to get this crap off me, and fast. My pink sweater, there was no way this sinister goo would ever come out. I tossed it back on my jeans and climbed into my sanctuary of a shower. The black mess smeared over me with every swipe of soap. About the time I rubbed my skin raw, Nic placed one small whack to the door and presto the locked popped open. Under the rush of the shower, I could hear him sliding out his clothes.

"Aubrey." Nic pulled the shower curtain back and joined me in the uninviting steaming shower. "Come here." In his hand, the smelly towel from the barn. He took the towel with the magical chemical of 'come clean' on it rubbing it over all my splattered non-removable grease spots. After a few rubs, my ivory white skin welled to blotchy streaks of red, bubbling, making it worse.

I crawled out of the shower not saying a word. I should have at least said thank you to him. But my greasy clothes stared pitifully at me as I wrapped myself in a towel. I'd seen his work clothes. I washed them, soaked them, but grease stains didn't wash out. I saw red welts rising on my hands, felt them on my face, I didn't bother to look in the mirror.

I blew out a long agonizing sigh while he dried off, "Any hope for my sweater?"

"No honey, not a chance." Genuinely filled with sympathy over my latest mishap, he waited for me to do something. "I wasn't laughing at you."

"Seriously, you…"

"Aubrey, you looked," his hands motioned around my towel covered breast, "the sweater, it fit you so," he grinned, "your jeans, all of you covered in grease. I could of just…" Nic's grin turned into a full fledged smile, "I just wanted to toss your greasy body on that work bench.

"Nic," I snapped back at him. "Make love to me all greasy? You've got to be kidding."

"Bre, you don't know what you do to me."

"This isn't sexy. Not even a bit arousing." My finger traced over a bubbling welt.

"Come on let's go have dinner. It smells great." He kissed a welt on my check.

"No," I kept shaking my head no, "I just want to go to bed." Moping. It wasn't me, but I couldn't help it. Less than a month of ranch life and I've started to doubt myself.

Buried under a pile of pillows my stomach sold me out, the rumbling growing louder. Dinner, the aroma of the slow cooked roast beef found its way up the steps to my nose. Mr. Perfect picked his fussy head up when I surfaced from my pillow cocoon. Another grumble from my empty tummy had the cat's head turning. Dad must have been watching a game on the big screen, it echoed up the staircase as I stopped in the bathroom to collect my pathetic clothes. Just my shoes sat on the carpet, only a stain of grease remained.

"Too bad his magic 'goo-be-gone' didn't work on clothes." I rambled, pride still hurt as Mr. Perfect circled my legs. "Nice." A few layers of my rubbed off skin flamed with pink in the mirror, the welts slowly receding. My housecoat, comfort food for the body, I wrapped myself tighter in it.

I spied on Dad, all caught up in the ballgame, "Aubrey, hey Cleveland, made it to the playoffs."

"That's good. Bet the city is rockin' tonight." Actually I hoped to escape him and Nic both, but luck wasn't on my side. I caught a bit of Nic's phone conversation, his face brightened into a smile, as I slipped past him into the kitchen.

"Saturday. 'Round ten. Nope. Good time. Yeah I'll have her … yeah them too. I'll make sure. Yep that's right," he answered the caller glancing around to find where I'd disappeared too.

While I waited for my tea to warm, I finished the rest of the dinner dishes hoping they at least saved me a small morsel of crumbs to eat. The microwave dinged and I exchanged hot tea for a plate of my roast beef, mashed potatoes, and gravy. Didn't think the vegetables would last, Dad loved candied carrots.

"Hey." Nic finished his call coming back in from the laundry room and planted himself in the chair next to my cup of tea. "Dinner. Outstanding as usual." He tried anything to make me feel better.

"Thanks," I slid my plate over, bumping my tea. "Do you want anything while I'm over here?" I didn't really wait for his response as I walked to the other side of the island.

"I'm good," he pulled the chair out beside him for me. "Aubrey, accidents happen."

My tea bag twirled on the end of the string as I played in the cup of hot water wishing to avoid discussion of the latest accident. "Once again, I'll be the laughing stock of the barn yard."

"No honey, come on. Just think, when I say I greased you, people's mind will fall to the gutter." Nic's attempt to cheer me up worked a little.

"Nic, they all know you're greasing me up in more ways than one." I smirked, even shook a giggle out. "You should've seen the look on your face."

"My god, Aubrey, I thought you were going to kill me." Nic laughed louder. "Hey, Saturday, ride into town with me. I got to pick up some stuff from the tack shop."

I appreciated his quick change of subject for once, "Tack shop? What's a tack shop?" I asked nibbling on my roast beef.

"Stuff for horses. You game?"

"As long as I don't have to be near a grease gun, we're good." I finally smiled.

Chapter 23

Polly Holiday

Under her stacked bee hive hair, Polly Holiday's mind planned away as she finished her conversation with Nic. The old wall phone, cord stretched to the max, kept her on a tight leash while she said her goodbyes to Nic along with a 'give my best to your dad.' Twisting free of the cord that had wrapped around her modestly large figure, she chuckled, thinking back of the days when Ruthie and she would talk. Hours upon hours spent gabbing away to each other.

Polly's hand searched her apron pocket at last grasping the 'cat eyed' bifocals from the bottom. She returned herself to her work. Mounds of fluffy white frosting sat in a bowl at her cupcake table. She grinned looking at the photo of her late partner, Ruthie Ravenwood.

"Ah, Ruthie, Ruthie, Ruthie, wish ya were still here. You'd of approved of this girl. Smart head on her shoulders. Pretty too. Nice sense of humor, she'll be needing it with your boy." Polly chuckled aloud. "Heard rumor she snatched Nic's heart with a smile and a dance. Your boy finally got it right. 'Bout time he did. Been worried about him, Ruthie, temper of his, always getting in the way. But got to say, he did good for himself. She's a sweet one Ruthie, a sweet one." Polly fidgeted. Her round bottom overlapped the wooden stool at her decorating table.

Polly squeezed a king sized mound of frosting from the icing bag, swirling it high on the muffin sized cupcake.

"I knew she had to be your Nic's bride when I saw her sittin' there in the airport crying her heart out to her sister. Lord, those girls look so alike."

Polly continued her conversation with the silent photo. "Just wanted to rush on over and hand her a tissue."

With the hands of a sculpting artist, Polly filled the tray with her trademark decadent cupcakes for the morning rush. "Had the pleasure of sitting 'cross the aisle from her on the flight home. Poor dear. Scared to death. But the excitement in her eyes, she'll fit in just fine, Ruthie. Just fine. You needn't worry, I'll be keeping my eye on her. Besides, I'm thinkin' about expanding the business." Polly winked at the picture of Ruthie. "Been thinking, nice little lunch café. I hear the new Mrs. Ravenwood is quite the chef. I sure could use her help."

Polly's nightly inventory of sparkling baked goods counted, and the rainbow of colored cupcake trays placed in the glass showcase. She double checked her materials to make fresh donuts at the five a.m. mark, and took a quick check of the coffee supply.

She returned to her paper littered desk, pulling her worn address book from the top drawer. Front page of the tattered old book, Ruthie's phone number. Polly's long polished nail tapped at the name. Ruthie and Polly had been best of friends all their lives. So it was no surprise, kind of always known, they would be partners in the 'Decadent House of Cupcakes.' Thirteen years of early morning baking together before Ruthie's untimely passing.

"Sure miss ya, Ruthie." Polly took a drink of her herbal tea, thumbing over the finger printed pages, dialing numbers, explaining how she'd be hosting a surprise shower for the new bride of her late friend's son. Between calls Polly jotted down her menu for this Saturday's gala. She asked each guest to bring their favorite recipe, something quirky, and she knew the new bride won't need.

Polly Holiday, a long, loved resident of the town, knew everyone and everything that slipped past her shop of deliciousness. Gossip held the bakery together better than her famous frosting and no secret got past the ears of Polly. Fifteen numbers dialed, fifteen yes's, she continued on until she had well over thirty women coming to the surprise shower.

Dear Al,

Allison, I'm not so sure I did the. No I know I, I did the right thing by marrying Nic, but the move, I can't get adjusted, and I'm so lonely. I'm sorry I'm so depressing, just not what you want to hear. The ranch is beautiful, I can't imagine ever living someplace else, but I miss the bright lights and hustle and bustle of the city life. I miss having you, Gram, and Gina at a finger tip reach. It's not like I don't have friends, Mimi and June El are great, but I feel kind of uncomfortable just showing up on their door step with a bottle of wine, wanting to whine. I know I can hear what you're thinking: "put your big girl panties on and make the best of it." When Nic's asleep, I curl up in the window seat and watch the quietness of outside. I'm so thankful Nic didn't fight me over Mr. Perfect, it's like the only link I have to home. I think he really likes the cat, but that dog of his drives me crazy.

I'm riding into town with him on Saturday. Got a big lunch date with him. Said he needed something from a tack shop, guess I'll see what that's all about. Have you been able to make plans for the holidays, please come? Really I'll cheer up soon, it's just hard to leave everything you've known and start fresh.

Love you, Aubrey ☺

Chapter 24

A Shower

"Aubrey." Nic yelled up the empty staircase.

Something I learned quickly about Nic, he never heard my footsteps unless I had soled shoes on. Mr. Perfect greeted him at the top of the stairs instead of me.

"Who called you, Fuzz Nuts?" Nic scolded the cat for peering down at him. "What did ya do with her this time?"

Nic had both hands planted on each side of the banister, a foot resting on the first step. In my ice skating style cotton socks, I pretended to skate over the shiny wood floors gliding right into the back of him. My arms circled his stomach as if I were trying to bear hug him.

"I hate when you do that, woman." Nic reeled around to face me.

"I hate when you call me woman." My nose wrinkled into sourness. "Did you lose me?"

"Saturday, woman. Tack shop. Town, you're goin' with me." He stated in an ordering tone.

"A tack shop? Is that like where you get tacks at? There's a drawer full of tacks in the kitchen." I wanted to babble on about this tack shop, but Nic interrupted, shortening my humor.

"City girl, it's a place to buy things for the horses and the ranch. Your new saddle is in." So carefully he said those last few words and my playful smile fell upside down.

"Saddle? Nic, I'm not...no. No horse." I shuddered with the sound of the word 'horse' ringing in my ears.

He wanted me to learn how to ride. Wanted me to see all fifty thousand acres on the back of a horse. He wanted to take me out and camp on the range…over night…under the stars. My kind of roughing it, let's try the Holiday Inn with an indoor pool. But learning to ride this horse meant one thing to me, Emergency Room. Just call ahead, have a bed ready for me. It's going to be an ugly lesson and I'd wormed my way out of it, until now. My horse's new saddle arrived. The horse Nic hand picked for me, waited patiently for me to even attempt to pet her.

"Aubrey?" Nic waved his hand in front of my eyes. "You're worrying too much."

"I can't even pet her yet, Nic. Think about it. Horse. Learn to ride. Add that together and it equals--visit to the ER. Now there's a trip I'm not looking forward to." There was no smile from me when I met Nic's eyes.

"Aubrey, Emerald Bay is a very gentle horse." He rubbed at the arms of my terrycloth housecoat. "I really want you to bond with her."

"Bond? Like you've bonded with Mr. Perfect?" I liked sarcasm, but Nic liked it better.

"Yep, like you an ole' Toby."

"The Super Wal. I need to stop there." I pulled one of his numbers, changing the subject.

"Sure," he started up the steps, taking my hand with him, so I had to follow. "Put one of those pretty dresses on, I'll take ya ta lunch."

"You throwing in dessert, too?" My playful mood swung back.

"You are dessert." Like leading one of his stray horses, I trailed him into our bedroom kicking the door shut. The only other breathing creature allowed in our bedroom, of course, Mr. Perfect, who slept peacefully on the window seat.

An early morning romp before Jack the rooster even crowed. And, well, before the rest of whomever on the ranch strolled into the kitchen in search of brewing coffee. Nic made sure no one or anything would interfere with his morning appetite for sex. A thick terrycloth housecoat covered my silky night gown and he knew what I had hidden under it. Boots, his life had to revolve around those damn boots. I started counting seconds to see how long it took him to remove them. Clunk one, clunk two, they hit the wood floor muffled by a throw rug in less than fifteen seconds. He reached for my lilac fluffy housecoat pulling the ties free. I held a hand out motioning him away pointing to his jeans. I enjoyed the rough sound of stripping blue jeans from his body. With a smirk, he tossed the jeans across the room purposely hitting the sleeping cat. Why bother to protest, when Mr. Perfect hissed at him. Drawing his attention back to me, I giggled when his hands felt up under my housecoat. He softly pulled it from my shoulders as I crawled over the bed. I hadn't even gotten the bed dressed and Nic was undressing me. He pulled me on top of his naked body, slipping his hands under my gown.

"You need some practice with your riding." He laughed, lifting the silky gown over my head.

The early morning sun danced into the darkened bedroom streaming a lace pattern through the new curtains I'd just hung. Still held in fascination, I outlined one of the tattoos on Nic's chest. He cringed slightly as my cold fingertips swept over his colorful skin. Warm hands stroked my back while I leaned down slowly licking his lips, enticing him into a deep kiss. In surprise, I gasped at how easily he entered me, and felt how deeply the sensation aroused me along with him. Firmly his hand gripped my hips relaxing me into a comfortable sitting position.

"First lesson. Slow 'n easy." Nic guided with words. "Just ease into the saddle. Break it in slowly."

In need of balance, I grabbed for his hands, steadying myself as we rocked our bodies smoothly, slowly back and forth. "Nic you're lying to me," my breath hinged and I gripped his hands tighter, "There's no way riding a horse would ever be this enjoyable."

Dress on, hair teased and tamed, I even touched my face with a splash of makeup, "That'll shock him," I kissed my lips together smearing my color of coco cream lipstick over them. "No barn work this morning?" I asked as I rounded the staircase into the living room.

"Nope. Guys can handle it without me today." Nic flipped off the TV. "You ready?" He followed me into my favorite part of the house, the kitchen. Well, one of my favorite places.

"Yes. Is Dad going with us?" I asked, while double checking my shopping list for the Super Wal.

"No. Said he had something else to do." Nic tugged at my sweater, running his hand over the snug wool skirt. "Ya look mighty pretty, Aubrey."

I flew around landing directly in his arms, "The last time you said I looked pretty, you greased me and made me cry." Still a sore and touchy subject with me. "Don't say another word."

Nic parked in front of some kind of coffee shop bakery. "The Decadent House of Cupcakes" in a pastel jeweled print was painted on the shop's window.

"Is there a reason why I can't go to this tack shop with you?" Not whining, I grumbled at him. "Seriously, what do you men do there?"

"You'd be totally bored. Nothing but old men, chewin' a wad and spiting in cans." Nic frowned trying to discourage me from wanting to go with him. "Besides, do you really want to sit around listening to them complain about what ails them and scratchin' themselves?"

I about gagged on the last explanation of why I shouldn't be there. "So let me get this straight, you're going to sit around and smoke, scratch, and chew."

Nic's eyes crinkled, a smile edged but he held back, "No, I'm not. Smoke yes. I got to load up on some supplies this time of year. Ya never know when the weather will turn. That new saddle of yours, you're going to break it in."

He winked at me and my mind flashed back to this morning's version of Nic's riding lesson. I felt the blush sear over my cheeks.

"So did I pass my first lesson this morning?" I pulled at the collar of his jacket, bringing myself to his lips, meeting for a kiss. "How about a second lesson?"

"Will ya just go in there and do your girly stuff. June El and Mimi said something about bein' here today. You'll like the place. I know the owner, she'll treat ya good." He walked back to the truck, leaving me standing alone on the sidewalk. "I'll call ya when I'm on my way back."

A kiss goodbye and he left. Just got in the truck and there I stood, alone, with Saturday shoppers buzzing by. On the busy sidewalk, I sulked; viewing what I hoped wouldn't be a dive of a place. Back home in Cleveland, coffee shops were practically on every corner and, oh, so good. Phone in hand, I pulled up Nic's number ready to dial. I didn't want to go in. My finger pressed his number.

"Bre, what's the problem?" Not even a hello, Nic and the big blue pickup truck waited at the first light on the corner.

"Nic, come get me. I don't want to go in."

"Why?" I could hear the heavy breath he heaved out. I'm sure filling the cab with cigar smoke.

"I feel like a stranger in this town, I didn't know a soul. This is a small town where everyone knows everyone. They all know everything about each other." I cringed, "Wonder what they already know, or better yet heard about me?" Still stuck at the red light, I could feel his eyes watching me from the review mirror.

"Bre, go inside. Get your fancy coffee and whatever they bake there. You'll be fine." The light had turned green and he pulled away in traffic. "Pretty sure Mimi and June El said something about being there today."

"Ok. I'll go. Just promise me, if I call, you'll come get me?"

"Aubrey, think you're goin' to love the place. Go on, check it out." He chuckled and hung up.

Like a forgotten puppy, I stood on the sidewalk and watched the truck disappear from sight. Facing the old stone building, the jeweled letters jumped out at me. Kind of a nice way of inviting me to come in off the street. One of those frilly half curtains dangled loosely under the neon glittery title. The door swung open with a jingle of bells bouncing and the aroma of fresh bakery followed two happily smiling ladies.

Today's cupcake specials, scribbled in neon pink called to all passersby on the slate blackboard.

"Come In and Sit, Sip and Indulge Yourself In Our Cupcakes"

Almond Joy
Sweet Coconut Cream
Seductive Dark Chocolate Raspberry
Peanut Butter Delight

    Hesitantly, I fingered the door handle, "I don't want to go in here," but the fresh brewed coffee tempted me even more. "All in the name of needing coffee, here goes nothing." Again, I whispered aloud.

    With a quickened heartbeat and a step, I found myself inside the decorative walls of The Decadent House of Cupcakes. "This isn't too bad." The heavenly scents of bakery clung to the walls and tickled my nose.

    "Good morning," called a familiar voice. With a lift of her tea cup, accompanied by a warm smile in welcome, "I see you've made your way into our slice of heaven." I found Mimi seated at one of the fancy tea tables.

    "Mimi." My nervous tension melted away, "Nic said you might be here. Is June El with you?" Delighted at seeing a familiar face, I joined her at the fancy table.

    "On her way. Had to pick something up from the tack shop." Mimi rolled her eyes. "Nic didn't take you there?"

    "No. Said something about a lot of chewin', spitin', and scratchin'. Why do men do that?" Sarcastically, I laughed.

    "Be with ya in a moment, sweetie." A well rounded lady brushed past me. I only saw the backside of her as she swaggered in and around the neatly placed tea tables that were dressed in pink and purple tablecloths. The robust lady disappeared behind the flowing pink curtains.

    I found, in my view, the display case filled with the most deliciously decorated cupcakes. "Mimi, what in the world are those?" The eye-catching colored frosting stopped me dead in my tracks. Truly, I was a sweet junkie through and through.

    "Trademark cupcakes. Place is known for it. Sure hope you're not doing the diet thing today." Mimi teased, enjoying a mouthful of something sweet.

"So, what do you think of our hideout?" June El appeared behind me. "From the outside, place looks like a dive. But inside, a sinful heaven of delights."

"I see you've escaped the 'tack' shop in one piece." I tried to hold my little snicker of laughter back.

"Yep. Had to drop Charlie off there and left my list with Nic. Glad to be here." June El pulled a chair out next to us.

"Charlie? Nic said he had something else to do."

"Changed his mind. Caught a ride in with us," June El, quick to switch me back to the sweets, "So what's tempting ya over there?"

"Aubrey says she's on some diet." Mimi mocked me.

"Diet? Not hardly," I protested. "I've got to snap a photo of those cupcakes. Gina would die to have a taste of one of those." That sugar plum thing that dances in your head on Christmas Eve, well a sugar fest of sweet treats was dancing right before my eyes. I left Mimi and June El sitting alone, following the site of the rainbow colors in the display case.

A young gal, not meaning to interrupt my fascination, startled me with her simple, "Can I help you?"

"I definitely need the largest cup of coffee you have and, and…" I couldn't pick a flavor of cupcake. "Surprise me. Just pick one for me." Happily, I told the sales girl.

In my midst of entertaining my sugar rush, I didn't realize how quickly the little shop filled with chatting woman. A Saturday morning gathering spot or just a popular place to gossip. Politely, I smiled and excused myself through the growing crowd. With cupcake and coffee in hand I wiggled my way back to my partners in 'sweet confection' crime.

"What a place to have a bridal shower," I plopped down next to Mini who had moved to a replica floral print Victorian sofa. "Look at that table." I pointed to the center of the room. Packages of all colors, shapes and sizes piled high.

"Someone's going to have fun opening all those." Mimi dunked her coffeecake into her cup showing a huge smile.

"Anyone you know?" I asked, still admiring all the wrapped gifts. Mimi grinned, hiding behind her mug of coffee, not answering me.

"Move it over," June El returned with her tempting treat. "Can't believe this place. Never this busy. Must be some kind of shower by the looks of that table." Her spiky head of hair bobbed towards the presents.

Lost in cupcake heaven, I never noticed how everyone chatting turned towards the three of us, mostly in my direction. A buzz of whispering went unheard as I dived into my morning delight.

Every single bite I took reminded me of when Gram would take us to the bakery, letting us pick out our own special donut. A 'never fail' after Sunday church treat. My eyes came to rest on the lady sporting the beehive in a shade of "Lucy" red who stepped from behind the counter. A thousand curls must have been stacked in her bobby pinned hair. Fuchsia cat rimmed glasses framed her plum rose face, accenting her emerald feline eyes. A gold tooth smile flashed at me from the lady with hair piled as high as she was wide.

Lips of cotton candy pink asked: "By chance, sweetie, are you Nic Ravenwood's new bride?"

The low hover of female conversation ceased, along with the clatter of teaspoons tinging the side of their tea cups.

"Polly. Polly Holiday." Frozen in my seat, I recalled the plane ride into Buffalo with this amazingly wonderful woman. "Polly. It's you."

Polly and her beehive shouted an introduction as I bounced up to hug her. "Ladies, let me be the first to introduce all of you to Aubrey Ravenwood." She glowed as if I were her own daughter-in-law. "She's here girls. Let's have our bridal shower."

"Bridal shower? What bridal shower? Nic didn't say a word about…" I squirmed as the sea of ladies weaved around me in greetings.

"Come on girls, let's meet our newest resident." Polly parted the sea of 'let's get to know Aubrey' women, taking me by the arm. I found myself seated in front of all those brilliantly wrapped packages.

"Let me guess, you two were in on this?" Mimi snapped a picture of Polly handing me a gift.

"Yep. Nic and Charlie, too." June El couldn't hold her grin back as she pushed another brightly wrapped package towards me.

"Wait, we forgot someone." Another pink apron lady interrupted. She ran behind the sparkling show case, smiling at the framed picture now in her hands. "Ruthie has to be here too."

"Ruthie?" I reached for the photo. "Nic's mom." Easily I recognized her from all the photos displayed of Nic's parents.

"We were partners in this sweet little establishment." Polly's eyes rolled with a smile from wall to wall. "Best friends from kindergarten 'til she passed." She caught a tear, hoping no one noticed her whisking it from her eye.

"How did you do all of this?" My mind whirled from face to face of all these ladies who wanted to know me. Or were just curious about the city woman Nic Ravenwood married.

Dear Allison,

 Remember me telling you about the lady I flew to Wyoming with? Her name is Polly Holiday, she said she owned the bake shop in town. You're not going to believe this, Polly called nearly, if not every, woman in town and hosted a surprise bridal shower at her bake shop for me. You'll love the name of her place, "The Decadent House of Cupcakes." Watch the mail box, I'm sending you and Gina some of Polly's fine creations. Come to find out, Nic's mom, Ruthie, and Polly were best of girlfriends. Ruthie was co-owner of the shop. I wish one of my two men would tell me a little more about Ruthie. They certainly didn't mind when I sat her pictures out, Charlie just glowed when I found him holding one.

 Sorry, rambling again, that hasn't changed, now, has it? The shower, the place from the sidewalk, looked like a dive, a hole in the wall. The only thing that kept my attention from running was the sign advertising that day's specials. Get a kick out of these cupcake names, Almond Joy, Sweet Coconut Cream, Seductive Dark Chocolate Raspberry and Peanut Butter Delight. Those were just that day's specials. Inside, Polly and Ruthie had transformed the little space to a step back into the Victorian age. Chairs, tables, linens, wall decorations all the way down to the tea cups, totally Victorian. To top it all off, Nic and Dad knew all about it. Nic bribed me into going to town with him. Told me if I wore a dress he'd take me to lunch. I'm so glad I listened to him for once and dressed up. I'll have to take you there when you come over Christmas. You're still coming, right? Please don't let me down, I just started feeling good about me again. This shower really helped, too. Nic has been hinting every night, after dinner, that he wants me to go pet that horse, Emerald Bay. Why would someone name an animal that? It's a horse, Allison. You know those big, four legged, hoofed creatures. She's so big, just sends me straight into a panic attack when Nic mentions it.

 Your turn to call on Friday, I'll be waiting to hear from you.

Love you, Aubrey ☺

Chapter 25

Emerald Bay, Nic, and Me

From the window, I could see her prancing around the corral as if she owned it. For several days now Nic's other woman kept his full attention. The morning air clung with the threat of snow as I stepped out on the front porch. Bitter cold pinched at my eyes, tearing them. A bone chilling cold that really did sting the nose. I hugged the deerskin shawl close to my body wrapping in its warmth. Another handy shower gift, wool socks, even in pink. My feet happily danced inside my girly boots. Sunday mornings became a laid back affair at the ranch. Nic usually slept past the crack of dawn, except for today. His four legged lady friend had been restlessly waiting for him. Toby, the dreaded bloodhound, trotted along beside me as if we were old buddies. Nic's dog was growing on me about as fast as Mr. Perfect grew on him.

"I don't like you. You know that don't you?" Toby, whose ears flopped along not giving a care about my sarcasm, brushed beside my leg. "Don't try to win me over with that head bobbing, tongue lopping smile of yours either."

Sarcasm with a dog. Kind of funny. But ole Toby kept right in time with my steps. I slowed my pace. Eyes glued to the beast Nic handle so delicately, I inched my way to the fence.

Over the forty-seven years of his life, the sun had drenched a leathering of creased lines into my new husband's face. Under his worn ten gallon black suede hat, sparkled eyes of mahogany, and a braided tail of raven black hair trailed down his blue plaid flannel shirt. Intently, he focused on training the honey bronze, four legged creature prancing before him. He didn't realize I'd draped myself over the wooden fence rail admiring him.

The sun hung droopily, trying to reach atop the mountains to start the day. The chill of the frosty morning clung steadfast, while man and the animal of beauty worked simultaneously together, bonding, and forging their trust to one another. I could only wish this animal would take to me as she did to Nic. Observing, noting, and mentally detailing how he moved, stroked, and tamed the animal, I continued my silent vigil.

Nic's gift to me, a quarter horse. She'd soon be left in the care of my incapable hands. Never in my wildest dreams did I believe that I would become one with a horse by the name of Emerald Bay. He hand selected my horse for her loyalty, gentleness, and even temperament.

"Well now, your mistress has come for her first lesson." I swear the horse smiled at the deep rasp in his husky voice.

By her reins, Nic slowly led his four legged companion in my direction. My new friend came too close, too fast, sensing my uneasiness with her. Fear flushed over my face, eyes teared from panic. I swayed, attempting to step away from the fence. Nic grabbed my hand, steadying me, coaxing me back to my living gift.

"Don't be scared. She won't hurt you, honey." Nic's voice patient, calming his student from city life.

Emerald Bay greeted me with a head shake and a stomp of a hoof. Her moist nose nudged at my trembling open hand. Deep dark chocolate eyes blinked a sign of comfort as if I were her foal. In her own mothering way, she guided my finger tips into feeling her silky coat.

"Aubrey come in the corral with us. Just pet her." Nic insisted.

"Not yet. I'm fine on this side of the fence." I continued to massage her neck, "I'm not ready. Didn't realize she'd be so soft."

Toby sat down, cramming his chubby fat-covered frame into my legs tilting me off balance. I felt myself falling. Not just a few staggered steps, I couldn't catch myself. My scream only had Toby flopping with me, falling towards the half frozen ground. From nowhere the painful slap to my shoulder had me bolting back to Nic's grabbing hand. Emerald Bay swung her head again, connecting another hard blow to my shoulder, knocking me back into both the fence and Nic. My chin slammed into Nic's forearm, better than the wood fence only inches from my face. Emerald Bay, my so called friend, bashed me on the back holding her head against me, pinning me between Nic and the fence. The weight of her enormous head held me captive. She stepped closer not allowing me to move. I clung to Nic waiting for her to free me or take another blow. But she didn't. She rested her massive velvety head on my throbbing shoulder.

"Nic, get her off me! Please get her off!" I begged, scared beyond tears. Toby my want-to-be body guard, pinned my legs between the fence and his lumpy body. Emerald Bay rubbed her head up and down my shawl, like I was her pet. "Nic. Get them off me!" I wailed into the sleeve of his jacket.

"Aubrey, don't move." For once I obeyed Nic's command. "Easy girl. Easy." He called to the horse slowly backing her away from me. "Easy girl." Emerald Bay side stepped, tossing her head from side to side. She pouted in disappointment being separated from me, while Nic attempted to steady both of us at the same time. "Aubrey. You're fine, honey." Emerald pushed at Nic coming towards me again. "Stay still. Just hold your hand out to her."

"No." I eased away from Nic's reach, shooing Toby off my legs. "She hates me. Your beast, she tried to attack me for being near you." My face turned whiter than the snow capping of the mountains in the distance.

"No, Aubrey. No. She tried to protect you from the fall." Nic pulled at my hand wanting me to pet her again, "Aubrey, just try."

"Protect me?" My hand resisted him; I curled back under my shawl, not wanting to touch her again. "No. That wasn't protective. The horse is obsessed with you."

"Aubrey, she not obsessed with me. Come on. Give me your hand." Nic held his hand out to me, his other wrapped around Emerald's lead.

I backed away, this time my hand on Toby's collar. The sparkle in Nic's eyes died like the embers of a fire smoldering out. His high expectations turned to a miserable disappointment in me.

"I'm going to start breakfast." I backed away from the fence feeling every ounce of his disapproval along with the riveting pain in my shoulder. Pathetically scared to death, I kept wondering if I'd ever be able to become one with Emerald Bay like Nic.

"Aubrey. Come on, honey. Stay. Just watch her work with me." Nic pleaded, trying to reason with the panic he saw in my eyes.

"Maybe another day." The words squished from my mouth. I couldn't believe I even said that much. I know he saw me wipe the tears from my eyes. "Don't be long, breakfast. OK?"

My faithful unwanted companion, Toby, double trotted along beside me. I didn't even look back to Nic when he called my name. All I wanted, the refuge of the house, the comfort of my kitchen.

Nearly all of Nic's spare time seemed to be tied up with the barn yard trollop named Emerald Bay. What did she have that I lacked? Well, let me list a few. 'Miss Goodie' four hooves, she listened to him. She followed his direction. And she usually obeyed Nic's every command. But Emerald Bay proved to Nic she had a mind of her own. Her temperamental disposition and rebellious manner, at times, ticked him off to no end. My favorite quote from Nic after a rough ride on Emerald, "Damn mare acts just like you." Wife and horse did share a driven spirit. I loved her spiteful demeanor when he demanded too much from her. After dinner, I heard the usual, 'Aubrey, ya need to go see the horse. Ya need to try again.' My reply back, a flat out 'NO.' Nic got annoyed with me, but after my first and only meeting with the giant four-legged beast, I hesitated returning to her. Eventually he'd win me over, but it won't be happening soon.

"Ya goin' out to the barn tonight, girly?" Bones crept in behind me, with the freshly baked cherry pie in his sight. "He's alone with that sweet tart of his. One with a tail and mane ya know."

"You're not winning brownie points or a piece of that pie rubbing my nose in the fact my husband, of how many months, has taken up with some broad ass bimbo." I snapped back at Bones grinning and slapped a healthy slice of pie on a plate for him.

"Go keep him company. Man's been a damn grump. Acting like he did before you came. Got that temper of his going again." Like a kid in a candy store, Bones' eyes dazzled at the two plates I handed him.

"Don't eat Charlie's piece, either," I pushed him out of my way heading for the stairs. "You sure he's alone out there?"

"Yep. Saturday night everyone but ole Moe went to town." The ballgame distracted his attention from me.

Plan 'A', get your husband away from the trouble making barn slut, even if she's a four legged animal. I bounced up the steps to our bedroom, Mr. Perfect following at my heels. "I need skimpy. No. No. Not that one either," Lingerie flung back over my shoulder as I dug deeper into my private world of female 'I want to get laid, honey' drawer. "Perfect."

I held up the plum lace teddy trimmed in black, another handy shower gift. "Sorry kitty, mommy's pretties don't do a thing for you." Mr. Perfect rolled over the silky bras, panties, and gowns I'd tossed on the bed. "Give me those."

I scooped up my mess tossing it carelessly back into the depths of the dresser drawer. Blue jeans, sweatshirt, they were the next to fly off my body. I shimmied the lace teddy over my naked pale curves. "Undies? No undies." Those to, off and on the pile of plain and boring. "Fishnet's," I giggled slipping the thigh high stockings over my toes, "Now this says, 'honey bang the hell out of me'." I snorted a laugh, digging in the closet for my satiny black heels. "Ok kitty, please pray nothing happens to mommy this time."

I scratched the cat's head, wrapping my housecoat over my 'me the surprise package' body. Baseball game, blaring loud, concealed my great escape from the house.

Carefully, I peeked in the living room, my housecoat wrapped securely. Charlie and Bones, still chewing away on the cherry pie, didn't even notice me. I bet that's slice number two as I padded softly into the kitchen. A bottle of wine, two glasses, and the laundry room was none the warmest. I exchanged my fussy housecoat for Nic's long duster. I loved stealing that thing from him. Ankle length, tough smell of leather laced with day old cigars, the inside, soft wool, better than my favorite housecoat. I cuddled myself deep inside the three sizes larger than me coat.

"Damn, I have to wear boots to get to the stupid barn." I muttered, shoving my stocking feet into them. Shoes, wine, glasses, I stepped out into the night. A blast of frigid air shot up under the bottom of the duster. "Holy shit, it's cold out here." Yes a simple reminder to get moving or freeze the goods off before you get to hubby.

"Please don't squeak, please don't squeak." I begged the door to the horse barn, slipping in as quietly as I could.

Clomping boots could be a dead giveaway and I kicked those

off, slipping into my heels. I barely even heard the tipping clicks from my own heels, "He can't possibly hear me."

Mental note, stop muttering to yourself as I practically tip-toed to the bright light in the back of the barn. I found Nic in the middle of hopefully finishing Emerald Bay's grooming. His shirt, the old flannel tossed over the gate of her stall. He exposed those muscles to her? Look at her, she doesn't' even appreciate his finely toned body. I did want to crack the bottle of Merlot and kick back enjoying my eye candy.

"Well I'm so glad to see the new ranch slut gets you all hot and bothered that you have to take your shirt off for her." I giggled under my breath startling Nic.

"Aubrey." Surprised? Shocked? Maybe even totally blown away, Nic dropped the grooming brush, along with his jaw.

"Listen up you savage. You're mine. So tell that big ass bitch, she's history." I popped open the cork and poured the wine. "Or you're not getting what's under this coat."

"What are you up to?" Nic pushed the horse out of his way locking the gate behind him.

I handed him a glass of wine. "I'm tired of competing with your four legged home wrecker. This tail wagging other woman of yours has you wrapped around her hoof. All four of them. You're with her all hours of the day. I'm sick of it. You've got to pick, either me or Cleopatra eyes."

Nic stood there wiping his hand on a towel, grinning. Grinning too much. The last time I called him a savage, I couldn't feel my lips for a week. Plus he did….oh never mind, I locked that memory in my mind, grinning back at him. I lifted the chilled bottle of wine offering him a refill. At his approach, ever so cleverly, I teased Nic sliding my fish netted leg through the slit in the duster.

"Now woman, what could you possibly want?" Nic let his eyes skim my coated body. He lingered longer on the black satin heels. He parted the duster open with one hand, slipping it around my waist, feeling nothing but silk covered flesh.

"Your attention." I demanded, "Little Miss Bay, she can't do what I can do to you." I handed Nic the bottle of wine. "Refill please."

Instead he took my glass, "Take the coat off Aubrey."

I could tease with this command. Gently, deliberately stalling, I slipped the coat off my shoulders, only to reveal the skinny spaghetti straps of the gown.

"All the way Aubrey." No more commands to play with.

Simple, I let the heavy duster that kept me warm, slip to the ground and stepped aside it.

"How the hell did you get out here in those shoes?" Nic's eyes landed on my feet. With a bounce, his eyes stopped midway up, hovering over my next to exposed chilled lady parts.

"Hey." His eyes bounced up from my protruding nipples finding mine. "Really you savage, does it matter? I'm here." A quick shiver went up my spine. "I suggest you keep me warm."

"Come on." Nic grabbed my hand giving me back the bottle of wine and glasses. He reached for Emerald Bay's saddle blanket yanking it off the gate. "This way."

"You've done this before?" I let him trot me along to the back of the barn.

"Don't ask questions you won't be happy with the answers to, woman." Nic conveniently stopped in front of where all the fresh hay was stored.

The wine found a home on the nearest bale of hay as Nic spread the blanket on a bed of loose hay. An instant romantic ambiance surrounded me as I crawled over the wool blanket. The artificial lighting had its own personal glow, the sweet smell of hay tickled my nose, the wine, relaxing. My heels, a distraction for a roll in the hay, got kicked off immediately. I had no super model pose; just propped myself up on my elbows, bending a knee, exposing what he'd hope to be true. I wore nothing under the silky night gown.

"Hair." My turn to give orders. He knew I had a fetish for his thick black tresses. He pulled out of the ponytail that kept it from me. "Pants…Drop them cowboy."

Nic's warm hands spread my thighs apart; his fingers lingered over my stockings. "I don't know what got into you woman, but I like it." He rolled to his back taking me with him until I sat straddled over his hips. "Take it off."

"Leave my stockings on." One silky gown tossed. Naked wasn't one of things I liked to be, especially in the brightness of overhead lighting.

"Beautiful." Nic's hand circled under my breast, "Simply beautiful," slowly playing over every inch of my full figure, sliding down my tummy, resting on the inside of my fleshy thigh. Another flip around, the hay padded my back, "Savage huh?" Nic's lips bit into mine.

Packed with hard lean muscle I enjoyed the view of my naked husband stepping back into his jeans. "Come here." Nic held his hand out pulling me up from the blanket. "Care to take this up back in the house?" Playfully, he asked squeezing my bottom like he was checking fresh vegetables.

"You're givin' up that four legged woman for me?" I smirked, arousing him with kisses to his bare chest. "How do you plan on sneaking me past Dad and Bones? They're watching the ballgame."

Nic slipped my teddy over my head, "Games on. They won't even notice us?"

I started to nibble on his lip, pulling him back towards the blanket, "Take another round, cowboy?"

He exhaled, his warm breath past over my bare shoulder, "Aubrey you're shivering. Grab the wine, I'll sneak ya back in."

"Will we get grounded if Dad and Bones catch us?" I cracked up laughing at Nic's sour expression.

While Nic sat on a hay bale putting his boots on, I gave him a little floor show of my own. Dancing around to the music in my head, I flashed him my naked body parts hiding under the teddy. Right in the center of the main aisle, I continued my show hysterically laughing.

"Chucky. Damn it boy. What the hell is goin' on out here?" Bellowed old Moe.

Immediately Nic threw me the blanket, stepping in front of me for extra cover. No shirt on, his pants not even zipped, I clung to Nic's back wrapping my arms around his chest.

"Shit. What the hell are you two doin' out here?" Moe barked again stalking closer. "Haven't I told ya not to bring your dates back here?"

I snuggled my whole body into the back side of Nic, peering over his shoulder at Moe, who didn't bother to stop his rampage towards us.

"What the…Nic, Miss Aubrey… you two?" Moe stopped dead

in this tracks. "What in the good heavens are ya doin' out here?" Slowly Moe's ears burned a bright red.

"Havin' a roll in the hay with my wife, ya dumb fool." Nic smarted off, annoyed for the distraction.

"Had no idea. Chucky, damn hose monster, always sneakin' a girl out here. Caught him three times this month. Three times. Even made it with the preacher's daughter."

"Reverend Miner's daughter? Which one?" Now amused, Nic inquired.

"That youngest one. Now that one, wild. Seen her bare ass a few times. And the set of knockers on the girl…" Moe laughed, catching a glimpse of me hiding behind Nic. "Oh. Oh, sorry there Miss Aubrey. If I'd known it was you two, wouldn't of barged in. Moe winked at Nic, "You two carry on." Bidding us a goodnight he left whistling.

"Great. Tell me, who on this ranch hasn't seen some naked part of my body yet?" My head dropped into Nic's back. "I can't believe this. I have to compete with the four legged monster for your attention. When I finally get it, I can't even get the hell banged out of me without someone busting us."

I started dancing, but it wasn't my fun dance of a few minutes ago. My fingers attacked my arms, legs, my whole body. I couldn't stop itching. "What is? What is this? Nic what's on me?" I screamed at Nic in a panic. Red welts bubbled surfacing all over me, from my feet to my face.

Nic whipped the blanket from me. "Turn around." Doing a full turn, not caring what on me showed I faced him again as the splotches kept popping with expansion. "Holy shit, woman," he stepped closer to me. "You're allergic to either the hay or the wool in the blanket." Nic ran his finger over my bubbling chest.

"Maybe I'm allergic to you." Sarcasm went well with the itching. "Can't be the blanket. It's wool." Welts bubbled with the intensity of itching. "Your duster. It's wool lined, I wear it all the time." I started scratching faster. "Just get me back to the house. I'll Google remedies and care for hives."

Never mind Emerald Bay or her pretty blanket that I just got my brains screwed out on, Nic shoved the coat around me, "Wait I need these," I kicked at my boots by the door. "How do you think I got out here?"

Using Nic to steady myself, between itches, I slipped from my pretty heels to the clumping of cowgirl boots.

"Nic, I'm itching in places that shouldn't be scratched." I shoved my arms into the duster, tightening the body of the coat closer to mine. "Don't think I'll be trying this again." I snorted sarcastically.

"Appreciate this little surprise." Nic grinned, sliding his shoulder gently into mine. "I'm impressed."

"Let me tell ya, the way I feel, you won't be getting surprise treatment for a long time." I cringed scratching at the outside of the coat. "Bones and Dad, they're still watching the game." My sigh, a long drawn out annoyed with the whole night kind of sigh.

"Why? Who put the bells on the back door?" I needed to slap them. The slightest jingle of bells brought ole Toby up from his slumber in front of the living room wood burner.

"Down Toby. Go lay down boy." Nic, firm with his old friend, the dog followed his command.

"My housecoat," I was so happy to see my old friend of comfort. "I left it here on the washer when I snuck out to play with you." At least I grinned at my past doings, tossing Nic his duster. But the soft terry was no comfort for my hives. 'I'm going to the computer, guard me."

"Stop." Nic was good at commands, "Feet." He motioned me to give him my boot covered foot.

"Thank you," I whispered heading to the corner of the kitchen. Clicking in the words 'hives', the Worldwide Web outdid itself with selection to choose from.

Nic, standing guard over my shoulder, pointed to the fourth one down, "Try this one." He tapped at the screen.

"Hey kids," Charlie switched the main kitchen lights on. "What are you two lookin' up at this hour."

"Aubrey." Dad's voice alarmed at the sight of me. Slowly he tilted my head towards the light. Next he took my hand from the keyboard, rolling up the sleeve to my housecoat.

"He went all savage on me, Dad." I chewed at the bottom of my lip, holding the laughter in.

"Nice son, nice." Charlie rolled his eyes. "Say it's a reaction from either the hay or the wool in the blanket." Charlie stated point blankly.

"What?" I turned my whole bubbled body facing Charlie, "How do you know?"

Charlie brushed the hair aside my forehead lightly fingering the bumps rising over my eyebrow. "They all over?"

"Yes." I twitched a little dance step in my chair

"Got any oatmeal and chamomile tea in this fancy kitchen of yours?"

"Yes. Why?" I waited to see what Doctor Charlie had up his sleeve next.

"Fill the tub with luke warm water. Sprinkle the oatmeal in. Add a little baking soda; it'll help with the itching." Charlie prescribed while I jumped up to get the ingredients.

"Dad how do you know all this? Is it going to work or is she going to smell like breakfast?" Nic questioned over his dad's recipe.

"Chamomile tea?" Charlie checked over my tea cupboard dropping the box on the counter, not with the rest in my arms. "Your mama would have a flare up of hives from time to time too." The smile reached Charlie's eyes.

"Really? This is what Ruthie did for it? Soak in all of this?" I fidgeted, trying not to scratch, dropping the box of baking soda on the counter.

"Not all. Tea's to sip on while you soak." Charlie tossed the box of tea at Nic, "Make her a cup of tea, with a touch of honey."

"Oatmeal. Just about a cup full. Won't clog the drain." Dad checked over the hives boiling on my face.

"I really need to get this soaking going." Right in the middle of the kitchen I peeled off my sexy hose right in front of Charlie eyes. "Sorry Dad I can't stop scratching."

"How'd you sneak out in that get up, girly?" Charlie asked as I retied the front of my house coat.

"Pie, ballgame. Dog, dead to world by the wood burner. Wasn't hard. You and Bones totally lost to the game and cherry pie. Just simple and slick. Now look at me." I moaned.

"Don't scratch honey." Dad chuckled. He reached for my hands, trying to stop my digging spree. "Every now and then, my Ruthie liked to have a little entertaining in the barn."

"Dad. You and mom? In the barn?" Tea kettle in hand, Nic stopped in the middle of the kitchen.

"Oh yes, yes." Charlie's smile couldn't get any bigger. "Your ma, she loved the smell of that hay. I could get her...." Charlie stopped meeting my gaping mouth and Nic's shifty grin. "Oh yes. Well, um, Ruthie, she never figured out which one it was that set the allergy off. But she made up this remedy. Should work for you too, honey."

"Dad you didn't?" Between scratches I cracked up laughing. "It was great, till this flared up." I looked over my skin, "But it got worse. We got busted."

Charlie, he couldn't stop the outburst of laughter, "Moe busted you two?"

"Yep," Nic grinned at me, winking. "This one thinks she's some little ballerina. Twirlin' her naked ass round and round. Moe comes in, yellin' out Chuckey's name. She starts screaming." Nic joined in his dad's laughter.

"Why am I the only one not finding this so funny?" My eyes drifted from one laughing hyena to the other.

"Ole Moe, think he's got the record for break'n up the rolls in the hay. Da you know how many times he interrupted Ruthie and me?" Charlie howled again. "Ruthie, she'd be so furious with him. Once she put a sign on the door, "Enter and I'll kick your ass. That means you, Moe.""

"Mom did that?" Nic laughed louder.

"Sure, sure. Never bothered us again." Charlie smiled.

"I'll remember that." Again, I started scratching.

"Get yourself up in the tub. Soak. Soak. And soak some more. Got some cream round here Ruthie use ta use too."

"Thanks Dad." I didn't think twice, gobbled up my boxes, and tossed my hose at Nic as I headed for the stairs.

The claw foot tub and I had become one. When the mood of loneliness played me out, I'd fill it up, nearly topping it over. I'd hide me and my mood deep in the water. One cup of oatmeal and half a box of baking soda mixed in the running water.

"Ahh, perfect." I exclaimed to the moisture rising from my porcelain safe haven.

Slowly, I submerged my entire welted bumpy body into the mixture. I sank to the bottom of the tub feeling like a freshly baked oatmeal cookie. A deep breath held, I dunked under letting the healing float freely over my face and hair.

"Hey." Nic's voice, all garbled under my sea, had me surfacing. "Here take this. Benadryl should calm the swelling way down."

I popped the pills, downing the whole glass of water he offered, noticing the tube of cream he sat on the vanity. "The magic cream?" I asked with baited breath.

"Some lavender ointment. Dad said Mom swore by it. She'd practically bathe herself in it." Nic chuckled. "This all makes sense now."

"What does?"

His grin broadened, "My parents. I remember seeing mom covered in hives. Never knew that Mom and Dad were getting it on in the barn. Got used to comin' in after carousing in town with the guys to hear their headboard banging."

"Ha, that's too funny. I'd say they had a very healthy appetite for each other." I giggled harder slipping down in the water till my lips were covered.

"Next time you want to play in the barn, make sure you post a sign on the door like Mom did." Nic laughed splashing water at me.

Dear Allison,

Late October blew in like a clipper sliding over Lake Erie. We've had a few dustings. The snow is sticking. In the distance, the mountains are fully covered in the white stuff. Guess what I learned? How to stack firewood. Yep, firewood. The entire front porch is completely covered with cut, split, and stacked firewood. I'm happy to report at no injury to my body. I can't believe how much wood they've stored. Nic said winter sometimes lasts well into April.

I've been walking the two mile track to the mailbox daily. I just get Toby, tagging along, da dump de dump beside my legs. The animal follows me all over. Guess he's not too bad, just his nose is so cold and wet, I'll keep to cats. Laugh of the letters, I hope you're sitting down, it's a whammy of a one. I found out I'm allergic to hay. Yes, hay. I've been whining to you about Nic spending too much time with the horse, his so called other woman. You'll love this. I put a skimpy outfit on and snuck out to the barn to surprise him. Dropped the coat and wham, had his attention from the four legged creature in no time flat. Had us a nice bottle of wine, warm blanket, matter of fact the horse's blanket. Then I learned what rolling in the hay meant. Did it in the barn. Yeah, yeah I know, said I won't, but I did. Just having a wonderful time till Ole Moe busted us. I was hiding behind Nic as Moe chewed us out. When he finally got closer and saw it was us, the look on his face, priceless. Guess one of the younger guys sneaks his girlfriend in...a lot. To add insult to injury, I started itching and itching. Huge blisters bubbled from my head to my feet. These big red splotches covered me from head to foot. You're laughing, I know you are. Tell Gina I took a roll in the hay. And for doing my wifely duties, we get busted and I get hives. Dad whipped up this quick fix that Ruthie used. Seems my in-laws got busted a lot for rolling in the hay. Nic's mom was allergic to the hay too.

Next insult to life for me that damn horse. Nic's still hounding me about her. Did I tell you she pinned me next to him and the fence the first time I tried to pet her. Nic claims she tried to protect me from falling. Toby's fat ass knocked me over. I'm terrified of her. Nic's getting annoyed with all my excuses, but he's kept his temper in check, so far. He's getting testy. I've even given him the 'I've got cramps' excuse to get out of touching that beast. Really I don't have the need to play cowgirl.

Have you made plans for Christmas? Please come. Gram has made arrangements already, she's coming for Thanksgiving. Charlie is really pleased. I know it's your busy season, but please come. I miss you so much.

Love, Aubrey ☺

Chapter 26

Saddle Up Baby

My hand screamed with writer's cramp at the thank you notes still left to be written. Polly must have invited the entire town, wait she did. Forty-seven white glossy envelopes sat in front of me in need of stamps, return address labels, and another twenty something to be finished.

"Woman." Nic shouted before the backdoor had a chance to slam behind him.

"Stop calling me that." I demand from my high perched chair at the island. "How would you like it if I called you 'Savage' all the time?"

My eyes pierced him while he stood in the kitchen doorway, a total ragged mess. Dirt marks smudged over his face. Favorite jeans, ripped, ready for the trash, and the tail of his braided hair spiraling lose. What was it about a flannel shirt that made him look so hot and appealing to me?

"You want to play savage with me, Bre?" The slightest smile barely creased his lips. He propped a plaid covered arm up on the doorway. A simple wink. He nearly had me melting off my chair.

"No." I whispered, swearing he could read my mind through my eyes. "What did you want?" My turn to play change the subject.

"Emerald Bay. Think ya could give her a little of your attention?" Nic's head went up. Chin stiffened. Stern glare, the one he used when he wanted me to be a part of his world. "Keep tellin' ya. Ya need to try again. Pet her, brush her."

Nic just dashed my moment of melting into a puddle and playing savage with him. He just had to bring up that damn horse.

I'd put him off for most of the week. Nic, he's so adamant about me bonding with this four legged creature.

"Nic, no. I'm not ready. She scares me. Can't I just keep practicing on you?" I tried a little pout, tilted head, and a little eye flirtation. Nothing doing, he still held onto his serious ground with me.

"You can ride me all night, sweetie." Another wink. "For now, I want you to come see the horse. Just pet her." His eyebrows went up trying to coax me along.

How was it, my husband could get me to do just about anything when he stood there filthy dirty, and flirted with me by just using those mahogany brown eyes. "Nic....I'm scared of her." I whined tapping the note cards in front of me.

"Grab your jacket. No one's in the barn. It'll be just me, you, and Emerald." Nic pulled my jacket from the coat rack behind him motioning me to fill it.

"Gee, no one to bust us playing with the horse?" Just had to smart that one off.

Another gift from Nic, he purposely had me fitted for a pair of boots for barn chores. Barn chores? I could barely deal with my flock of chickens. Now he wants me to play nice with a horse who has a bad ass attitude towards me. Resentfully, I shoved my stocking feet into the brown rose print patterned boots. Girly, I insisted on it, and I clomped down the back steps with him nervously playing with the zipper on my jacket.

A coyote ripped out its evening howl. Nic chuckled at my expense when I grabbed his hand stepping closer to him as we walked. "I don't think I'll ever get used to those things. Did Bones tell you, he shot one right outside my chickens' house the other day?"

"Coop." Nic rolled his eyes, "You watch yourself now. They're coming in close, its gettin' cold, food supply, it's dwindling."

I hated his little stern glares down the nose at me. It's not like I can't take care of myself. Correction, he's right, but I wouldn't say that out loud.

"Third one this week. Old Moe took one out. I got one behind the cattle barn." Nic shook his head. No one had anything good to say about a hungry roaming coyote.

The horse barn was the farthest from the house, but it seemed only steps away. The side door creaked opened with Nic's pull and he ushered me into the waiting darkness. Behind me, the door slammed shut with a thud, "Nic?" I was lost in the pitch blackness.

"Hold on city girl." Presto. A flip of a switch and four overhead lights warmed to their illuminated brightness.

"Should I put a note on the door?" I giggled.

"No. Don't be playing in the hay. Think the bedroom is a better place for you, woman." He smacked my bottom side, enjoying my snarl of protest.

Out of all the buildings, the horse barn intrigued me the most. Not because of the horses. Just the way it has to be kept. I'd expected it to be dirty. Hay all over the floors. Horse equipment hanging off a beam. Just a mess of a place. Totally opposite. Nic and June El had an understanding, this place was a home. Each horse had its own stall and their name on the outside gate. Directly beside each stall the horse's saddle, blanket and grooming brushes were kept. Everyday each horse had a maintenance schedule of grooming, riding time, stall cleaning, and pasture time. Even a bathing stall. I thought my kitchen was a spotlessly clean environment; the horse barn could rival it. A daily chart kept tabs on what each horse ate. Also, all actives were charted.

"She hears you." Nic said as Emerald Bay's head hung out over her open gate.

"How does she know it's me? I've never been near her since she attacked me?" I slowed the pace of our walk.

"Aubrey, I'm telling you, she was protecting you. Haven't you noticed when you're out by the corral she'll head right to you? She hears you. See's you. She'll go to the edge to get your attention." Nic grinned nearly pulling me along now. "Look at her. She's excited that you've finally come for her." The horse pranced in its stall making strange noises and shaking her head.

"Great, not only are you a cat whisperer, you're a horse whisperer too." I hid behind Nic as he rubbed Emerald Bay's nose reintroducing us.

"Give me your hand, Aubrey." Nic reached back feeling me resist. "Aubrey, she won't hurt you."

"She's so big." I gave in, thinking Nic's in front of me she can't hurt me this way. "She feels like velvet." I squirmed closer to Nic's back reaching a little deeper, stroking Emerald Bay's face. "Stay between us, please." I whispered inching Nic a little closer to her.

Emerald's huge, lean body stretched trying to get past Nic. Hesitantly, my fingers felt around her long narrow face. Huge eye lashes blinked covering her deep onyx eyes. My hand trailed the velvet texture of softness down her neck and I stepped beside Nic still needing the protection of his body. Emerald Bay twitched an ear cozying closer to me.

"Not so close now. I'm not sure about this friendship. You scare me." Listen to me, talking to a horse. Why not? I talk to Mr. Perfect.

"Once you two get comfortable, we'll start working on grooming her together." Nic stepped behind me, his hands tight on my hips. A deep firm grip to yank me away if my so-called girlfriend really did have an obsession for him. Instead, he steadily pushed me closer to the horse.

"In time you'll find yourself out here instead of hiding in the bathtub when life gets you down." Nic rubbed his chest against my back.

"You noticed?" I asked still playing with the textured velvet on Emerald's neck.

"I notice everything about you, Aubrey. I notice how quiet you get after you talk to Allison, or Gram, even Gina. I know you miss home, Aubrey."

"I miss my family. I get lonely."

"Lonely? You've got all of us. How could you feel lonely?"

"Ever been the new kid trying to fit in?" I asked him. "Things are so different here. I had everything I needed at a finger tips reach. I'm trying."

"I know." Nic inched me closer to Emerald. "You ok?"

"Yeah. This is close enough for now." I stroked the length of her long soft neck letting her put her head over my shoulder.

Nic's hands released me. "Let her in Aubrey. You might not feel so lonely."

Chapter 27

Wine and Whiskey Don't Mix

"Girls comin' up tonight?" Nic savored a mouthful of grilled salmon.

"Yep. You joinin' the 'Click Chick' club or playin' with the boys?"

"Haven't played a good hand with the boys for long while." He indulged in a second helping.

"Ohhh, then you can dish up all the gossip about me when you get back."

"They won't say shit about you when I'm around. Unless you've done somethin' again." Nic grinned, he knew how it irritated me.

"They tattle on me all the time. Can't even walk down to the mail box without one of them tellin' ya where I am. Your ranch boys are nothing but gossipy old hens." I spouted, actually ticked off.

"Gossip? Men don't gossip." Nic scowled at me. "We drink, spit, smoke…"

"And scratch." I chimed in unison with him. That's just…not over dinner. Two gross for me.

"Using your new patio?" Nic appreciated the way I breathed new life back into his mom's old stone patio.

"Yep. Nice evening to be sitting out there. Sure you won't join us?"

"You need your female bonding time. Do me a favor; don't be bonding too much with those two. I like ya the way you are." Easily he slipped his hand up my thigh. "Haven't played a good game of poker since I got you here."

"Then again we won't hear you boys whoppin' and hollarin' over who made who go broke. Or is it, who got laid and who got caught?"

"Why don't you and the other girls come on down and play a little strip poker with us." He nudged my arm, offering an enticing grin.

I wasn't so sure if Nic was kidding or not as we cleared the table.

"Seriously? Think about what you just said. The bosses' wife and two gay ladies joining the 'good ole boys' for a game of strip poker." I scratched the remains of the salmon skin into Mr. Perfect's dish. "You boys would be going home in nothing but boxers. If even that."

"You think you can take me, woman?" With a simple pull, I found myself in Nic arms.

"If ya don't stay out too late, just might let ya play a little game of poker with me." Dirty dinner dishes scattered falling into the sink when Nic sat me on the countertop. "Honey, the girls, they'll be here…"

A little rough at play, Nic locked his hands around the base of my head. A little thrust of the hips and I curved close into his body. My legs wrapped instantly around his waist. His moist lips wondered down my neck, while my hands desperately tugged at his shirt.

"Nic, we can't…" another bite to my collarbone and he stripped my flannel shirt down to my wrists. "Remember what happened the last time…"

"Bre, shut-up." Nic's hands ran up under my tank top, scooping and pinching at my lace bra.

I did as I was told, but I let my hands attack his belt buckle, "It's six. They won't be here till like…Ow…be careful." He yanked my jeans down past my hips as I unzipped his pants. "Did you lock the backdoor?"

"Christ woman, stop with the questions."

Another plate, or dish, or something glass crashed into the sink. The frenzy of countertop sex had started. The game, get it done without getting caught.

"Knock knock. It's us. Ready for Sangria and…" Mimi and June El let themselves in through the unlocked backdoor. "Well, well still enjoying dessert?"

"Get out." Nic ordered. Not even missing a beat, he planned on finishing what he started.

"Busted. Game over." I whispered in his ear.

"On the countertop? Don't you two have a bedroom for that kinky sex stuff?" With arms folded over her chest, June El lectured. "You know anyone could walk in here."

"Maybe we should come back?" Mimi's delicate voice followed as she sat a huge cheese plate on the island. "Nic are you going to be long with Aubrey? We've got town gossip to share."

Neither woman seemed ruffled by our countertop quickie. They even waited for his response.

"For Christ sake can't a man get a piece of ass in his own home?" Nic roughly yanked up his jeans. Not caring, he faced June El and Mimi tucking in his shirt and readjusting his deflated manhood.

"You didn't lock the door." Straight faced, June El pointed out to him. "Ya know, if ya don't want anyone surprisin' ya, lock the damn door."

I slid off the countertop, redressing myself behind Nic's shielding body. "See, I asked ya if ya locked the door." I tugged at his braid, "Next time I'll post a sign, 'Nic's getting laid don't come in.'"

"I'll finish with you later, woman." Nic grabbed my chin with sheer roughness he laced my lips with a deep long kiss.

"Enjoy your Sangria, ladies." Nic slapped his hat on his head, still disgusted. "Why don't ya ask these two about joining us for poker?" He grinned slyly, as he pretended to be nice, "You better be awake when I get back, woman."

"Savage," I muttered lovingly under my breath.

"I heard that." The backdoor rattled on its hinges as he left.

"He's in rare form. What's his problem?" June El scoffed.

"Problem? He never locks the backdoor. Every time he sits my naked ass on that counter top, we get busted." My reply, sarcastic, but truthful. "If he'd just lock a door."

"You ain't going to teach that dog a new trick. Man just wants in your pants."

"Oh, ha ha June El. My pants won't fit him." I laughed harder at my off the wall comments.

"You finished the patio." Mimi noticed all the twinkling lights through the window.

"Wait 'til you see it. And the treasures I found in the old storage barn. I love it. Come on grab up this stuff and let's go enjoy. I want to hear all the gossip about town. Am I in it?" With three bottles of wine in hand, I lead the way to the patio.

My new patio resembled an outdoor eatery. Nic couldn't believe that I put it all together by myself. More importantly, I didn't hurt myself. The tea table and chairs that I formally used as my kitchen table found a new home on the patio. Rustic chairs and tables dating back to the sixties, I polished, shined, and restored back to their luminous state of colors. Neon yellow, lime green, and orange orange radiated under the less than a thousand twinkling lights I'd strung up.

"Oh my gosh, Aubrey, I can't believe you did all of this." June El, stopped in the dead center admiring our new place for gossip and wine. "Unbelievable."

"Never thought anyone would do anything with this place again." Mimi uncorked our first bottle of chilled Sangria. "You've really changed Nic, Aubrey."

"Changed him? How?" I didn't know the Nic Ravenwood they knew. "I know he's got a temper, but…"

"You're the best thing that ever happened to that man." Mimi shot an unsure questioning glance to June El.

"Ok someone's got to dish." My head bounced back and forth waiting to hear more.

"June El, you've known him longer," Mimi passed me the bottle of wine, "Some of it's not pretty, Aubrey."

"Pretty, how ugly?" I nearly poured the wine over the brim of my goblet.

"Got himself into all kinds of fights in town. Tossed his ass in jail, just a few times. He was a lot younger. Charlie go bail him out every time." June El's spiked hair followed her every bobbing head shake. "Shouldn't be telling ya this."

"You should tell me. What pisses him off so bad?" I wanted to know. Curiosity never killed this cat.

"He was one of those bad boys women just wanted to be loved by." Mimi giggled.

"Known him, seems forever. Went to high school together." June El announced.

"You went to high school with Nic? I don't remember him in high school." Stunned, Mimi questioned.

"Remember you're five years younger than us, Miss Captain of the Glee Club." June El picked back at Mimi.

"Glee Club?" My head whipped back to Mimi. It was definitely going to be a night of surprises.

"Yeah, we can just call her Prancer." June El took another stab.

"Oh I could just break out in song. Or, how about a little dance number?" Mimi played back. "Just keep my glass filled and I'll sing ya any show tune, but someone has to dance with me.

"Ok, Ok, Ok. Back to Nic." I waved my hands in the air, snapping my figures getting their attention back, "Start the gossip, Juney bug."

"Nic wasn't too popular in school. Not a big ball player. Mr. Agriculture. After school he went off to college, double majored."

"No, not Nic," Mimi interrupted, "Three degrees. A Bachelor of Veterinary Science. One in Agriculture and, of course, let's round it off with a degree in Business."

June El patiently waited for her partner to finish. "Came back here to take over the ranch. That's when he and I hooked up. Couldn't keep a horse trainer out here for nothing." June El took her time getting to the good stuff.

"I know all of that." I opened the second bottle of sweet red wine. "Chocolates?"

"Your husband got himself a good reputation of a bad boy." Mimi of all people started to dish the dirt.

"Mimi." June El tried to stop her.

"Juney, if you're not going to tell her…I will." I'd never seen Mimi so firm with her partner before. "I just don't want one of his so called 'ex-bimbo's' coming up and sayin' something inappropriate to Aubrey. That's all."

"Tell me what?" I wasn't sure I wanted to know anymore.

"Nic used to be known for his Saturday night banging's." June El stole back the conversation.

"His 'banging' nights? It sounds, sounds like…"

"He was known to be quite the stud in bed. Weekends come you didn't see Nic till late Sunday afternoon. He'd carouse with any willing female, drink a little too much and well…you know. Don't think I have to spell it out for ya." Kicked back in the lime green metal lawn chair, June El shook her head.

My head dropped and I stared down at the table. Something a new wife really doesn't want to know is how many females her husband's tagged over the years. I played with my wine glass, took a deep breath in and let it out.

"So you're telling me my husband was a male slut?" From nowhere we all erupted in laughter. "He banged the hell out of whatever female would give it up. Got into fights. Got himself thrown in jail. How long did this go on?"

"Till his mom got sick. Then it all stopped." Mimi spoke softly. "It really messed with him seeing how sick his mama got."

"That temper of his tore into everyone after she died. No one ever thought he'd get himself married off. Then you came along. Tellin' ya Aubrey, you brought him back to life." June El lightened the conversation. "And I'm tellin' ya one more thing. Don't be sayin' to him we told ya this stuff, either."

"Secrets stay safe on the patio." My glass raised, "A toast to the secrets of the patio and all other girl talk we have out here." A chiming of glasses, another round poured, and we passed the plate of chocolates. "Here, all this time, I thought my stud muffin grew up a geek boy."

"How did it get to be eleven already?" Mimi pointed at her watch. "Are you joining us for church in the morning, Aubrey?"

"Depends. My cowboy hasn't ridden back in. If I'm up in time, I'll drop over. Remember he was spouting something off about me waiting up for him. Might be needing a Saturday night banging." Endless laughter did the soul good and I found it with Mimi and June El.

Clean up was a breeze. Empty wine bottles, empty cheese and cracker plates, and a whole box of chocolates, all devoured in just a few hours. "Guess I'll have to be doubling my walk," I said as the empty candy box hit the trash can.

"Hey girly." Charlie snuck in the backdoor. "Wine party over already?"

"Hi Dad. Mimi and June El are getting up early for church. Have a good time with all the boys?"

"Sure, sure. If ya like watchin' other men lie to each other." Dad sighed, "Nic's cleanin' the table again. Guess I taught him good there. I'm headed to bed, sweetie. See ya in the morning."

"Night, Dad." I watched Charlie climb the steps with Mr. Perfect tossed over his shoulder like a baby.

I finished cleaning up the kitchen, left a light on for Nic, and went upstairs myself. I had no clue how much longer he'd be playin', smokin', and scratchin'. For the fun of it, I pulled out a thinner t-shirt night gown. Nothing overly sexy, but it hung snuggly on my curves. My magazine would keep me company till Nic drug himself in or I feel asleep.

"Bre, you up yet?" Nic's voice echoed up the staircase in the silence of night.

Instead of me meeting him on the landing, as usual, it was the cat. "You're not the pussy I want ta play with," he scolded the cat with slurred words.

"Did you just call me a pussy?" I picked up my cat, stroking his back. "How was poker night?"

"You're lookin' tempting, Bre." Nic took three steps at a time not even out of breath when he landed in front of me.

"Yuck. Who was smoking what? You smell."

Before I could escape his clutching reach, Nic grabbed me around the waist, "Don't you run away from me, woman." A shove with too much power behind it had me flush against the wall with the weight of his body pinning me tightly.

"Ow. Nic that hurts. A little breathing room would be good."

"I didn't finish what I started earlier. Your girly girlfriends put a stop to that."

"Bed would be a more comfortable spot for this attack." I playfully suggested.

"Right here suits me fine, woman."

When I attempted to move toward the bedroom, I got round two of a hard slam back into the wall. With a bouncing thump off the wall, I cracked my forehead into his chin.

"Nic stop it. You're playing too rough." I was no match for his body weight as I tried to shove him off me.

"Who said I'm playing, woman?" Again, another painful shove to the wall.

Nic's lips burned on mine. The biting pain seared deeper. "Stop it." I screamed, hitting his shoulder with my fist as hard as I could. My free hand raked through his tangled hair, yanking his lips free of mine. My aggressive struggling was taken by him as willingness to play.

"You like it rough and hard don't you Bre?" Nic's words slurred as he took another bite at my neck.

"NO! I don't like it. Stop." Bodies pinned together and my protesting wasn't about to stop him. "Nic. Stop." I screamed half begging him. "Please Nic, stop. You're hurting me."

Nic's rough blue jeans chafed my legs that were tangled between his. How his clod-hopper boots missed my bare toes, I'll never know. He only laughed when my knee missed hitting the bulging lump in his jeans. My body conformed into the stiff wall that helped to hold me captive as his entire body crushed down on mine. Nic yanked my hand free of his hair and started his biting descent down my neck. The eerie sound of my t-shirt style nightgown ripping echoed with another scream of pain from me. I screamed louder, not caring if I woke the whole ranch up. Then again who would help? They were all drunk from poker night. The taste of blood lingered in my mouth from where he bit my lip so hard.

"Nic. Stop. Please stop." Struggling to get free of his attack, I begged him to let me go, crying this time.

My self-appointed guard dog, Toby, heaved his rubbery old frame into the back of Nic's legs. Each pass by, Toby howled in a hideous sadness.

"Nic." Charlie's hands tore Nic's weighted body from mine. "What the hell are you doing?"

A shock of sober reality woke Nic from his drunken rage. A thin trickle of blood dripped from my battered lips to my torn nightgown. Decorations of pink and purple bruises lined my neck and chest from his game of biting. Toby sat his old body in front of me, pushing his weight back on my legs, lending me his support.

"Nic? What the hell is wrong with you?" The back of my hand caught another dribble of blood. Oddly enough, I wasn't an ounce scared of him. Just pissed off and deeply hurt.

"Oh god, Bre? Your," in a mind crushing moment Nic realized the damage he'd inflicted on me. "Your neck…I'm…god, Aubrey, I'm sorry." Nic stepped forward to cradle me in his arms of apologies. But his father stopped him before he could lay another hand or lip on me.

"Ya don't treat no woman like that, especially your wife." Charlie snapped. "Sleep it off in the tub. Deal with you in the mornin' boy." Nic actually stumbled when Dad yanked him down the hall to the bathroom with a continuous line of cursing words.

"Aubrey. Please, I'm so sorry. Bre…" Words still slurred, Nic called as his father gave him another shove into the bathroom.

My sniffling turned to sobbing as I sat on the top step, slumping into the rail for support. Mr. Perfect wound around me purring in a comforting tone. Toby, bless his furry heart, came to my aid with a wet kiss to my face.

"Shouldn't you be consoling your master?" I saved the sarcasm on Toby as he licked my swelling face again. "Come on guys," I took each step very gingerly, as I headed down to the kitchen, "a little ice should help."

It had become a game between Nic and me when I called him a savage. Rough kissing, tossing me on the bed, this I thought was his so called rough play. There would be no way I'd be letting him get a crack at a repeat performance. I filled a zip lock bag with ice and climbed the staircase.

"Come on my furry kids," with a wave, I motioned for the cat and dog to join me. Comforted by my furry companions, I crept slowly down the hall to our bedroom. I could hear Charlie giving Nic another thrashing of nasty words as I passed by the bathroom.

Toby, folded his furry body inside the threshold of the door, just daring anyone to cross it. The only one curled tight to me was Mr. Perfect, one eye opened checking on my stirring movement.

Not even six a.m. yet, I tossed the covers off, feeling each and every prickle of rippling pain, and made my way to the bathroom. I rubbed the bump on the back of my head, entering the bathroom to find Nic snoring in the tub. Toby, who appointed himself my watch guard, followed me licking at Nic's face.

"Crap. Get the hell off me Toby." Nic snorted. "Damn, my head's killing me."

"Really? Remember me?"

Nic's eyes snapped open. He didn't expect to find me sitting on the toilet glaring at him.

"Aubrey," The bright bathroom light didn't hide a single mark on me. "Honey. I'm sorry. I'm so sorry." Nic tried to sit himself upright. A leg tossed over the side of the tub didn't help with his balance as he slid down into the deep walls of the claw foot tub.

"Don't say a word to me. You got drunk and turn into a psycho animal? Don't talk to me till you've cleaned yourself up." I flipped the shower knob to cold letting the spray of icy water hit him full force.

"Aubrey." Nic scrambled to get himself up as I yanked the shower curtain closed around him.

"I don't even know if I want to talk to you. You're terrible." The bathroom door slammed behind me before he could holler another word.

It made me feel a little better, not much. My head still hurt. My shoulders were stiff, and I sure the hell didn't want to see what my lips and neck looked like. I landed myself in the kitchen. Coffee would be a must today. Not only did I need a cup, Nic would be needing the whole pot. The loud knocking at the backdoor startled my already jumpy nerves.

"Who would be…oh never mind?" I knew. June El and Mimi, I'm sure. They wanted to go to breakfast and then church. "It's open." I called out.

"Hey, you up for breakfast before church?" June El all 'morning perky' bounced in.

"I'll be skipping this Sunday." I kept my back to her acting like I was making the already brewed coffee. "I'm not feeling so good."

"Aubrey what happened to your neck?"

My housecoat didn't hide the bruises. "Nothing, I'm fine, just slept wrong." June El grabbed my arm, forcing me to face her.

"Oh my god. Did Nic do this? He hit you?" June El reached for my housecoat, but I stopped her before she could view more of my new bruised designs.

"Juney, keep your voice down. Dad's still asleep. Nic was passed out in the tub. I turned the cold water on him. And, no, he didn't hit me. His lips attacked me." I clutched my housecoat close to my neck. I didn't want June El to see anymore of Nic's handy lip or so called love bites on my body.

"Aubrey, what did he do to you?"

Guess too much whiskey, and, um, he likes to play a little too rough for my delicate skin…"

"Where is he? You said tub?" June El started for the doorway.

"Juney, stop." I caught her by the elbow. "This isn't for you to fix. It's between me and Nic. His hangover is beating on his brain. Believe you-me, he's already seen his handy work. And I'm not done with him."

"I can't leave you here." June El stepped into protective mode.

"Yes, you can. I'm not afraid of Nic. He knows it."

"How the hell did you get away from him? You're not all that strong." June El eyed me up and down as her temper slowly simmered down.

"Dad. Woke him up with all my screaming and hitting the wall. Toby howled in horror."

"Nic had you pinned to the wall?"

"Yep. Thought I was some kind of midnight snack." I smiled at her in an attempt to ease the awkwardness.

"You two go. Have breakfast. I'm fine. He won't ever do this again." I poured myself a cup of coffee. "I know you'll tell Mimi. I want to see how Nic's going to explain to the boys how his wife got all banged up."

"Aubrey. I…I don't know what to say. Other than I'd like to go kick his ass."

The creaking of the steps signaled us that we had company approaching.

"Bre, you down here?" Nic called, his voice had lost all anger.

He stepped into the kitchen meeting June El's ugly demeanor.

"June El just stopped to see if I wanted to go to breakfast and church with them. What do ya think?" Sarcastically, I glared at Nic and pointed to my colorful face.

June El shook her finger at Nic. Words didn't pass her lips. She left, slamming the backdoor behind her.

I took my cup of coffee heading the same way June El left. My favorite refuge, the claw foot tub, wasn't going to help me this time. I clopped, in my so called fashionable cowgirl boots, to the patio. I didn't care who saw me. My tea set welcomed me as I curled my housecoat closer to me.

"Aubrey." Nic stood quietly at the edge of the patio.

"Nic." Best answer I could come up with.

"It's a little chilly out here. Come back in."

"No." Small words seemed to help my growing anger.

"Then I'll join you." He sat across from me and waited. "Aubrey. You don't know how sorry I am. I can't even blame the whiskey. When I saw you on the steps. My mind went wild. The thoughts. The stuff I wanted to do to you. Right there. Right then."

"Shut up, Nic." I ordered. And it shocked him. "No. No. No. No excuse is going to make these bruises go away."

"Aubrey, please. I'm so sorry."

"Easy for you to say. You weren't pinned to a wall. You weren't being bit. You weren't the one begging you to stop. Your dog even tried to rescue me. Yeah, your dog. But the best, your father had to pull you off me."

"Aubrey, all I can say is I'm sorry." Nic offered another plea for forgiveness. "Swear to you, it won't happen again. I'll never, ever pull another stunt like that again."

"Let me see if I can get this statement into your hung over brain. It's real simple." Instantly, I grabbed his still wet hair yanking him closer to my colorful shaded face. "I'm your wife. Not some chick you pick up at the bar and bang the hell out of for enjoyment." Another yank to his hair had him even closer to swollen lips. "You will never handle me that way again. Or there will be no more Mrs. Ravenwood in your life. Got it?" My fingers untwisted from his black mane of hair as I settled back into my chair. "I'll be gone. But not before I hurt you. Understand?"

Slowly, Nic slid back to his side of the table, "I got it, Bre. I got it." He lit up his cigar, "Aubrey, I didn't mean to hurt you. I love you. I'm so sorry." His eyes never left mine as he reached for my hand.

Chapter 28

I Want To Go Home

    For the first weekend in November, the temperatures soared into the low seventies. A warm front, pushing in the California winds, had Bones claiming a huge storm would be hitting next. A teaser of nice weather. Then wham. You're up to your eyeballs in drifting snow. Bones should try a winter in Cleveland and face the Lake Erie snow machine. The warmth of the day perked my spirits, reminding me of how we'd get unseasonably high temperatures in late November back home. Indian summer, I missed it. I took full advantage of the warmth and sunshine. Laundry hit the lines. All the bed linens and comforters stripped off, washed, and hung out to absorb the last of the windy sunshine.
    Directly off the back steps sat my patio tucked behind the house. My patio with a panoramic view of the mountains became another private retreat for me. My old kitchen table, the wrought iron tea set, found a new home on the large slate stone patio. Mimi, June El, and I enjoyed our wine and cheese parties there until the weather turned, causing us to retreat to the comforts of the house. Empty flower boxes framed the edge of the patio, waiting for flowers to be planted next spring. My herb garden safely transplanted to the inside kitchen window box, I pretty much had my 'girly' patio tucked away for the winter.
    Something I didn't have access to while living in an apartment, a clothes line. Thrilled at being able to string everything out just one more time, I mindlessly hung my pretty little lacy unmentionables on the line with the bedding. The warm breeze tousled around my hair and old Toby rolled to his back enjoying the sunshine on his arthritic bones. I thought Emerald Bay was

obsessed with Nic. However, his dog gave obsession a new meaning towards me.

"Toby. Go on. Let me finish." Kindness, just for the moment, I patted the old dog's head while I sorted out my bras to hang. I didn't pay Toby much attention as his head bobbed after my hands.

"Toby. Get your lobby-legged self out of my basket." I snapped, shooing him away with the wave of a hand.

At the same time I bent down to pick up a new garment, Toby snatched one of my lace bras. With the speed of a track star, he took off with it. As if my bra was some kind of junior bungee cord, he shook it madly. One purple lace strap fell over a flopping ear as Toby made a break with his soft stretchy toy.

"Toby. You monster. Come back." My scream pierced in the carrying wind.

I rounded the side of the house stopping in mid run. Tail high and wagging at me, Toby darted further down the drive dragging my chewed on bra with him. My hysterical screams brought two ranch hands from the equipment barn. Joe, the oldest of the ranch hands, got to me first. And Jimmy, rubbing his eyes at the sight of what Toby bounced over the dirt with.

"Good god, woman, what the hell are ya hollerin 'bout?" Joe stood beside me, panting worse than Toby.

Horrified, I unclasped one hand from my reddening face, stretching my arm out pointing towards Toby and his new chew toy. My bra. No words needed, but Joe did his best to stifle his laughter.

"Jimmy, grab that damn animal." Joe ordered. "Now Miss Aubrey, calm down. Just a stupid dog bein' stupid."

Between the anger and humiliation of my favorite bra running free in the dog's teeth, the tears fell down my cheeks.

"No harm here, Miss Aubrey. Jimmy, he'll fetch it for ya." Joe tried to console me with a half hearted pat on the shoulder.

I shrugged his hand off watching Jimmy wrestle in the dirt with Toby for what was left of my bra. Let's just say adjusting to ranch life wasn't hitting me with the full 'Howdy Partner' force Nic had hoped it would. Seeing my pretty delicate lace bra, directly ordered from the Victoria Secret catalog, being stretched, slobbered on, and dragged through the dirt, just slapped my unhappy ass into emotional overload, but the worst was hollered from Jimmy's lips.

"Got it, Miss Aubrey." Jimmy held the one end of the strap high into the air. It swung in his hand like a prize for winning the fight with the hound.

"No." My mouth formed the words. The low growl that rumbled from my throat, the scream that flew from me, had Joe stepping back. I'm sure he wanted to save his own skin. Tears gushed liked a spiting geyser, blowing high in the sky.

"Oh, Miss Aubrey? Now. Now, it's not that bad." Joe's hands tried to pat me into some kind of a hug. "We've all seen…seen lady's under things before."

Joe's words of consolation inched me over the edge. "Not mine, you haven't." I screamed at him.

"Jimmy find Nic. Find 'em fast." Joe gave up with the hug, yelling orders to Jimmy again. His hand pinched tightly into my arm, trying to keep hold of me till they found Nic.

Joe had dealt with a few crazy women in his life. He knew directly by the glare in my eyes to let go. I ran for the safe haven of my kitchen. The back door slammed so hard behind me, that Mr. Perfect skidded from the sunny window seat to get away from me and my brewing racket.

I threw myself into a kitchen chair sobbing uncontrollably. My feet on the edge of the chair, I hugged my legs sobbing harder into my knees. I barely heard the shuffle of words outside the back door through all my hideous crying. Something about Old Toby, my bra, and the blood curdling scream.

"You better take this to Miss Aubrey, Mr. Nic. She's real upset." I heard Jimmy recreating my horrified ordeal with Toby.

The back door squeaked open, as if to ask 'do I dare let anyone in?' I heard Nic's boots clicking on the floor, hesitating step by step.

"Bre?" He waited with uncertainty. "Aubrey? Honey, you ok?"

"Go away." I sobbed at him, not moving from my cradle wrapped position on the wood chair.

Nic slid a chair over in front of my rocking body. From the corner of my tear stained eye, I saw him lay what was left of my purple bra on the kitchen table.

"Aubrey heard there was a little incident with Toby and...this." Nic's hand fingered the gooey slobber marks of Toby's teeth print. "We'll just get a new one." Confident that his last sentence would comfort me, Nic tried to unfold me from curled security, while he too stifled his laughter.

"You're laughing?" My whimper of a voice choked out.

"No, honey." Nic broke; he couldn't hide his laughter anymore. "Bre, I got to admit, it's pretty funny."

"Funny? Everything that happens to me is so damn funny to you." I screeched at him, nothing seemed to be tickling my funny bone. I kept sobbing; tears soaked the knees of my jeans from where I wrapped myself so tightly into them. "I want to go home." I cried harder, grabbing onto Nic, burying my head in his chest.

Nic's hands sank into my shoulders with tightness, sitting me upright. "You are home." The annoyance in his voice showed. No sympathy for my latest mishap, and my tears got put on hold from the anger in his tone.

"No, this is your home." My eyes welled with running tears as I tried to struggle free, escaping his grip. "Let go of me."

I tried to shove Nic away, but he caught me mid shove with one arm around my stomach reeling me back to him before I could even step one foot down. Easily he sat me down on his lap. "Don't run from me, Aubrey."

My eyes swiveled to meet the budding anger in his.

"Nic. Let me go." I whispered, pushing at his shoulder. "This isn't working."

"Aubrey you haven't even been here two months. You're ready to pack up and leave cause Toby swiped your bra?" Nic snapped crushing my heart. "Not working? You want to leave me?"

Nic's words stung. But I couldn't answer him. No reply seemed to say it all. He dumped me back on my chair leaning over me. One hand resting on the chair the other trapped me between him and the table. "You want to leave? Your call. I won't stop you."

"I gave up everything for you. I left everyone I knew. I came here for you. I never asked you to give anything up for me." I cringed, jumping when he moved away from me. Did he mean it? Would he let me go without a fight?

"Aubrey." My heart pounded hearing his ill-tempered voice. "This is your home." He stopped in the doorway of the laundry room, "You make the call, woman."

He slammed the backdoor behind him, rattling the wall hangings in the kitchen.

"*Failure. Failure. I told you so.*" Phil's voice echoed in my ears. What the hell was I thinking? "Rancher's wife. I'm not cut out for this job." I sobbed to my empty kitchen.

The floor boards in the living room squeaked, a softer footstep came looking for me. A pile of tissues mound high on the kitchen table. Half an empty box sat in my hand. I didn't hear the intruder, till she spoke.

"Aubrey." June El's manly voice sent me sky rocketing. "Aubrey, you ok?'

"Where did you come from?" I gasped turning to face her. "I didn't hear you come in. I'm, I'm..."

"Just wanted to check on you. I um, well, I gave Nic...no, I ripped your husband a new asshole." June El boasted with confidence rocking back on her boots.

"You did what? You know? You heard us?" Not even surprised that June El already knew, she seated herself across the table from me and my piled high tissues.

"Well, hate to tell ya. The dog. Your bra. Everyone knows. Stuff like that, can't keep it under your hat." She sighed. "I came to see if ya were alright. Heard what he said to ya about leaving. Didn't mean to be eaves dropping. He had no right..."

"I told him I wanted to go home. Home. You know Cleveland." I brushed a tear away. "You want tea?"

"Get the wine. You need it." June El smiled crossing the kitchen for the glasses.

"What did you say to him? His temper is beyond pissed off." I plopped back down in the wood chair.

"Man's got no right to be pissed at you. Bringin' a city girl to ranch land. You're clueless, but you catch on fast. Ole Nic, he don't take orders well. Not from anyone. Gave him a friendly reminder you're not one of the boys." She sipped her wine. "You do have good wine, Aubrey. Plus a few other not so...let's just say it wasn't very lady like." June El chuckled softly. "All I can say is, I hope you stay."

"Thank you. Refill?" I pointed to the bottle of Merlot.

"Nope. One's good. Got to get back there before Nic chew's me a new ass."

"Thanks, Juney Bug." I actually smiled.

"Any time. Us woman of ranch land…we got to stick together." June El left as quietly as she came in.

My refugee, the claw foot tub. The water steamed up filling the bathroom with the scent of lavender. I slipped my 'sorry for me self' into the bubbles and slid under the water. My fingers lightly skimmed the bubbles resting on the side edge of the tub, waiting to pull me up when my air supply depleted itself. I left the bathroom door open in hopes my cat, the only thing I had left from city life, would wander in. My lungs burned for oxygen and I surfaced to find Nic standing in the doorway. I padded my eyes dry, leaning back resting my head on the tub, and waited.

"Figured I'd find ya here." Nic leaned heavily into the doorframe.

"Go away." I mumbled from under the wash cloth hiding my face.

"Aubrey, so you hit some bumps."

I cut Nic short sitting up in my steamy non-relaxing bath. "Hit some bumps? Let see, you're right, I haven't even been here two months. In that short time, I've been attacked by chickens. Fell off a fence knocking myself out cold. Let's not forget the exploding grease gun, remember?" I couldn't stop. "How about the hives? Total enjoyment there. Everyone on this ranch has seen my ass, my boobs, or my girly underwear."

"Aubrey I get it. It's not easy."

"Not easy? Oh, I'm not done. This horse you want me to bond with," I rolled my eyes. "She pinned me down. Smacked me even. You think I have to be its new playmate. And what about the night when you came home so drunk from poker night?"

"Bre, you're startin' to tick me off."

"You're ticked off? You were so drunk, your father had to pull you off me. Do I need to remind you what my lips and neck looked like? No wonder you slept in the tub that night."

"Aubrey." Nic put his anger on hold for a second. "I've apologized over and over for doing that to you. I promised you it will never, ever happen again. I still feel guilty for hurting you."

"You ever pull shit on me like that I will pack up and go home."

Nic gripped the side of the door, channeling all his anger into the wood. Mahogany eyes glared fiercely back at me.

"For Christ's sake woman I came up here to try talk some sense into ya. Why don't ya pack your shit up and go back to your prissy ass chef life?" Nic yelled, shutting me up.

"Really? Prissy ass chef? That's what you think of me?" I hissed back at him.

"If you were one of the hands, I'd of fired your ass."

"Well I'm not one of your hired hands. I'm your wife." Screaming seemed to help me. "Get out." The bar of soap in my hand aimed for the back of his head, but ricocheted off the door frame with a thumping crack. Officially over, the honeymoon ended as I sat crying in my bubble bath listening to Nic's boots stomping down the steps.

Chapter 29

Horse Care 101
By The Way Of Cyber Space

The printer kicked out the tenth and final piece of paper on Horse Care 101. I didn't need Nic to show me anything about my beast in the barn. Ok, I lied to myself, again.

"Why am I doing this? I don't even know if I'm...." I couldn't finish my sentence out loud.

Staying or not, it hurt deep down in my heart just hearing the words burning in my brain. The last page dropped into the paper tray. Impressed by the handy dandy Google everything site, I did my research and hopefully could tackle Emerald Bay on my own. Somehow I was going to prove to Nic, and all of them, I just wasn't some dumb, prissy city girl. Horse care and bonding with Emerald Bay rated high on my 'I don't want to do this list' along with the flippin' chicken coop. At least the chickens, I had a small grip on, but it didn't make things any easier for me. Lost deep in my own thoughts, I didn't hear the back door open, till I heard Nic's voice.

"Aubrey," Panicked by his intrusion, I turned facing him looking like the cat who ate the last kitty treat. "What are ya reading?" He peered from the center of the kitchen around my shoulder.

"New recipe," I lied. Not really. It was a recipe on horse care, but Nic didn't need to know that. I swung back around in my chair, clicking into a culinary web site.

"Going into town, picking up supplies. Ya coming?" Nic waited for me to face him again.

I shook my head no before the answer even came out. "List's on the table." I really did look for a recipe as his foot steps closed behind me.

"Aubrey." I stopped typing seeing his reflection in the computer screen. "Sure you won't change your mind?" Nic's fingers played lightly with the ends of my hair.

"No." It wasn't a harsh no, it was just a no. "I'm sure your dad would enjoy going." I wimped out on him not wanting to face down the escalating question that loomed in both our minds.

A deep sigh of frustration unveiled itself from his lungs, "Ok."

The back door didn't slam this time. It creaked in defeat and Toby's big furry head flopped on my lap.

"Shouldn't you be sucking up to Nic?" I petted my floppy eared shadow. "Come on, we've got work to do." I collected my papers and tromped up the stairs.

If I planned on spending the day in the barn with Nic's other woman, I needed warmer clothes. Jeans, wool socks, heavy flannel, I stole one of Nic's. He'd be gone half the day, why not? I shoved my feet into the flower printed pink rubber boots instead of the fashionable cowgirl boots Nic got for. Mimi helped me pick out the rubber soled ones on one of our shopping trips to the Super Wal.

"Why do you follow me?" I stuck my tongue out at Toby opening the door. I laughed at myself. "Ha, I invited you, how stupid am I?"

He bolted past me howling like a fog horn and signaling anyone who cared, that I was on the move. "No need to tell me why I love cats."

Just my truck left in the driveway, sitting alone next to where Nic's had been parked. I'm sure he'd be spending time at the tack shop, especially with Dad along. My coast was clear. No one to see what I was up to. Don't know why I worried about any of the hands seeing me out here, they tell Nic every move I make. The usual circuit, I walked straight towards the horse barn, still hurling insults at Toby.

The midmorning sun filtered through the open door, the barn, dark and empty. "Great. No one is here."

I grinned at Toby as I flipped on the overhead lights. My furry sidekick and I headed for Emerald Bay's stall. One single paper slipped from my packet, reliable Toby didn't even realize I had dropped it. "Don't even think you're growing on me, mutt."

At the sound of my voice, my majestic beauty appeared, hanging her long sleek neck over the open gate.

"Listen up, home wrecker; I've got the World Wide Web info on how to take care of you." I swear she nodded her head in agreement. "Let's just start with page one here," and I read it aloud to my student. "You're the student right? No, I'm the student? Well, one of us is."

Bones, his footsteps as silent as a cat, came up behind us, I never heard him. Even Toby didn't alert me with his howling of hellos. Bones ducked into an empty stall observing my class in horse care.

"This is your brush. See the picture shows how to hold it and how to stroke you with it. Look at that, there's more than one. You've got, hold on a sec. Let me match it up. This one is for your tail. Curry brush. Oh, so when you get dirt caked on ya," I held the printed off copy of instruction for Emerald's inspection. "Ok, tramp, let's see what else we've got."

Maybe I should rethink my hostile insults to the horse. She's just a tad bit bigger than me. I'm sure one knock from that big caboose of a behind of hers would send me flying.

"Page three, food. Nic said something about a feed room. Did you eat today?" Convenient, no answer, "Like talking ta Nic lately," I muttered, taking a fast look into her stall. Then strolled myself over to the feed room.

"Ok, Princess, we've got something called sweet grain, mixed with oats. I can read labels, too, ya know. Then for dessert, which I know you like these." I held up a carrot to her large lips. "Fine, fine, where are your manners?" Emerald yanked the carrots from my hand chomping and chewing, spraying orange shreds of carrots all over me.

"Anybody scoop the poop out of this massive kitty litter pan of yours?" Why I asked the horse questions? No clue. "You're not much help. You need water. You got stuff…oh yuck. What did ya do? Sneeze in here?"

Toby, another dead beat helper, planted himself in an empty stall across from Emerald's. He took to rolling in the saw dust bedding. "Ok chick, let's see what's on the next few pages. Great, halter, lead rope, saddle, pad, aka horse blanket, bit, rein. A girth. What in the world? Oh look Emerald, it goes under your tummy to tie the saddle to." Once again I held the sheet of printed information up to her. "See, just Google horse care. And look at all I've taught you. Oh yeah. You're all girl. Look at the hardware and accessories you've got. You need a bow in your hair too."

Emerald brushed her head up against my shoulder. A giggle shot from me. Where did that come from? Another one slipped out. "I guess you're not so bad. Don't tell Nic we had a play date. I think you're the only one who won't tell on me."

"We got some basic stuff out of the way. I'm going to have to give in and ask him for help. This whole saddle, bridle, girth, all your lady stuff here, I don't get. Let's check out that brushing thing again." I flipped back to the beginning of my package. "Crap I have to come in there with you." I frowned, hanging my head to my chest, nothing like sucking the air out of your own sail. My biggest fear, being in the stall with the horse.

Immediately, Emerald nudged me with her head. Then nibbled at my arm that held the brush. Instead of opening the half gate and letting myself in with her, I crawled up on her saddle stand, sitting sideways. She made a funny snicker sound at me, showing her teeth in disapproval that I moved so far away from her.

"You want me to come back over? I had more fun riding Nic, then sitting in this saddle of yours. Kind of stiff. No motion." Emerald's personality matched mine, we're both moody females. As if someone flipped a switch my hormonal rage surged. The weakness kicked in. I was so home sick for my family and the lights of a big city.

"Emerald, I'm a real failure. Your boyfriend, you know him, my husband. It's been a nightmare the last few days. Barely even talking since dumb ass here took off with my bra." Like an old school teacher I shook my finger at Toby. "I told him I wanted to go home."

The horse stretched her neck out waiting for my hands to wrap around her. "I'm not cut out for here, Emerald. I'm a chef, for crying out loud. Not a ranch hand. I design and create with food.

I used to be a chef." I frowned at Emerald. "Look you've adapted to your new home, why can't I?" My hand slowly glided up and down Emerald's velvet nose. "Can ya see if I do go back to Cleveland? Butt wipe of a brother will be rubbing my nose in the 'I told ya so' every chance he gets. That would be a living hell. Lived through it before. But if I do stay, I'm nothing more than the laughing stock of the barn yard. Even caught some of the guys making bets on me. How's that for more humiliation? Think Nic would be better off without me." Emerald Bay nudged closer letting me pet her ears and neck as my tears slipped down between our heads.

"Aubrey." Bones' gravely voice extinguished our private moment. "Nic would be one miserable man if you left."

"How long have you been spying on us?" Emerald trotted back into her stall as annoyed as me by the interruption of Bones.

"Came in to get one of the horses. Ya dropped this." He handed me back page eight of my classroom training packet. "Didn't mean to listen in."

"Perfect. Just perfect." Sarcasm, I spit it out well. "You're Nic's right hand man. Suppose you're going to call 'em up and tell on me. Just like everyone else." I glared Bones down, swiping the paper from his hand without a thank you.

"I'll have a talk with the men taking bets on ya. Don't approve of that kind of behavior." Bones, his lips twisted in and out like he wanted to say more to me. "You fixin' to brush this horse or not?" He asked instead.

"Page two has a step by step grooming list." I held the paper up for Bones to view. "I was trying to show Emerald that I'm not that stupid of a city girl."

He opened the gate to Emerald's stall. "Get on in here. I'll show ya what I know. Just for the record Aubrey, you're one brave woman for takin' on all this. Not many would've lasted this long. Don't think you're prissy, either."

"Thanks Bones." Emerald's tail swatted me for attention. "Wait, I need my notepad. I'm not going to remember it all."

Bones wasn't a man of many words, but his talent with horses didn't need words. "Surprised ya didn't ask June El for help." Bones tried a little conversation on me.

"When you're the laugh of the barn yard, I just started staying away from everyone." I gently brushed out Emerald's long tail. "I don't know why I'm doing this. It's not going to get me anywhere."

"Aubrey, you're far from stupid. Look what you've done here. Ya used cyber space to your advantage. Ya came out on your own determined to make it work." Bones smiled. "What else's troubling ya?"

My hand stopped in mid brush. A little shocked by Bones compliment and he wanted to know what was troubling me. "I'm sure you heard. Seems no one can have privacy around here." I picked up the softer brush working it over the horses back in the manner Bones instructed. "I made the mistake of telling Nic, I wanted to go home. Meaning Cleveland."

"Yep, heard about that. Nic, he's a control type person. Can't control you, that's for sure. Boy's met his match with you." Bones grinned at me then spit his tobacco juice to the corner of the stall. "Don't know the rest. Takes a lot to get under Nic's skin. You must have nailed his rotten hide to the wall on something." Bones handed me a different brush, showing me how to circle over Emerald's coat. "Figure if ya planned to leave, ya won't be taken the time to get to know Emerald here. You know how to braid hair?"

"Yes. Why?" Intrigued, I asked as Bones moved his round body to Emerald's back side.

"Nice job on brushing her tail out. Show ya how to braid it down." Bones' pudgy fingers threaded over the hair, separating and twisting it perfectly.

"Where did you learn how to braid hair like that?" Speechless, Bones left me amazed at how his hands worked so freely through the length of the horse's coarse hair.

"Raised four girls of my own. Me and the Mrs." A robust smile filled in over his rosy cheeks. You'd swear Santa Claus was standing there in jeans, a flannel, and work boots.

"You've got four girls?" I gasped smiling back at him.

"They're all over the states now. Went off to college. Never came back here. After our last girl went off to college, the wife wanted ta move ta town. Didn't want ta stay out here anymore. Believe you can see why." Bones glanced up to me, no need to answer there. "She lives with her sister in town. I get, what is it those young people call it?" Bones racked his brains for the right words. "You know when ya make a visit. What did my girls call that?"

"A booty call." I cracked up laughing.

"Yeah that's it. A booty call. It works for us." Bones out laughed me. "Kind of fun. Like we're dating again. She does her thing. I do mine. We meet in the middle."

"Bones, that's a riot." Fat chance. Who would've thought that Bones and I would actually have a bonding moment?

"Yep, me and the Mrs. been married over forty some years. Just think things over. All I'm sayin'. Come on; let's put her out to pasture."

Bones slipped the halter over her long muzzle, giving direction on how to properly fit Emerald with girly accessories as I liked to call them. We walked her out to the open pasture were Emerald could stretch her long legs and graze all afternoon.

"Ya did a good job, Aubrey. Think Nic would be impressed with what ya tried here. Ya going to tell him?"

"No. And don't you either." I shook my head as we walked back through the empty barn.

"Aubrey, I'm not one for all this mushy stuff. Just sayin' when you came up to Nic in that little bar, ya changed his whole world."

"Really? Don't think I've ever made that kind of an impression on anyone."

"Well, ya did. Never seen that man fall like that." Bones grinned and shoved a wad of chew into his mouth.

"Thanks, Bones. For all of this." Like hugging a big ole stuffed teddy bear, Bones he's not one much for any physical contact, but he accepted my hug.

"Got time for one more question?" I asked, watching his wad of black slime form in his jaw.

"What's that?" We stopped by Emerald's stall.

"To me, this looks like a giant size kitty litter pan. How do I clean it?"

"Ya don't. That's Jimmy's job. He'll be round here pretty soon." Bones chuckled.

I could only image what was running through the jelly bellied man's mind. I crawled back up on Emerald's saddle. Thing was stiffer than a board. Don't know how Nic thought I was going to ride on something so uncomfortable. I skimmed over the pages of notes I took while Bones coached me. Sorting and resorting. I had to keep my horse care training class organized. Next question of the day, would I tell Nic what I was up to? Guess it depends on the mood he finds me in when he gets back.

Chapter 30

Betty Davis Eyes

"Left ya some bacon, honey. Ya need to eat, girly." Dad buttoned up his heavier fleece jacket. "Feelin' any better?"

"No. Not really, Dad. Nic made sure he was out of the bed before I woke." I crunched on the crisp bacon.

"Ya try say'n anything to him?" He plucked gloves from the coat pocket.

"Dad, he told me to pack." Why did I always have to cry?

"Don't see no bags packed, now do I, girly?" Charlie grinned. "It'll blow over, honey. Always will."

What did Charlie know that I didn't? Never took sides, a well preserved, patient man who wasn't afraid to stick his nose into our business.

"You make sure ya eat something. Not just that cookie and coffee stuff I've seen ya do." Charlie waved a gloved finger at me heading out to master his daily chore list.

"Stop following me. You caused this mess." I scolded Toby for just being Toby. Funny how Nic's damn animal traipses after me instead of him. I dumped Toby out the back door whether he wanted out or not. The chill in the air matched the mood I sported, bitter cold. From the screen door window I watched Nic working on a tractor with his dad. Again, a wave of the all girly mushy stuff hit, I didn't want to leave.

"Damn this crying," my sweatshirt cushioned the swipe of tears.

Why was it so hard for me to adjust to this life style? Silly question to be asking one's self, I'm from the city. Nothing or no one could have ever prepared me for this culture shock. I closed the door behind me in search of another piece of bacon. Home grown piggy did taste sweet. I licked the grease off my fingers on my way for that morning wake up cup of coffee when the phone rang.

"Gina." I love caller I.D. "How are you?"

"You tell me? What the hell? He's kicking you out? I'm flying out now to string up those stud muffin balls of his till he apologizes to you." All that in one breath shouted over the phone line.

"Glad to see Allison passed my love along." My coffee cup and I planted ourselves at the island. "I don't know what I want to do."

"Stand up to him. Call his bluff. Don't you dare give in to sex. They think if they get a piece of ass, problem solved." Good advice from a woman who knows the ropes.

"Gina, we're barely even speaking." I slumped in my chair. "He was out of bed before I even opened one eye this morning. You'll love this one; I threw a bar of soap at him after he called me a prissy ass chef and told me to pack."

A spree of giggles flooded over the phone line, "Did ya hit him?"

"No. I don't even think he heard it hit the wall, he was stomping down the steps so hard."

"First thing, sleep in another bed. It'll piss him off. Get a note pad you'll forget all this by the time we hang up." Gina ordered while continuing her rant on Nic.

"All sex, completely and I mean even a kiss, boob rub, smack on the ass, it all stops."

I giggled, "Gina I woke up through the night to find his arm around me and Mr. Perfect sleeping on his shoulder."

"Good for the cat. Now pay attention. I'm telling you. Get him by the balls. Yank till he drops to his knees." Gina's rave marched on.

"Gina. Nic isn't like one of your boy toys you tame, then you parade them around on a leash." I sipped my coffee trying not to laugh.

"Oh, my gosh, Aubrey, haven't I taught you anything?' She barked back into my ear.

The door alarmed me with a creaky crack as to whomever was entering my haven of a kitchen. Toby brushed past me, sitting by the treat bucket, hoping I'd give him a treat for being in my way. Then Nic's rugged body filled the doorway.

"Gina, honey I'll call ya a little later."

"Why? He's there isn't he? Put that rotten bastard on the phone." She screamed in the receiver, practically killing my ear drum.

"I love you too. Call ya later." I hung up the phone, kind of hoping Nic heard Gina's viscous attack.

"Gina?" He snorted walking past me to the fresh dripping coffee pot.

"Yes."

"Day light back there. Little early for her to be up and on the prowl?" Nic backed himself against the kitchen sink. "What'd she want?"

"You're a little snappy this morning." I glared over my coffee cup at him. "She told me to cut your balls off."

I swallowed my gulp of coffee with the air of confidence, while Nic nearly spit his.

"She what? Some friend ya got there woman." He snickered knowing how I hated it when he called me 'woman'.

"Did you come in for a reason?" I didn't really want to hear what I thought it would be. "Or are you just back to try and make me feel worse than I already do?"

Nic poured himself another cup of coffee, then smugly walked over to refill my cup. He cocked his head to the one side, almost ready to tear into me by the scrutinizing look in his eye.

"What'd you throw at me the other day?" He shifted his weight leaning back on the sink again, relaxing a little too much.

My confidence slipped, but I squared my shoulders, sitting myself tall in the chair.

"You're lucky I've got good aim. The bar of soup hit the door instead of the back of your head." I glared back, arching an eyebrow, not moving an inch from my pedestal seat at the island.

His eyes brightened, amused by my awful aim. I waited for Nic to ask me the dreaded question, if I planned on returning to Cleveland. "Ow. Toby. Stop it." The over-grown fur bag pushed on my legs. Poor pitiful dog. All he wanted was for me to pet him. His howl reminded me of nails down a chalkboard.

"I hate your mutt." The venom rolled from my lips.

"Yeah, well I guess ya won't be missing him much when ya move back home." Nic hammered the word home back in my direction.

I jolted as if he slapped me up along side the head, "You really want me to leave?" Instantly my eyes drained huge droplets of tears, splashing on the granite countertop.

"Geez, god, no, Aubrey. Stop with the tears." Nic hissed facing me from the opposite side of the island. "No, I don't want you to go. It's up to you. No, just…" The tone of his voice softened, "Here." He slid a box of tissues over to me. "Just don't be rushin' out the door. Think about it. I don't…I don't want you to go."

"Why is your coat getting all wet?" I wiped my eyes, not sure if I really saw the wet mark appearing on Nic's jacket.

"Damn cat." The zipper on Nic's coat flew open, revealing a long haired kitten. The little mess couldn't have been more than six months old.

"She's a misfit. Been beat on pretty bad by the other cats. They won't accept her. Found her hiding in Emerald's stall shaking worse than a leaf." A small meow squeaked from the little hairball. "Check this out." Nic held her little leg out for me to see. "Only has three toes on her right front paw and look at these eyes." He shoved the cat across the counter at me still miffed about the wet spot on his coat.

This little bundle of fur became an instant tear stopper. Once again Nic knew how to change a very touchy subject.

"She has Betty Davis eyes." I scooped her up. "Look at this hair. You're a prissy girl aren't you?" I smirked at Nic. Another feline relaxed some of the tension in the air between us. "Drop your jacket in the laundry room. I'll run it through the wash later."

"So can you love a misfit?" Nic's voice hinged on a hidden meaning as he shrugged out of the peed on jacket.

"Can you love one back?" I curled little Betty Davis under my chin still nursing my bruised ego.

Chapter 31

She's Gone

"Dad, you seen Aubrey?" A hidden concern hinged in Nic's voice as he bounded down the staircase. "She's not upstairs."

"Saw her leaving early this morning. She didn't say anything to ya?" Charlie wiped a hand over his jaw, flushed with a sudden worry. "Not like her not to say something. Town. Bet she went to town. Saw her list on the table." He paused, taking a deep breath. "Startin' to snow out there, too.

"Should've been back by now, don't ya think?" Nic glanced at his watch, not wanting to alarm his dad. "Sure Aubrey remembers how to drive in snow. Guess Ohio can get some flakes."

"You show her how to kick the truck into four wheel?" Charlie drew the curtain back from the kitchen window watching the drifting flakes.

"Not yet." Nic hesitated.

"Polly. Let me ring up Polly. Ya know Aubrey and her hit it off real nice. Maybe she's there." Charlie waited for Polly to answer, still watching the scattered flakes of snow.

Nic raided the refrigerator looking for leftovers. Cold dish of pasta in hand, he could hear Aubrey's voice of reminder, 'Heat that up. Tastes better warm.' Slowly, he finally realized how much he'd become so dependent on his new wife. The intensity swelled around him as he listened in on his dad's conversation with Polly. Aubrey had to be there. Where else would she have gone? Nic tried to ignore the obvious. Did she really leave him?

"Let me guess, Aubrey's there makin' damn fancy cupcakes with Polly and didn't hear her phone." Nic spouted off as Charlie hung up.

"Polly hasn't seen her, son." Charlie pulled a fork from the drawer, eating the cold, day old ravioli dish with his son.

"Mimi. Bet she met her someplace in town for lunch." Nic couldn't hide his worry from his dad. "I'll try her number."

"Son, Mimi's home. Got that bad cold." Charlie let a distraught sigh fill the worry between them. He didn't want to ask, but he did. "Nic, ya don't think she left, do ya?" Charlie's dark eyes clouded with concern for his new daughter-in-law.

"No." Nic shook his head. "All her stuff's here. She won't just up and leave. Not without a fight." He pulled out his cell phone and dialed Aubrey's number again. "Aubrey, will ya pick up the damn phone. Been try'n to reach ya. Where are ya, woman?" Nic shoved the phone in his back pocket while his dad reheated the pasta dish.

"She's right. This is much better next day. Better yet, when it's warm." Charlie stood in front of the microwave. "No answer yet?"

"Naw. Just dumped into her voice mail." Nic impatiently tapped his fork on the granite countertop. "She won't up and leave. Woman's got too much damn spirit in her." Subconsciously, Nic stroked the back of Mr. Perfect's fur coat. "Aubrey wouldn't leave without this fur bag, that's for sure."

"Hoped you two would've patched things up a little." Dad added, sitting the dish between them on the counter.

"Thought we did. She loved the kitty. Hasn't said much to me the last couple days though." Mr. Perfect batted at Nic's hand for another petting. "Aubrey's been ending her phone calls as soon as I walk in the room. I know she's talkin' to one of three. Hope to hell it's not Gina."

"Why?" Charlie asked through a mouthful of pasta.

"She'd be the one to fill Aubrey's head with crap. That woman had the nerve to tell her to cut my balls off."

"A little harsh." Charlie cringed sliding his hand over the private area tucked away in his jeans. "Now that one. Gina. She's a spiteful woman. I know she's Aubrey's best friend, but she's trouble for you two." Charlie chewed on the pasta shaking his head slowly.

"You think Gina would try to convince her to go home?" Worried, Nic asked his dad.

"Won't put it past her. My money's on Aubrey. She'll get it worked out." Charlie grinned at Nic. "Maybe she just needs to, ya know, clear her head so she can think straight. You got her all upset."

"Ya don't need to remind me dad." Nic stabbed an innocent ravioli with his fork. "Left her about ten messages. She won't pick up. Probably went shopping." Nic picked up the cat, "Where'd she go Fuzz Nuts? You know all her secrets? Maybe I should go lookin' for her. It's getting late. She doesn't know the roads. Snow's startin' to stick, too."

"Here, I'll try her cell. If she don't want to talk to you, maybe she'll talk to me." Charlie dialed Aubrey's cell number only to be immediately switched into her voice mail. "You pressin' her about this stayin' or leavin' thing? Did ya ask her ta stay or did ya fly off the handle at her again?" Charlie folded his aging arms over his chest, testing his son's temper.

"No. No. Before I gave her the cat, we talked, some. Told her I didn't want her to go. I asked her to think about it. Be really sure of what she wants. Cat's the only thing that's made her smile in days." Nic knew his temper took a toll on his wife's emotions. "I'm going to head to town. See if I can find her." He went for the keys to his truck.

"Hold on son. Don't be going off half cocked. She'll call when she's ready to. Wasn't too pretty of a fight ya had with her. Ya crushed her heart. Just let her sort things out in her head." Charlie put his arm around his son's shoulder. "I'd say your wife is just plain outright homesick. Remember she left her life ta join yours. Not an easy thing ta do for a city girl, son. She'll call. When she's ready, Nic."

"Homesick? I'm sure she is." Nic scratched his head looking at his dad for further help. "Guess she wasn't prepared for what life on a ranch is like."

Charlie pulled a chair out at the breakfast nook. "Why don't ya sit down for a moment with me? Got a story about your mama and me. Just might make ya feel better."

Nic turned the chair around sitting on it backwards. "You and Mom had a great marriage."

Charlie laughed, "Not always." He chuckled reminding himself of their rocky beginning. "Your mama was a townie girl. Pretty dresses. Silk hose. Never canned a vegetable in her life. How you call Aubrey prissy. That was your mama too. Just down right a beautiful woman." Charlie flushed with a glow remembering his late wife. "Anyways, when we got married I moved her out here. Your mama wasn't about to have no part of a house that didn't have indoor plumbing, or running water. Didn't even have a phone line. She stuck it out a week. Poor woman. She was miserable. Packed her bags, took the truck, and dove back to stay with her parents. Left me the sorriest note. Told me she loved me. If I wanted her to live here, I'd better do something about this house or she wasn't coming back." Charlie caught sight of the photograph that Aubrey had put up of Ruthie bringing an instant smile to his face.

"Mom left you after one week?" A wave of disbelief crossed Nic's face. "Hell, Aubrey's damn near made it two months."

"That's what I'm sayin' Nic. Look at the damndest things that happened to her. We all expected something from her. Not thinkin' that she grew up in city life. We all expected Aubrey to be a farm girl right off. You pushin' that horse on her. Hives for rollin' around with you in the hay. Can't forget the way she looked after ya greased her." Charlie's smiled faded quickly. "Your little night playin' poker." Charlie's voice went stern. "Got yourself so stinkin' drunk leaving me to pull ya off her. What the hell where you thinkin' boy?" Charlie chastised Nic for his drunken behavior again. "Taught you better than that. Thought for sure she'd leave you after that." He exhaled a long breath, "Woman loves you. Ya fool."

"Dad. I know. I know. I've begged her to forgive me. Promised her. She could've left then. But she didn't." Nic rubbed a hand over his forehead scarcely remembering how he had his wife pinned to the wall before his own father pulled him off.

"You're lucky my boy. Damn lucky." Charlie passed a silent warning to his son again. "But this last one with the dog, Nic, it just sent the poor woman over the edge."

"Yeah, that. She's right. No matter where she is or what she's doing, someone has to tell me. I'm surprised she didn't flip out when Ole Moe busted us in the barn."

"Your mama would be so damn mad when that old coot stuck his nose in." Charlie chuckled.

"Toby." Nic scratched the big old dog's ears. "Come on Dad, you've got to admit, it was as funny as hell. Big ole mutt running off with a bra." Nic erupted with laughter.

"Yep. It was pretty damn funny. But it humiliated your wife."

"You caused this." Nic tamed his smile petting Toby, "Wish she'd just call."

Nic's elbow knocked a file folder off the corner of the table scattering the paperwork over the floor. "Dad. Take a look at this." He held up Aubrey's 'Horse Care 101' notes. "I'll be damned. Aubrey goggled how to care for Emerald." Nic handed his dad some of the papers with his mouth hanging open.

"No wonder she's been so quiet. Tryin' to learn this stuff by herself." Charlie thumbed over the papers.

"Looks like she had herself a little help." Nic pointed to Aubrey's handwritten notes. "That won't be how June El would handle things."

"Only one man in this county who'd have that much patience when dealing with the female kind." Charlie noted.

"Bones?" Nic asked. "Bones has been helping Aubrey with the horse."

"Damn straight I have," came the gravely voice of Bones standing in the shadows behind them. He crossed the kitchen pulling another chair out, joining the waiting party. "She ain't back, is she? Ya better not run my best student off. Ya dumb ass."

"Why didn't ya say something to me?" Nic asked pissed off, but still surprised.

"Why should I?" Bones cracked the top on his beer. "Woman ain't got no privacy around here. Everyone runin' and tell ya what she's doin'. Did you know some of the boys were taken bets on how long she'd stay with ya?

"What the hell? Who?" Nic's temper flared.

"Settle yourself down. Handled it." Bones took a long gulp of his cool beer. "She asked me not to tell ya. Found her out there accidently. She dropped a page from her notes. Let me tell ya. Not only can your wife cook, she's damn good with that horse. Best learner I've taught since my girls."

"She went to you for help and not me." Nic's pride just took a hard punching hit.

"Aubrey didn't come to me. Found her out there cryin' with Emerald's head draped over her shoulder. Damn pathetic sight. Offered her some help. Seeing you're too busy lickin' your wounds."

"Damn it Bones…" Nic never completed his sentence. The hard hitting steps from his boots laid into the slate as he walked towards the backdoor. "Dad, if she calls…"

"You'll be the first one to know, son." Charlie watched helplessly as his son's pride withered in the late afternoon snow flurries.

Chapter 32

We Play For Keeps

My bag of chocolates flew half way over the overgrown truck as I ripped into them. "Damn. I hate these bags." Still miffed, I collected the flying candy. "I hate this truck, too. My Escape. I want my Escape back. Now." I mouthed off to no one but me, knowing full well that I gave my Escape to Allison. "Target. I want to go to Target, you stupid machine." One more time I reentered the address of Target into the GPS while sitting in the Super Wal's parking lot, pouting.

Cat shopping. One cat bed, a cat condo, cat food, and cat litter. You name it. I bought anything that said cat on it for Mr. Perfect and Betty Davis. My day out for shopping, wish Allison or Gina could be here with me. My thick depression of homesickness had me slumped over the steering wheel in tears. I felt so tiny sitting in the huge leather seats of the truck, missing my family. My family, even my brother. Talk about feeling alone and in the dumps. My hand dug deeper into the bag of chocolate searching for instant relief. Again, my phone buzzed inside my purse. I knew who they'd be from, but I looked anyway. Nine phone calls from Nic and three from Dad. I suppose I should call them back. Naw, I'm not done being pissed, hurt, sad, lonely, how about all of the above. Besides, I'd just start crying when Nic would answer.

"Proceed to nearest route." The GPS unit was up and waiting to escort me to my next shopping destination.

"Target, here I come." Candy bar in one hand. Coffee cooling in the cup holder, I proceed to my next shopping spree.

Shopping, charging, sucking down candy bar after candy bar, I was on a roll with one heck of a sugar rush. Target, the GPS calculated it's only a forty five minute drive by highway. I pointed the truck in the direction that was given and planned on spending till my heart stopped aching. Driving can cause thinking. Thinking can cause me to be reasonable. Great, I was reasoning with myself. I didn't want to go back to the ranch, but I didn't want to leave Nic. I really wanted to hop a plane to Cleveland. I really wanted to see if Nic was a man of his word, 'drag my ass back to ranch land.' In a way, I hoped he would, if I was stupid enough to do that. A quick stop at the Get Up and Go Truck Stop for a super large coffee, a refill on candy, and of course a refill for the gas tank. I couldn't believe how this hog of a truck sucked the gas down. My cell rang again. Nope, wasn't picking it up, I didn't even take it out of my purse.

"Turn right onto Steeple Drive," the GPS announced.

"Oh yes, Target." I barely smiled or laughed since Nic and I knocked it out a few days ago. Even when he gave me Betty Davis, I still felt the emptiness. "At last, I'm here, my Target." My feel good place awaited me. I switched the phone to off. No ringing. No vibrating, nothing or no one was going to intrude on my little dance of happiness.

It was well after three when I piled all the bags in the cab of the truck. I re-plugged in my GPS. It was a nice gift from Nic, once I learned how to use it. Nearly two and a half hours of driving.

"Great, maybe I should just stop and get a room. Now wouldn't that be a pisser if I didn't show up tonight." My own cruel remark had me laughing. "Couldn't do that to Dad, but Nic…maybe."

The GPS waited for me to press the home button. "Home? Were was home?" The review mirror reflected the saddest eyes staring back at me. "I guess this is home. A ranch. Animals. People who, I think, care about me. Yeah, they do care." The reasonable me won the one sided conversation.

My daytime adventure ended in the parking lot of Target. I pressed the home button while scattered snow flakes drifted in the gloomy sky. Home was no longer in Cleveland. I grew up there. Had worked there, and lived there all my life until now. Home, home is with Nic here in Wyoming. I pulled out on the highway dialing his number. He answered on the first ring.

"Aubrey. Where the hell are you?" Scared, worried, and ticked off all rolled into one voice pierced my ear.

"Nic." The silent pause between us seemed like a light year. "I'm on my way home."

"Aubrey, tell me where you are. I'll come get you." Nic pleaded with me. "Whatever you do, don't get on that plane. Just wait for me there."

"Plane?" Static on the line hissed between us. "Nic, I, I went…" He cut me off before I could finish.

"Do not get on that plane. Aubrey please, I'm begging you…don't leave."

I could hear the click of his boots, pacing as he came unwound at hearing my voice.

"I'm not at the airport. I went shopping. All the way out here to Target." My voice cracked. I didn't want to start crying on him. "GPS says I should be home by six forty-eight."

"You went shopping? Why the hell didn't you tell me?" Agitation blew in his words while worrying about me got put on hold. "Aubrey, you scared the hell out of me. Dad said he saw you leave this morning. You didn't answer my calls. No note even. Ya got Dad all worked up." Nic's stressed voice told on him.

"Nic I had to….I needed to…" I whispered, not wanting to say I needed to clear my head, of him.

"Shop? Aubrey, ya could have called me to say you went shopping." Aggravation thickened deeper in Nic's voice now as his temper pended.

"Nic. Don't be…don't be giving me your shitty temper." I scolded right back.

"For Christ's sake woman, I thought you…" Nic stopped in midsentence.

"You thought I left you?" A stray tear rolled down my cheek.

"No," his voice stilled, temper tamed, and back in check. "Thought crossed my mind. Knew ya won't of left Fuzz Nuts here."

"Nic, you know I wouldn't leave without a fight." Another tear followed the first one.

"Aubrey, I wouldn't expect anything less from you." He sighed and I felt his relief over the phone. "I'll be waiting for ya. Probably going to call ya in a while, so answer."

"I will."

"Be careful. Roads could be getting slick with the snow. You're crying. Please stop crying, Aubrey."

"I'll be home soon." Home, that's what this entire fight had been over. "Nic…I really do love you."

"Aubrey." I loved the way he said my name, perfect smoothness. "Love ya too. Stop with the cryin', I'll be here. This will give ya something to chew on while ya drive."

"Chew on? I don't have anything but coffee. Chew on what?" Confused, I questioned.

"Think about it city girl. Think about it." Nic's laughter filled the phone line.

"Think about what? You didn't toss Mr. Perfect out?" I sniffled. "Nic?"

"No, I didn't throw your damn cat out." He laughed harder. "Polly called this morning lookin' for ya. Wants to talk to ya. Something about expanding the business. A lunch café. Said she needs a chef."

"Really? A café. She wants me to cook for her?" My excitement drowned out my loneliness.

"Yeah, a café. Said she wanted to call it 'Ruthie's' after mom. Ya got yourself a cookin' job if ya want it."

"That's wonderful. I, I don't know what to say. I mean yes, yes I want it."

"Tell ya more when ya get here. Just, next time ya want to disappear, tell someone. You've got Dad's blood pressure all up." Nic's way of dealing with stress, blame Dad.

Nic pocketed his cell phone walking towards the back steps, a mug of coffee in one hand, a cigar for relief in the other. Mr. Perfect, fluffed with attitude, blocked his path, glaring him down. With clear sky blue eyes, the cat conveyed his warning to Nic.

Come here Fuzz Nuts. You're lucky your mama's comin' home, or it would be the barnyard for you." Nic scratched the cat's ears, listening to the vibrating purrs.

Again, my phone sang a happy melody; another call from Nic came in.

"Still waiting for me?" This time I was happy to hear from him.

"Yep. So you do listen?"

"I told you'd I'd answer."

"Where ya at now?"

I liked his concern for me better than his ticked off mood.

"'Bout an hour away. Are you going to call me every five minutes?" I just had to ask.

"Yep. Get used to it."

"You're a hard one to get used to, Nic Ravenwood."

"That's what ya love about me. So tell me about these notes you left on the kitchen table." Cursorily, he changed the subject.

Caught cold, I choked on my reply, "Notes. Just, um, cooking notes. Why?" I knew what he'd found.

"Cyberspace. Impressive, Aubrey. Hear you're the best student ole Bones has had in a long time."

"I guess nothing is a secret around ranch town. Now is it?" My disappointment showed.

"Bones didn't sell ya out. I knocked the folder on the floor." Nic paused. "Why didn't ya ask me, Bre?"

"Ask you? You weren't exactly talking to me. Unless it was necessary." I reminded him. "Wanted to prove to ya that I'm not the stupid, prissy city girl your hired hands keep taking bets on."

"Heard about that too. Matter's been taken care of." Annoyed, Nic cleared his throat.

"You and Bones must have had a real nice chat about me." My blood started to boil. I think Nic's temper was wearing off on me.

"Yep. Me, Dad, and Bones. All sitting around the kitchen table worrin' about you."

"Well now, that should've been educational. Ya learn anything?" I snapped at him in defense.

"Yeah Bre, learned a lot tonight. I know one thing, you're one amazing woman."

Nic caught me off guard. I didn't expect praise from him. Not now. I thought we were headed for another round of unpleasant phone conversation.

"Aubrey, you still there?"

"Yeah, just surprised. Nic, I'm not fitting into your world very well." My tears fell at the appropriate time.

"Tissues are in the console between the seats." He offered. "You shake this place up. Won't have ya any other way, woman. You fit into my world just fine."

"Thanks. But, I just didn't think it'd be so hard for me." Now tissues were added to my pile of empty coffee cups and chocolate wrappers. "Ok, I just exited the highway. I'm back on the bumpy county roads."

"Good. I got to finish up here in the barn. Keep the phone on. I'll be callin' ya."

I lost count of how many times Nic had phoned me. I swear every time he stopped doing something animal related he dialed my number. I pieced together this image of Nic in my mind as I drove along. Nic chewing on the end of his cigar and shoveling cow shit. Not a pretty picture to visualize, but it did make me laugh.

The day's sunset long past and I didn't think the night sky could get so black so fast. For a long stretch I had the peaking mountain range to drive with. But it, too, was swallowed by the night. The snow steadily picked up and collected on the open fields.

The ringing of my phone didn't even startle me, "Hi Nic."

"Aubrey, I know you can drive in the snow. But it's a different kind of snow here in Wyoming."

"Really? Ya ever take a drive up 480 back in Cleveland in a snow storm?" I knew how to drive in snow.

"Aubrey, get serious." Guess I was a little too chirpy for him.

"Snow is snow, Nic. It's white. Collects on whatever it pleases and it's wet. Cold too."

"You know how to kick the truck into four wheel drive?" Nic ignored my sarcasm and tried to stump me.

"Honey, there's this knob, glowing in green, says 4x4."

"If the roads get bad, or too slippery for you, just switch it over. Real simple." His voice still rang with worry.

"Got it. You still in the barn?" I could hear the snorting of a horse in the background.

"Yep. Dad and Bones, they're gettin' on my nerves." His mood swung from worry to irritated.

"Oh. Hiding out?"

"Bre, you got everyone around here worried with this little stunt of yours."

"Little stunt? I don't need your permission to go shopping, Nic." For once I kept my nerve without tears. "Don't forget you're the one who told me to pack. Then not to pack. Wait, then pack, again."

"Aubrey, I don't want to fight with you. I'm sorry you're homesick. I get it." Nic's attitude changed drastically. "Just if ya feel like taking a little road trip, tell someone."

"Sorry. I just…I needed to clear my head. I don't know if you understand, but shopping, chocolate, it helps me think." I popped another bite of chocolate in my mouth. "I miss my family. Even my jackass brother."

"I know Bre, I know. How about I take a weekend off. Take ya back to Cleveland?"

"You'd really do that for me?" Nic's offer sweetened the moment.

"Good chance. Winter months are slow around here. What's that GPS tellin' ya?"

"I should be hitting Route 82 in about three miles."

"Be careful. It's not like driving in Ohio, Aubrey."

County Road 82 seemed endless to drive in the pitch blackness of night. The open land that traveled beside me was nothing but desolate, empty, and barren. Not even a sliver of a moon beam for a little guidance. Streetlights, another thing I missed about living in the city. Nic had called me three times reminding me to keep my wits about me. Oh ha ha. I didn't mention that I'm high on caffeine and sugar. Each phone call, he reminded me to keep my eyes open for roaming wildlife. Nothing like having a 'deer crossing' at any moment, add to that the possibility of a stray elk or two.

In the distance I could make out the huge 'Ravenwood Ranch' sign. I pulled into the driveway stopping in front of the sign, letting the headlights reflect off the wrought iron name.

"Wonder if they got the mail?" A slick cold slap in the face delivered by the wind hit me when I opened the truck door. "Nope. No one brave enough to come get it." I scooped up the mail and crawled back in the truck.

All I had to do is put the truck in drive and I'd be home. Instead, I sat there pretending to warm up from the blast of cold air. Not really, I guess I just wanted to ponder my thoughts a little longer.

"My name is Ravenwood. Ok, hyphenated Hunter-Ravenwood. I'm still one of them." I chewed on the edge of my empty coffee cup. I shifted the truck into drive and slowly drove up the lane, unsure of what I'd find waiting for me.

After I told Nic I was about fifteen minutes away, he stopped calling. It seemed we had talked every single 'Aubrey life upsetting' episode out over cell phones. The reassurance in his voice convinced me that once again I had made the right decision. A flickering bluish glow filled the living room window as I slowly drove by the front of the house. I'm sure Dad had his feet up, dog under them, cat curled into the crook of his arm, and a ballgame to watch. A little off my scheduled due in time, I parked the big ass truck around back next to the other ones. My sugar rush and caffeine buzz wore itself off about half hour ago. I was back to being me again and hoped there'd be no sugar rush withdrawal. Candy wrappers littered the floor boards and I gathered up all the empties, shoving them into my drained coffee cups before I started to unload my day of treasure hunting.

The backdoor squeaked in the cold night's air, I expected to see Nic.

"You're back," Charlie grabbed me into one of his almighty bear hugs. "Let me help ya with all those bags. Ya leave anything at the store?"

"Found ya a few of those nice quilted flannels you like, Dad." Charlie smiled at me, as if the day was only about shopping. "Got ya a new heating pad, too."

"Ya spoil me, girly. Glad you're home." He leaned over and kissed my cheek. "Good heavens, what did ya buy those animals this time? Dog treats? That ole mutt don't need no treats." Arms full of 'Target' bags Charlie muttered going in the house.

The illuminated lights on the outskirts of the barnyard showed no other shadows of humans lurking around. Slightly miffed Nic wasn't here to meet me I went back to cleaning all my candy wrappers off the floor. I kept stuffing wrapper after wrapper in my empty coffee cup.

"Aubrey." Nic's voice in the dark startled me and I dropped the evidence I tried to hide from him.

His image appeared in the blackness. The reddish orange glow from his lit cigar left his lips to hang between his fingers. With the dim light from the truck cap I could see him a little clearer as he stopped at the end of the truck bed.

"Hi." I stood there shivering in the frigid night air, wishing I had grabbed a heavier coat. "Have you been out here waiting on me all this time?"

"Yeah." He tossed the end of the cigar butt down, the heel of his boot grinding it into the cold earth. "Checked the horses."

"Nic....I'm"

"Aubrey, I meant what I said before. I'd drag your ass back here, if ya left me."

"Nic. I'm not some piece of property. And I'm definitely not some branded livestock you own. I'm me."

He chuckled out loud, "Bre, that's why I love you. If you left me, I'd find anyway possible to win your heart back."

"You really thought I left you?" My hand reached for the side of the truck to help steady me from the emotional impact.

"For a minute." He stepped closer to me. "Didn't think ya'd just hop a plane and go."

"I...I had to clear my head. Needed room to think. I didn't mean to scare you." A single tear just had to reflect off the light from the cab.

"You did." He took another step, but stopped short of me. "Don't like not bein' able to talk to you. Findin' out what's makin' you tick."

"Your temper scares me. That's why I stopped talking. Kept it all to me." Close enough for me to see the lines creased in his eyes with worry, Nic drew me into his arms.

"Figured ya won't leave that damn nut less animal with me."

"Dad won't let you hurt Mr. Perfect." Lightheartedly, I joked.

Nic whisked away my stray tears. His thumb rough, skin cracked and dry, I didn't care. His body rock hard under all that flannel. I cradled myself into his hug never wanting to let go.

"You've been chain smoking. Haven't you?" Cigar smoke lingered in his hair, embedded thick in his clothes.

"I believe I told you once woman, I'd be keepin' ya forever. No matter what happens, you're mine." Nic's lips softly pressed on mine. His fingers slipped under my sweater and rubbed the small of my back. The evening coyote sang his song, as I took a deeper kiss from Nic.

"Next time ya need a shopping spree," he glanced at the front seat of the truck rolling his eyes, "Would ya at least tell me, Aubrey. Tell someone."

The End

SUMMER 2013

LOVE ON THE RANCH

The Sequel to The Rancher's Wife

Chapter One,
Nerves That Aren't Made of Steel

A battered piece of paper caught my eye on the countertop. Nic's chicken scratch handwriting scrawled over the crumpled note in thick black ink. Edged deeply with his annoyance, the plain sheet of paper took his beating. I could tell, even before I read the damaged note, that something or someone ticked him off, royally. Gently, my hands smoothed over the wrinkled edges as I read the note. Then again. And again. After, I think the fourth time of reading the black inked words began to sink in. Not even pushing the chair back to sit down, I squeezed my body into the seat. Message in hand, I reread the tattered note Nic left for me.

"Ya goin' to call that rat bastard back?" Startled by Nic, he popped the top off a beer bottle and sat down next to me. "Your mind go blank readin' those few words?"

"No. Just shocked." Puzzled, annoyed, and still in disbelief, I took a swig of Nic's beer. "Why did he call?"

"Just said he wanted to talk to ya."

"Why?"

"Bre, my crystal ball," Nic's hand circled around an unexciting globe, "ain't workin' on that whack jobs mind." He retrieved his beer back from my hands chuckling.

"But you talked to him." I rolled my eyes over to meet Nic's sarcastic grin, "He didn't tell you what he wanted? Money? Did he ask for money?"

"Nope." A loud wet burp left his lips. "Why don't ya call? Find out what the hell he wants."

The cracking of thunder couldn't have sat me this straight in my chair. My head turned like an ordered robot as I stared Nic in the eyes. "Holy shit. I'd lay money on it. I'll even bet you." My painted chipped nails sank deeply into Nic's plaid covered arm. "Phil. He's on his way here for the holidays."

"Bre. Nails." Nic pried each of my fingers from his arm laughing. "Take ya up on this little gamble of yours. You're goin' to loose to me, woman." His eyebrow perked in a way I knew too well. "No way would brother, Phil, spend the money to come out here. He won't step foot on this ranch."

"I'll take you up on the bet mister. Terms of the gamble?" Betting had gotten to be a fun habit for us.

"Anyway I want it. Where I want it." Nic's description of 'want' meant only one thing…sex. "You?"

"Full body massage. Feet included." I grinned like the cat, "Plus, no sex involved."

"Hard bargain there woman. You'll be beggin' me ta please ya." Nic, always so sure of himself. "You know I'm going to win."

"Don't be so sure. Grams and Allison are coming for Thanksgiving. Plus Christmas. And Gina, she'll be here in time for New Year's Eve. You don't have a prayer."

"So pecker head is goin' to be alone for the holidays." Another gulp of beer slid down his throat. "Ya really think he'll be runnin' out here to be with his kid sisters?" Nic's hand squeezed my kneecap. "Jumpy there, woman?"

I slapped at his hand for pinching my knee so hard. "You'd be jumpy too if you had a brother like mine." Sheer panic kicked in at the thought that Phil could possibly be coming to Wyoming. "No. No. No. Crap, I don't even want to think about it."

"You're over playin' it Bre. Got yourself all uptight for no good reason." Again the squeeze to the kneecap. "Think about it. Cost of flying. Phil won't pay out that kind of money." Nic did make a good argument.

"Point taken. But still, I'm telling you. He'll be here. Christmas for sure." The panic already started to teeter in my mind.

"You'll be payin' me come January first. Gets cold outside, baby."

"Outside? You're crazy." Sex on a snow drift just won't be happening. The wall phone rang out a friendly chime terrorizing me even more. "I'm not getting that." I shouted at the phone.

"Chicken shit of a woman." Nic slid his beer in front of me as he went to answer the ringing terror.

Sheer displeasure smeared over his unshaven face. Nic really did wear a five o'clock shadow with appeal. Nervously, I watched him handle the unknown caller. My mind raced with agony. I just couldn't imagine spending my first Christmas with Nic and my brother. Like firecrackers popping on the fourth of July, my mind went up in flames. Phil. His holiness. All high and mighty. He'd display his commanding performance around the Christmas tree. My Christmas tree. My head hit the top of the granite island with a thump loud enough to turn Nic's head.

"Oh, that hurt." Propped on my elbows, I rubbed at the forming knot on my forehead.

"Bre. What the hell, woman?" Nic interrupted his conversation to scold with no sympathy.

"Who is it?" I mouthed with no voice. "Please don't let it be Phil."

Nic shook his head at me while I applied his ice cold beer bottle to my damaged skin. Life had been so happy. No Phil. No drama. Just my own drama that created around me. I'm sure Nic was right. I'm just over playing the whole subject of Phil coming to terrorize the holidays.

"Yeah, Phil. She's sitin' right here. Havin' a beer with me." Nic could only mouth 'sorry' as he motioned for me to come take the phone.

"No." I whispered back, not budging from my chair. "No." Slowly, with dragging feet I made my way over to Nic and the dangling phone in his hand. Eye to eye with him, again I whispered, "I'd rather ride the horse than talk to him."

One angry swipe and I had the phone in hand, with Nic's freehand swatting my back side for the sheer joy of aggravating me even more.

"Be taken ya up on that woman." Another smirk and he, with beer in hand, left for the living room.

Deep breathe in. Deep breathe out. In all seriousness, I'm sure Emerald would be easier to learn to ride than having a conversation with my brother.

"Phil." Surprise contained, I gave it my best shot for a hopefully pleasant conversation. "How's it going back there in Ohio?"

"Aubrey. What took ya so long to get to the phone? Damn savage got his hands all over you?"

"Well, yes." I paused not giving him time to answer. "Phil, it's so good to see your pleasant side is preceding you. What do you want?"

"What makes you think I always want something, Aubrey? Can't I just call to talk to you?"

"Phil, this is the first time you've called me. If you remember, I called you to say I got here safely and I never heard from you. Until now."

"Yeah, well you know I've got a life. Don't have Dee and her baggage to kick around."

"Yep. I know. Dee's moved on." I felt the need to slam him back. "I hear from her more now than when you two were married."

"She calls you?" The shocked mode clouded Phil's mind.

"She calls. Mostly e-mails me. Seems she's doing great with her new career and all." I waited for another blow of nastiness from him, but nothing. Silence wasn't Phil's style. "You still there?"

"Yeah. Yeah I'm here."

"What did you need?" Same question, let's see if I get an answer.

"Take it that husband of yours gave you my message?"

"Yes. Found it laying here waiting for me when I got home. What did you need, Phil?"

"Just thinking. You know, thought maybe I'd come out over the holidays. Maybe spend sometime there over Christmas."

I slid down the wall shaking my head no. Glad to see my so called 'over doing it' really paid off. My butt hit the floor with a thud and Toby took that as an invite to sit on my lap.

"Toby, ya big lug." I squirmed under the weight of the flabby animal.

"Who's Toby?" Phil demanded.

"Nic's dog. I'm sitting here on the floor. Toby wants to play."

"You hate dogs." Phil reminded me.

"Toby isn't bad. You'd like him. So when are you coming out?"

"Oh, don't know. Just thinking about it. You know with this new job and all, I don't know if I can get off work. I'm in management. Got a crew under me. Really like the job."

"Great. Glad things are going well. Got a new woman, yet?" I snorted a little laugh.

"No." Phil's answer bit my head off. "No, I'm not seeing anyone. I'll let ya know if and when I'll be coming out there. I know Gram and Allison have you all booked up. Didn't think you'd have time for me, too."

"You can come out anytime and stay with us. I know Nic would love to have you." I let my voice reach Nic's ears. In retaliation the words 'bullshit' floated in a sloppy burp back to me.

"Yeah right. Well if I decide to come, I'll just let ya know."

"Sounds good, Phil. Get your airline tickets soon. You know, holiday time. They're more expensive. I'll even pick you up at the airport."

"Gee, thanks. Wouldn't want you to go out of your way for me."

"Sure, no problem. I'll send Nic if you prefer." I had to shove that at him.

"Well, I got to get going. Got work in the morning."

"Nice talking with you Phil." No goodbye. No nothing. Just a click and then the dial tone buzzing in my ear.

I sat on the kitchen floor letting the phone hum in my hand. Toby inched his massive flabby frame closer to me and licked my face. Kind of like to say "Ah, mom, I'm sorry." The dog did have potential with me. The clicking of boots drew my eyes to the man halted in the doorway. There I sat, with his dog, feeling defeated and the holidays weren't even here yet.

"Why do you let him get to you like that?"

"Some emotions just die hard." I offered up with a semi smile.

"So, when's pecker head gettin' here?" Without a command, Toby jumped to his feet and bounced over to Nic.

"Not sure." I pulled myself up from the floor and returned the humming phone to the wall. "Said he'd let me know. I offered you as taxi service. He can't wait to be picked up from the airport by you." My cheesy cat grin met his.

"Hell, I'd just send old Moe. Maybe Joe. Yeah, Joe." Nic shook his head, "No that would just be plain cruel ta any human."

"Well there went my little fantasy of the perfect first Christmas together. Yep, right out the window. Smashed into the bitter cold of night." My frown of disappointment wasn't missed by Nic.

"Like I told ya, Bre, you're goin' to loose the bet. He won't show. Money. If you're not payin' for him to come, he won't show." Very simple and plain as day in Nic's mind.

"Ha. Money." I threw my head back laughing at Nic. "Oh, he's management now, ya know? Got a crew under him." I mocked my brother's bragging words. "You'd go and fetch him for me wouldn't you?"

"You talkin' about a little bargaining here?" Nic wanted to negotiate another deal with me. "You'll be makin' that up to me how, woman?"

"Making what up?" I loved the roll of playing 'what' with him. "Don't you love your brother-in-law?"

"Nope. I don't." Nic reached for my hand. "Couldn't give a flyin' shit about him. Believe you owe me."

"Owe you for what?" This time he lost me as he pulled at my hand.

"Had ta deal with him on the phone."

"No, no, I'm the one stressing. You dumped him on me." He yanked harder on my hand pulling me towards the staircase.

"Fine. You win. Takin' your lily white ass up to the tub. Relieve that stress."

"Lead the way cowboy." For some odd reason, I loved the way Nic would take my hand and lead me around. Actually, I think I'd follow him just about anywhere, anytime, and possibly anyplace.

"Fill the tub, woman. Don't be puttin' that girly lavender stuff in the water either."

"Why? Guys pickin' on you for smelling too flowery?" His hand felt around my tummy, pulling at my jeans as I bent over the tub. "We need water if you're going to soak with me, mister."

Nic had himself striped down to nothing but a buffed tattooed body by the time I got turned around to face him.

"How do you do that so fast?" I yanked my own sweatshirt over my head and tossed it at him.

There was nothing neat about the way Nic undressed himself. Bathroom door wide open with his jeans and boots lying in the threshold. Who knows where his shirt ended up. Mr. Perfect wound in and around my neatly placed clothes purring as he rubbed Nic's leg. The bright lights of the bathroom seemed to accent Nic's tattoos. The urge of an instant pull on my fingers, I couldn't help myself. I had to touch his artwork. My finger tips seared over his warm hard body. First, I outlined the dragon, my favorite. Eyes of piercing red, orange flames breathed from its unruly mouth. Nic's eyes followed my fascination in amusement. One last sweep over the wings of the dragon, I let my fingers rest on his bare chest.

"Feel better?" The smirk on his face instantly pushed a rush of color over my cheeks.

"Candles?" I ignored my blush. The match burned with brightness as I lit the candle and Nic slipped into the hot water.

"Holy hell, woman. How do you stand this water so hot?"

"You're such a pansy." On the edge of the vanity, the glow of a single candle filled the bathroom.

Water slipped and slopped over the rim of the tub as I settled my body in between Nic's legs. Toby's large head plopped up on the edge of the tub, hoping for an invite to our private splash party.

"Go lay down, boy. Momma's all mine." A whimper from man's best friend, and Toby curled up on Nic's clothes in the doorway.

Soapy, callused hands rubbed with gentle circles over my shoulders. My fingers squeezed into his kneecaps propped beside me. "Oh," my moaning 'oh' signaled Nic's hands to roam freely. "Your hands are magic. Ah, please don't stop."

"Bre, you've got to give up trying to please your brother." Nic continued his soft pattern down my back. "Lean forward."

"I'm not trying to please him." I rested my chin on his knee. Arms wrapped around his thighs, I enjoyed the back rub. "Just clinging to the hope that maybe, possibly, we could have some kind of decent relationship. Everything with Phil, it's like in hidden code." Nic's hand rubbed down my spin and back up. "I really think he'll show. But it'll be unannounced."

Nic handed me a glass of wine. "Drink some. Help ta calm you. I see why you do this bath thing. Kind of like it myself."

"You feel good." Easily I rested my back against his chest. My fingers outlined the tattoos running down his arm. "Are you going to get anymore of these?"

"Love your little obsession, Bre. Love watchin' your eyes light up. Those long fingers tracin' over my skin." He slipped the empty wine glass from my hand.

"When you took your shirt off the first night we slept together, I couldn't take my eyes off of them. The color alone. To me, totally sexy."

"Let me see if I've got this straight. Ya like the smell of my cigars. Like playin' with my body."

"Artwork on your body." I blurted out, "And yes, your body too."

"Still can't believe ya married me in less than seven days. You're a breed all your own, Mrs. Ravenwood."

"That's what I like about you. Your strangeness suites me." I rolled to my side slopping water over the edge of the tub. My lips next to Nic's, I let my fingers play on all the tattoos covering his chest.

"How'd we get the house to ourselves?" Bathroom door still wide open just in case any of the other wildlife in the house cared to join us.

"Dad and Bones went ta town. Some movie Dad wanted to see. Think he's stayin' there with Bones and his wife tonight."

"Seems Dad and Gram have taken to e-mailing each other." I gave myself another self guided tour of Nic's chest. "He asked if we could get a webcam. Said he'd like to be able to see Gram when they chat."

"Ole man's got it bad for your Gram. Surprised he hasn't flown back to visit her." Nic slipped lower in the tub.

Water gushed and splashed as we slopped along trying to get comfortable in the old porcelain tub.

"Take this to dry ground?" Nic casually asked between our heated kisses.

"No. Not yet. Here, just a little longer." I used Nic's body like a surfboard, letting my breast slide up his chest. Lips locked tight I managed to crawl, swim my way on top of him.

"Goin' ta get yourself in trouble, woman." Nic's hands slid over my warm, silky wet skin.

"Hoping too." Fingernails tipped in carnation pink polish outlined his face.

Lost in the taste of his lustful kiss, we never noticed Toby's advances. Two extra large paws clawed at the side of the tub. The old dog's pathetic whine didn't even interrupt us.

"Get the hell out of here, Toby." Nic freed a hand from me to swat at the dog.

"Toby. No." My playful bath of two, turned into a threesome. Uninvited, he joined us anyway. "Get out of my tub." I shoved a half wet dog off my back and slid to Nic's side. Toby only sank down in the heat of the warm water. "Nic. Get your beast out of here."

"Damn it Toby." Nic's sopping wet hound replaced me on his chest. "Christ sake, get out."

On that note, I ended up being shoved to the foot of the tub while the wrestling match continued. My long legs dangled over the tubs rim as I pulled myself to semi-dry land.

"Give me his collar. You shove, I'll pull." Completely naked, pissed off at the intruder, I reached for Toby's collar. "Oh crap." As Nic shoved on Toby's big behind, my wet feet slipped on the drenched floor. Instead of pulling Toby, my bare feet skated right back to the tub. His claws dug deep into the old tub with the last hoist out. A howl of 'I don't want to get out' yelped from the dog. "Stop. Toby, stop." Another helpless shout from me as Toby shot between my legs. His great escape, knocked me right back in the tub on top of Nic. "Damn it, Toby." Nearly upside down, smack dab over Nic's shoulders, my legs waved like a flying flag in the air.

"I got ya. Just slide back." His fear of laughing at me, well, it didn't stop him. Firm hands gripped my hips in hopes to balance me.

I did as he suggested. Wet floor, wet dog, wet body, down I went. I thought this night couldn't get any worse as I sat bare ass naked on the cold wet tile. But luck wasn't on my side. Toby, being a dog, went into a wild 'let me shower you with wet love' shake. Water flung up the wall, over me, over Nic, and I swear it hit the ceiling.

"For Christ sake, Toby. Get the hell out." Nic bellowed at him as he exited our so-called evening swimming hole. "Ya ok?" He offered a wet hand, still laughing.

"Fine. My ass hurts." A towel wrapped around me with Nic's hand patting my bruised bottom. "Damn animal of yours has the worst flipping timing."

In the bathroom doorway, Toby sat happily waiting for his turn to be toweled off.

Made in the USA
Charleston, SC
08 April 2013